the longest night

KARA BRADEN

sourcebooks
casablanca

Published by Sourcebooks Casablanca, an imprint of Sourcebooks, Inc.
P.O. Box 4410, Naperville, Illinois 60567-4410
(630) 961-3900
Fax: (630) 961-2168
www.sourcebooks.com

Printed and bound in Canada.
WC 10 9 8 7 6 5 4 3 2 1

To the most important men in my life: my father, who taught me to love words, and my husband, who gave me the chance to fly.

Chapter 1

October 19

AFTERNOON SUNLIGHT BATHED THE PATIENT SUITE
with a dull gold hue. Outside, pools of shadow darkened
the carefully tended lawn as broken clouds passed before the sun. It was five minutes past four, another gorgeous New England October day. The view did little to
soothe Preston's taut-strung nerves. He turned to regard
his brother, Ian, who sat stiffly in an armchair beside the
hospital bed.

Ian met his gaze with weary resignation. "I know,"
he said, his once-theatrical baritone gone thin and quiet.
"I look like shit."

"You do," Preston admitted.

Ian sighed and let the white hospital blanket fall from
his shoulders. "Kind of you to agree."

Preston caught the edge of the logo on Ian's T-shirt, a
pair of crossed blue scimitars, and smiled affectionately.
"Nice shirt."

Ian lowered the blanket enough to reveal *Samaritan*
written under the scimitars. "If anyone catches me
wearing this old thing, my reputation will be ruined," he
teased, though the humor was bleak.

Preston studied Ian's face, wishing he knew what his
brother was thinking. They were close, but this addiction had become a chasm between them. Ian had fifteen

more days to go as an inpatient, followed by another three months of planned outpatient counseling. The program had an excellent rate of success, but only if the patient stuck through to the end, which had always been Preston's biggest concern. Ian blamed himself for his addiction. He tended to think he could do everything on his own.

"That's why I'm here: your reputation."

A hint of the old sharpness came to Ian's blue-gray eyes. "The firm contacted you."

Preston nodded. "They've reassigned your cases. You're on six months' leave—"

"Six months?" Ian sat forward, stubbled jaw set. "I have active cases. Trials—"

"And an addiction to painkillers," Preston interrupted ruthlessly. Guilt twisted through him as Ian sat back, going pale, but the time for gentle handling had passed. Since his postsurgical discharge nine months ago, Ian had sailed in and out of rehab programs, doing the minimum to satisfy the partners at his law firm. Painkillers had given him the false strength to handle a full caseload, but also to put himself back into physical therapy to try and fix the new damage he'd done to his still-healing back.

Ian glared at Preston. "What the hell am I supposed to do for six months?"

"Get clean. Get yourself squared away."

With a resentful huff, Ian snapped, "Fine. I need to catch up on continuing education credits."

"You'll have to do distance learning. One of their conditions was that you stay away from Manhattan."

The sharpness in Ian's eyes gave way to fire; he'd

loved Manhattan since the day he'd first toured NYU in his senior year of high school. "*What?*"

Calmly, Preston reminded him, "You're a criminal lawyer, Ian. If you want to get painkillers, you know people."

Ian's jaw clenched. "I *live* in Manhattan. What the *fuck* am I supposed to do? Sleep on your damned couch?"

"You think I want you on my couch? Bad enough I have Ray crashing there between missions." Preston shook his head, hiding his horror at the thought of putting his brother and his business partner in the same room for more than an hour. "I have another plan."

Ian huffed and pushed up out of his armchair, abandoning the blanket. He steadied himself with a hand on the back of the chair and then walked to the window. His back was noticeably stiff, but once he had his balance, his steps were smooth. "If it's a round-the-world trip on your boat, you can forget it. I just got through withdrawal. I've had enough nausea to last a lifetime without seasickness."

Even before the law firm's partners had made their request that Ian stay away from the temptations of Manhattan, Preston had been thinking about how best to help his brother. Ian was both brilliant and arrogant. He'd pounce on any hint of weakness, which made rehab—especially group therapy—all but worthless. And while he had the willpower to avoid drugs for recreation, he was too good at justifying one more pill to get him through a tough case, never realizing that all those "one mores" added up to an addiction that would destroy his life.

Ian needed time to heal, to learn how not to push himself. He needed someone who could win, and hold, his respect. And after days of thinking about it, only one name came to Preston's mind, the single person who might be able to stand firm against one of Manhattan's most promising criminal defense lawyers.

Preston smiled reassuringly. "I promise, you'll be nowhere near the ocean."

For long, heavy seconds, Ian studied Preston's face. Then he closed his eyes and turned his face to the sun. "All right," he finally agreed, looking back at Preston. "Make whatever arrangements you need. I'll tell the staff I'm leaving."

———

Cecily Knight walked up the creaking wooden steps and opened the door to the double-wide trailer. Over one shoulder, she carried a large frame backpack filled with groceries and supplies. Her parka was unzipped, despite the chill wind that blew through the mountain town. She'd had years to get used to the cold.

"Mark?" she called, pushing her sunglasses up onto her head.

The back door opened, and the airfield manager, Mark Wallace, grinned at her across the combination office, lobby, and kitchen. "Just finished refueling. You're set to go."

"Thanks." Cecily held the door for Chuck, the kid from Pinelake Grocery and Feed, who was carrying a sixty-pound sack of chicken feed. He shifted the bag in his arms and trudged after her, exuding the teenage resentment that came with being required to do any work.

Pinelake Airfield hardly deserved the name. It had a single hundred-foot-wide runway paved with gravel that trailed off into weeds at the edges. Cecily's own aircraft, a blue-and-gray two-seater, was already parked at the end of the runway, puffing exhaust out into the crisp midday air. Overhead, the steel blue sky seemed to stretch into infinity.

Mark fell in beside Cecily, saying, "I did a full check on the engines, changed out the fluids, all that. You're ready for winter."

"I appreciate it. Put it on my card?"

"Already done."

She nodded as she swung her heavy pack off her shoulders. "Toss the feed in the passenger seat," she told Chuck as they reached the little aircraft. He nodded and jogged around to the other side while she opened the cargo hatch. She stowed the frame pack behind her seat, keeping an eye on Chuck as he strapped the sack securely in place.

"Think you'll make it back down before winter really sets in?" Mark asked.

Cecily shrugged. "Might."

"If not, see you next spring." Mark gave her a friendly smile. "You take care of yourself."

Cecily returned the smile and opened the cockpit door. She leaned across to pass Chuck a five-dollar bill and then climbed into her seat. "Thanks, Chuck."

"See ya, Miss Knight," he answered, shoving the five into his pocket and slamming the door.

She put on her headset, adjusted her sunglasses, and keyed the mic. "Charlie Foxtrot X-ray Lima Niner requesting permission for takeoff."

Mark took the radio from his belt and waved to her as he led Chuck off the runway. "All clear, Charlie Lima Niner. See you around."

In ten minutes, she was up in the sky. She'd never meant to be a pilot, but she'd never meant to be a lot of things. By now, she was supposed to be a major in the Corps or maybe dead in the desert—not living in the backwoods of Canada in a place so remote that she needed a plane or snowmobile to reach the nearest grocery store.

The radio crackled to life, startling her. "Charlie Foxtrot X-ray Lima Niner, this is Pinelake tower, over," Mark said.

Baffled, she toggled the mic. "Pinelake, this is Charlie Lima Niner. What's up, Mark?"

"Can you swing back around? Got a phone call for you. The guy says he'll hold to talk to you."

"Seriously?" She glanced out at the ridge of pine trees that hid the blue ribbon that was her highway home, upriver of Pinelake. The only thing she could imagine was that the Veterans Administration needed to get hold of her—possibly some issue with her disability payments—but that sort of thing could be handled through the mail. "What the hell?"

"Uh, says to tell you it's Samaritan?" Mark said uncertainly.

Cecily's hands clenched the controls. Her mouth went dry as she remembered smoke and gunfire before the flashbangs had rendered her temporarily blind and deaf. The first thing she'd seen when her vision cleared was a silvery badge, not from a nation but from a corporation. Two blue scimitars. *Samaritan*.

Numbly, Cecily answered, "Roger, Pinelake. Charlie Lima Niner turning back to the runway. Request clearance for priority landing."

"Pinelake acknowledges. Charlie Lima Niner, you are cleared to land. Drive safely, Cecily."

"Out." She keyed off the mic and took deep breaths as she eased the plane around. She circled wide and studied the brilliant, endless blue sky, so pale and different from the sky in her nightmares. Only when her hands were rock-steady did she turn fully and begin the descent back to Pinelake.

Chapter 2

October 21

FIVE HOURS ON A PLANE, EVEN IN THE LUXURY OF A first-class seat with Internet access and personal service, was a living hell for Ian. Despite a year and a half of surgery and physical therapy, his back still hurt if he sat still for more than an hour. He'd walked up and down the aisle as much as the stewards would permit, though eventually they'd asked him to sit down and please get out of the way of the other passengers.

His spine felt like it was on fire. He washed down two more ibuprofen with a Coke, wishing he dared order something stronger. Every time he closed his eyes, though, he remembered the hell of getting off Percocet. While he'd never had problems with after-dinner drinks or going to the bar on weekends, he was terrified of replacing one addiction with another.

Preston was probably right, damn him. Ian was in no condition to be anywhere but rehab or therapy.

It had taken Preston two days to make all the arrangements. Somehow, Ian survived the flight to Calgary International Airport, where he went through customs with a delightful lack of issues. From Calgary, he took a sixteen-passenger jet to the ominously named Little Prairie Airport, which was hardly an airport at all. It was a single-story terminal with no jet bridges. Instead, passengers disembarked via a wheeled staircase, which presented an interminable challenge to Ian's back after spending the whole day in the air.

When booking the flights, Preston had delicately asked if Ian wanted to be listed as a special-needs passenger so he could have access to a wheelchair. Proudly, Ian had refused, and now he was paying the price. The terminal couldn't have been more than a hundred yards away, but it felt like miles. Delaying, he put down his carry-on suitcase, eased the laptop bag off his shoulder, and flexed his back until the pain made him wince. Ibuprofen wouldn't help. He knew he needed something stronger, but he had nothing.

As he waited for his bags to be off-loaded, he huddled into his wool overcoat and looked around with growing horror at the thought of being trapped here. The air traffic control tower was three stories high, little more than a room perched atop a cement post. There were two runways and one L-shaped concrete building with small windows.

The airport wasn't fenced off, though the nearby cows were. Beyond the field, he could see a distant cluster of small buildings. There wasn't a single structure taller than the control tower. And this *wasn't* his destination.

He had more baggage than any of the other three passengers: a carry-on suitcase, his laptop bag, a garment bag, and a larger wheeled suitcase. Preston had told him to pack for an extended stay. Ian had envisioned Switzerland and had, in fact, spent three days researching the various ski resorts he might want to visit. Just because he'd injured his back didn't mean he couldn't take advantage of other amenities.

Now, seeing the grim reality of his future, he decided he'd have to find a way to get back to the East Coast as soon as possible. He needed to have a long talk with Preston about his ideas for recuperation.

As he stood on the tarmac, wondering how to handle all of his luggage, a handy airport steward ran over. At least, Ian assumed he was a steward. No one would willingly wear that much navy blue polyester unless it was a uniform.

The steward consulted a rumpled sticky note taken from his pocket. "Mr. Fairchild?"

Glad of the assistance, Ian picked up his laptop bag. "Yes. If you can take that"—he waved at the carry-on— "I'd appreciate it."

Obligingly, the steward picked up the bag. "I've got your luggage ready."

"Thank you." Ian nodded and started toward the concrete bunker that passed for a local airport, anticipating the warmth and a hot cup of coffee, if there was any to be found.

The steward ran a couple of steps to catch up. "Uh, your plane's here, if you want to go right to it."

Ian turned and saw him pointing toward the sixteen-seater commuter jet. "I just *arrived* on that plane," he said, wondering if he'd been meant to stay aboard. But no, his ticket had listed Little Prairie as his destination. From here, he was supposed to be picked up for the last leg of the trip.

"Not that one. *That* one," the steward clarified, ducking to point under the front end of the jet.

Frowning, Ian took a few steps—he didn't think his back could handle bending over—and spotted a little toy plane a short distance away. It was gray on top and blue underneath, with C-FXL9 painted in black on the tail. It wasn't *quite* miniature, but it was definitely close. How the hell was he supposed to actually sit in that thing, with his back? Was it even *safe*?

"That toy isn't a plane," he objected.

"Oh, sure it is. I'll just grab your other bags," the steward said and jogged off to the stack of luggage beneath the commuter jet, leaving Ian to slowly cross the tarmac. He circled the nose of the commuter plane and got his first good look at the plane and the person leaning against one wing.

The person proved to be a woman with a shock of fire-red hair pulled back into a short, tight ponytail. Her skin was flushed from the cold, with a light dusting of freckles over her nose and cheekbones. She wore a battered leather jacket, faded blue jeans that hugged her hips, and work boots. She turned and looked in his direction, dark sunglasses obscuring her eyes.

She was ruggedly attractive, far from the usual type who would've caught Ian's eye, and he wondered if she was his unknown hostess, Cecily Knight. If so, his exile might have just become a lot more interesting. Then again, Ian never let first impressions fool him. Whoever this woman was, she chose to live *here*, which could well indicate some deep flaw in her. Beyond the attractive facade, she was probably boring or antisocial, and Ian had high expectations even for one-night stands.

The steward reached the plane well ahead of Ian. Over the sound of rattling suitcase wheels, he shouted, "That's your passenger, captain!" He pointed back at Ian.

"To be a proper captain, one must have a proper airplane," Ian muttered under his breath, pushing himself to catch up.

"How much luggage did you bring?" the so-called "captain" asked sharply, looking Ian up and down before turning her attention to the luggage the steward had piled beside the plane.

"I have absolutely no intention of taxing that *thing's* cargo capacity with anything I value more than my socks," Ian countered.

Instead of getting angry, the captain barked out a laugh. "Suit yourself," she invited, fishing around in her jeans pocket for a moment. She pulled out a roll of brightly colored money, peeled off a blue bill, and handed it over to the steward.

"Is this thing even built to carry a passenger?" Ian asked with growing apprehension. He was trapped in the middle of nowhere, but even that was better than risking his life in a glorified toy plane.

The captain grinned and pulled open two doors on the side of the plane. Through the front one, Ian could see a seat; the back appeared to be a cargo compartment. "Guess we'll find out. Hurry up and stow your gear. It's almost four hundred miles back home, give or take. You probably don't want to walk."

"Four *hundred*—we're already *nowhere*," he protested.

She gave another short laugh and climbed up into the little aircraft. Her jacket rode up enough to show a black pistol holstered at her right hip. Ian stared. Having grown up in a military family, Ian was no stranger to guns but wondered what she needed it for. Out here, the only threats were boredom, snow, and bears.

"I don't think this'll all fit," the steward told him, looking between the little cargo compartment and the suitcases. The whole plane rocked as the captain slammed her door closed.

Ian sighed and turned to regard his belongings critically. He'd gone from the clinic straight to the airport, so he'd asked his assistant to pack his bags. He had specified that he'd be gone at least three months, possibly as many as six, and that he'd be staying with "a friend," which was all Preston had told him. That might have been a tactical error, as Preston would say.

"Right. Carry-on first, then garment bag," he told the steward, who obligingly did as directed. Draped over the carry-on, the garment bag provided a clean surface. Ian knelt down slowly and carefully to unzip his suitcase. He found an array of dress shirts, ties, socks, and underwear, along with a full kit of toiletries.

"Just pile everything on top," he finally said, getting back to his feet. He picked up his laptop bag.

"The suitcase won't fit, though."

"Keep it." Ian took the money clip from his pocket and passed the steward an American twenty-dollar bill for the extra trouble.

"Thanks!"

Ian walked around to the other side of the plane and pulled open the door. He had to brace himself to climb up into the passenger seat. He couldn't quite hide his grunt of effort as his back twinged in protest. The laptop bag barely fit into the space by his feet.

The captain looked at him but then twisted around to watch the steward start shoveling armloads of Ian's clothing out of the suitcase and into the cargo compartment. Dark red-brown eyebrows shot up over her sunglasses.

Then she laughed. "Good call," she said and turned to the instrument panel, grinning.

—⁓—

Twenty minutes later they were over the trees and away from civilization. Cecily was glad her passenger seemed content to stay quiet, though he obviously wasn't admiring the view. Once they leveled off to cruising altitude, he took a cell phone out of his overcoat and started pressing buttons.

Cecily frowned as she glanced over, only then realizing she hadn't seen another jacket in the luggage piled in back. The overcoat was nice for city wear, but he'd need something much warmer if he were going to make it through the winter. It was already snowy up at Pinelake.

"Fairchild said you're staying—"

"*I'm* Fairchild. Ian Fairchild," he interrupted. He turned and gave her a sharp, narrow-eyed look through his polarized designer sunglasses. Behind them, she could just make out eyes that were either blue or gray. "Consider it a reminder that you have yet to introduce yourself."

Amused, she answered, "Cecily Knight. The *other* Fairchild said you were staying through the end of the year."

Ian's answer was a huff through flared nostrils as he turned his attention back to his cell phone. "Perhaps. This may not work out as my brother had planned."

The thought of having an outsider in her space made her chest go tight, but she took a deep breath and concentrated on the sensitive flight controls. In fact, she realized that Ian was going to be the first person, other than Mags, to see the inside of her house since she'd had it built. She owed Preston Fairchild her life, and if it took an unwanted houseguest to clear that debt, so be it.

She snuck a look at her passenger, glad her sunglasses were the conventional type, with lenses that stayed dark. It didn't help that the houseguest in question was absolutely gorgeous, just over six feet tall and lithe, with dark blond hair that framed his cheekbones and brushed over one eye. He kept lifting a gloved hand to push it back, but the hair fell right back down to touch his sunglasses. She had the mad urge to move one hand from the controls, strip off her glove, and touch the strands.

Instead, she turned away to concentrate on flying. The silence was surprisingly comfortable, broken only near the end of the first leg, when she keyed the mic. "Pinelake tower, this is Charlie Foxtrot X-ray Lima Niner, requesting weather report and landing clearance to refuel."

"Charlie Lima Niner, this is Pinelake tower. Weather is cloudy with light snow, decent visibility. You are clear to land whenever you like. How was Little Prairie? Over."

"The usual, Mark. Glad to be home. Should be wheels-down in twenty, with a passenger."

"I'll put up the coffee, Cecily. Pinelake tower out."

She glanced over at Ian, who was staring at her so intently that she asked, "Something wrong?"

"Where exactly are we going?" he asked in that deep baritone of his. With a voice like that, she'd be content to listen to him read the phone book.

"Pinelake," she answered, reminding herself that she was supposed to be piloting, not ogling her passenger. "The house is another forty minutes' flying time north of the airfield."

"You *fly* home. Don't you have a car?"

She laughed and shook her head. "No roads up to my property. You can take a boat, if the draft is shallow enough, but I don't enjoy rowing." She resisted the urge to rub her shoulder and kept her hands on the controls instead. "The only other option is a quad or snowmobile."

Instead of answering, he turned his attention back to his cell phone. "I'm not going to get any signal out here, am I?"

"Not out here."

———

If Little Prairie had been tiny, Pinelake was surreal. The lake itself was pretty enough, surrounded by deep green pine trees dusted with snow. A small cluster of buildings stretched into the trees away from where a dock jutted out into the lake. It took seconds to follow a gravel road through the town, if it could be called that, to the airfield.

The runway was nothing but a gravel strip next to a flimsy-looking mobile home. "Where's the tower?" Ian asked.

Cecily laughed briefly. "No tower here, unless you count hunting stands."

After a landing that jolted every bone in Ian's body, she circled the plane at the end of the runway and drove toward an open-sided hangar. Three small planes and a helicopter were parked underneath. All four looked sturdier than her aircraft, and he wondered what it would cost to buy one for the duration of his stay. Not that he knew how to fly.

And then, there was the snow.

Snow in the part of Virginia where he'd grown up was a rare occurrence. An inch of snow could shut down the whole DC metro area. Snow here was thick and steady and blindingly white even with the heavy cloud cover that turned day into dusk. Ian shivered as he watched it build up on the windscreen; the chill outside would be knife-sharp and biting. Uncomfortably, he recalled family vacations in Europe, back when he and Preston had a proper family, before they'd all gone their separate ways. He thought of fires and warm blankets and playing chess with Preston and their younger sister, Amelia.

Cecily stopped the plane and waved at a man walking toward them through the snow. He was obviously insane, wearing a parka zipped only halfway up, hood down, with a radio microphone clipped to the front pocket. Snow dusted his graying brown hair and beard. Like Cecily, he wore sunglasses, and he was carrying two paper cups in his gloved hands.

"You need to get out, stretch your legs?" she asked as she turned off the plane's engine.

Ian almost said yes, because he felt as though he'd been trapped in a coffin, but he wasn't certain his back would stand the strain of climbing out of the plane and back inside. "Thank you, but no."

"Suit yourself." Cecily exited the aircraft in a blast of cold air as the man walked up to her door. "Mark, Ian. Ian, Mark."

"Welcome to Pinelake," Mark said, reaching across Cecily's seat to offer Ian the other paper cup.

"Thanks," he said gratefully, taking it. With a nod, Mark closed the door, though the icy air lingered.

Ian sipped and found the cup held vile-tasting coffee laced with artificial creamer, but it was still hot, and right now he'd drink diesel fuel if it would help him warm up. Even his spine felt cold.

Eight interminable minutes passed while Cecily and Mark stood outside, refueling the plane. Ian had finished the coffee by the time Cecily got back into the pilot's seat and started the engine. Cold air blasted through the vents. The cabin began to warm up too slowly for Ian's liking.

"You all right?" she asked as she started her instrument check.

"Fine," he lied. The plane jolted forward, making Ian flinch from the pain that shot through his back, though he turned away from Cecily to hide his wince.

Once she'd steered the plane around the other parked aircraft to the end of the runway, she keyed her mic and asked for permission to take off. Ian didn't hear the response, but a moment later, the plane accelerated toward the not-so-distant trees. At what felt like the last moment, the plane slowly swept up into the sky.

"We're almost home," she said, sounding relieved.

He glanced at her, noting the way her posture had relaxed. The tight lines at the corners of her mouth had all but disappeared, and he revised his estimate of her age downward by five years. Her sudden ease was curious, though. She'd been self-confident and comfortable dealing with the baggage handler at Little Prairie and with Mark, but she had apparently maintained a level of tension. Defensiveness. Was she relaxed at the thought of going home, as most people would be, or was it something else?

Whatever the answer, Ian would probably have it figured out soon enough. More than his skills at logic and rhetoric, his ability to read people made him a top-notch criminal defense attorney. At first glance, he might've thought Cecily Knight to be a recluse, but his instincts told him there was more to her than a desire to live a simple life in isolation. And given the crushing boredom that probably awaited him at their final destination, he was glad to have a mystery to solve—especially one so attractive.

— ~~~ —

Cecily's property had been in the family for generations, a remnant of an old mineral claim her great-grandfather had staked. At various times, it had been used for gold panning, hunting, and fishing, but it hadn't actually been developed until her father had retired from his medical practice just after she'd enlisted in the Marine Corps. He'd built a small dock for the shallow motorboat he used to take upriver from Pinelake and had cleared land for a cabin he'd never managed to build.

When she'd moved to Pinelake, she'd gotten rid of the boat and demolished the dock. She'd let the cleared land go wild and instead hired an architect and building crew to construct her small cabin on higher ground set far back in the trees. She'd also had them clear land for a short dirt airstrip and a shed that served as a hangar and garage.

The cabin itself had four habitable rooms, a small attic, and a basement that allowed access to the pipes for repairs. It was built of tightly chinked logs, double-pane windows, and a sturdy stone roof meant to withstand the weight of thick, wet snow. Her team of hired engineers had designed a redundant system for power and heating: a bank of batteries charged by diesel and propane generator systems. The fuel tanks for the generator and the propane heating system were safely stored in a shed well away from the house.

"City boy, aren't you?" she asked sympathetically. Her first couple of years out here, the snow had intimidated her. Winter had been absolutely terrifying, in fact, but she'd survived—thrived, even.

Huddled in his chic wool overcoat, gloved hands tucked under his arms, Ian let out a breath that showed faintly despite the best efforts of the plane's heater. "You could say that," he muttered.

She nodded her understanding and taxied the plane as close to the house as she could get. Preston had said his brother had been injured. He seemed fine now, except for a little stiffness to his gait, but there was no sense in risking a fall. Dress shoes didn't mix with snow.

"Go on in," she said as she engaged the wheel brakes. "I'll carry your stuff."

He looked at her directly, catching her gaze for a long, silent moment. In the twilight, his glasses had finally gone completely transparent, and she saw his eyes were the silver-blue of the bright winter sky at midday. She regretted putting her own sunglasses up on top of her head, feeling exposed under his sharp gaze.

"Thank you," he said and fumbled with his safety harness. His fingers were clumsy beneath his gloves.

Sympathetic, she reached over, pressed the catch,

and then tugged the straps to retract them. He nodded in thanks and let himself out into the cold, shivering. "Go on in," she told him and looked back at the clothes that had shifted during flight. She'd need to get a bag for them, so she hopped out and went around the plane, grinning to herself. At least he hadn't put up a fuss about losing his suitcase back at Little Prairie.

Despite her invitation to get inside out of the cold, he was waiting for her on the back porch. She gave him a curious look and pushed the kitchen door open, gesturing him inside.

"You don't lock your door?"

"A polite visitor will knock. Anyone else would just break a window if they couldn't get in through a door. Do you know what a bitch it is to get new windows out here?" Cecily answered, not mentioning that she welcomed anyone to try, as long as she was home. And if she wasn't home, she really didn't care. Her few valuables were in the bedroom safe, and it would take explosives to open it without the proper combination.

The door led into the kitchen and dining area that filled the back part of the cabin. A tiny table, currently with just one chair, sat by the back door. To the left was a small, well-appointed kitchen. Beyond the pantry, a door led to the bathroom, which also let out into the bedroom in the front corner of the cabin. A living room filled the rest of the front half of the cabin.

Taking pity on her guest, Cecily stomped her feet to clear off the snow and then went right to the potbellied stove. She stripped off her gloves, pocketed them, and then knelt down to build up the fire. She'd banked it before leaving.

"Where's the light?"

"Oh. Sorry," she apologized, getting to her feet to retrieve the oil lantern hanging on a hook over the sink. She lit the wick and put the lamp on the kitchen table where Ian sat, watching her.

"Don't you have electricity?" he asked, sounding worried.

"I do. I try to minimize using fuel to run the generators," she explained as she went back to the fire. The stove was more efficient, putting out almost enough heat to fill the whole cabin. She'd had the architect put fireplaces in the bedroom and living room, though. Even after all these years of living out here, she loved curling up under blankets in front of a crackling fire.

"If you don't mind my asking, why are you doing this?"

"Which 'this'?" she asked, coaxing the fire in the stove to life.

She heard the scrape of the glass oil lamp on the table. "Allowing me to stay here. You're not one of Preston's soldiers."

She froze, swallowing against the lump that lodged in her throat. She wasn't *anyone's* soldier anymore. "No. I'm not."

Ian made a thoughtful, quiet sound, accepting her nonanswer without question. Instead, he asked, "What's there to do around here?"

She shrugged and rose, closing the stove door. "Whatever you want." She went to the back door and picked up her empty frame pack. "Do you fish?"

"Do I—no."

She snorted. "Why *are* you here then?" she asked, shouldering the pack.

"What did Preston tell you?" he countered.

The evasive answer made her turn to study his face. He was even more attractive in the soft lamplight than he'd been in direct sunlight, but there was something stiff and defensive in his expression.

When Preston Fairchild had called her two days earlier, he'd tried to elaborate about the reasons behind the favor he needed from her. He'd said his brother had been in an accident and needed to get away after a series of back surgeries had led to a problem with painkillers. The whole thing felt like an invasion of this unknown brother's privacy, so she'd interrupted to ask if the brother was a security risk. When Preston assured her that he wasn't, she'd agreed to let him stay and cut the conversation short.

"It doesn't really matter, does it?" she asked. "You're a grown man. Stay as long as you want, and do whatever you'd like."

Ian went very quiet and still, and the controlled mask slipped, revealing a vulnerable expression of surprise that made her wonder if she'd said the wrong thing. "My brother must be a very good friend of yours," he finally said.

Cecily thought about the desert, about a man who was smart enough to follow an impossible trail of clues and determined enough to risk everything rescuing soldiers who weren't even his own. She remembered the pain and blood and screams. Her men. Her enemies. Herself.

"You can put on a kettle of water if you want something hot to drink," she said, rather than answering. She went to the back door and pushed it open. Cold air gusted inside. "I'll get your stuff."

—⁓—

Intrigued, Ian folded his arms and watched her leave. Already, his mind was cataloging everything he'd picked up about her, analyzing and assessing. What kind of person carried a handgun but left the house unlocked? If she hadn't been a part of Samaritan International Security, then she must have been military—American military rather than Canadian, judging by her Midwestern accent. But what branch? How had she met Preston? Had she been stationed in a war zone?

And for the love of God, why did she live like this?

He got up, feeling the strain in his back. The chill had settled into his bones, knotting up his muscles even more tightly than the successive plane trips had done. A hot drink would help, so he picked up the heavy iron kettle and brought it to the sink. He turned on the tap and was relieved when water flowed without him having to turn on a pump somewhere.

Despite the primitive surroundings, the kitchen was actually beautiful and neat and well-crafted, with loving attention to quality showing in every detail. In one corner of the kitchen, there was a trapdoor in the ceiling, with a long rope handle to pull it open. There were three doors that led to a pantry, a small bathroom, and a narrow set of stairs down into a dark cellar.

Curious about the rest of the cabin that was to be his home for the next few months, he picked up the oil lamp and walked through a river stone archway into the living room. The walls were lined with bookshelves packed with chewed-up old paperbacks. There was a single sofa—a wood frame with thick, dark brown cushions on the seat and back—and a matching rustic coffee table. A battered old desk was pushed up against the front window, with a secretary's chair wheeled up in front of it. Instead of a computer, it held an old-fashioned manual typewriter between two stacks of paper.

The fireplace here was also river stone, a massive construction with an empty slate mantel where there should have been photos or keepsakes. Frowning, he looked around and realized the entire room lacked any sort of personal touch. No photographs, no paintings, no mementos. There wasn't even a deer's head or a rifle on the wall.

The woodstove in the kitchen put out a surprising amount of heat, already driving off the chill. He felt comfortable enough to take off his overcoat, which he hung on a hook by the front door, next to an intimidatingly thick parka with a fur-edged hood. He tucked his gloves into the pocket of his coat. They were thin leather, not even insulated. If he did stay, he'd need warmer clothing.

The back door banged open, bringing with it a blast of icy air. Shivering, Ian carried the oil lamp back into the kitchen. Cecily set down the frame pack and disappeared out into the gloom once more without a word. He switched the lantern to his left hand, picked up the pack with his right, and grunted in surprise at the weight. Stubbornly, he shouldered the pack and carried it into the living room; then he stopped, mentally putting together a floor plan of the cabin.

There was only one more door he hadn't explored. He nudged it open with his foot and saw a bedroom— *the* bedroom, perhaps, since there didn't seem to be any empty space left in the cabin. A large bed filled the room, with a fireplace off to one side. A dresser and massive gun safe took up one wall, with a closet built in the corner to the left. When he checked the door beyond the closet, he found it let into the tiny bathroom that connected to the kitchen.

Where was he meant to sleep? Maybe she had a bed in the attic, though he doubted he could make it up a ladder or steep staircase. If he stayed in the living room, he'd last about two hours on the sofa before wanting to steal her gun and shoot himself from what it would do to his back, but he didn't want to complain or throw her out of her bed. And she hadn't given any hint that she'd be interested in sharing.

He finally set the frame pack down just inside the living room. She'd brought his carry-on and garment bag into the kitchen, along with a second kitchen chair that looked weathered and dusty. "Where should I—"

"Let me go stow the plane," she interrupted, glancing at the kettle on the stove. "If that boils, put it on the counter, okay?" Before he could answer, she disappeared outside once more. He was tempted to follow, but the thought of the cold kept him safely inside.

Finally, he replaced the oil lamp on its hook over the sink and started rummaging through the upper row of cupboards. One held plates, cups, and mugs; all the rest had canned goods. Cecily had apparently stocked for an apocalypse, but she didn't seem a survivalist or militia type. They usually lived in walled, guarded compounds, didn't they?

He took down a glass, filled it at the sink, and used it to wash down two more ibuprofen. The bottle was almost empty, and while he had another in his bag, he was going to need to resupply. At this rate, he'd be lucky to make it a month.

Cecily finally returned, stamping her boots on the mat just inside the door. She gave Ian a quick nod and went to the living room. Then she came back into the kitchen without her leather jacket and gloves. Underneath the jacket, she was wearing a cream-colored button-down shirt that looked like thick brushed cotton. He took in her body in a single glance—strong shoulders, small breasts, flat abdomen—before his gaze stopped at the holster she still wore.

Seconds dripped by, glacially slow, as he watched the comfortable, confident way she carried herself. She wasn't at all alarmed at having a strange man in the house with her, despite the isolation. Of course, she was also still armed. He might have taken offense, but judging by the wear on the holster and the way her belt was twisted slightly under its weight, he had the feeling it was habit.

"If you want the bedroom, that's fine," she said, finally crossing the kitchen to go to the refrigerator.

"Thanks, but where will you sleep?"

She shrugged, unconcerned. "The couch is fine. I don't sleep much."

"Neither do I, lately."

She looked back over her shoulder as she took a plastic container out of the fridge. "Just don't sneak up on me while I'm sleeping. I'm not used to having anyone else here," she said, bringing it over to the counter. When she peeled back the lid, he saw some sort of red meat. "Venison all right?"

He nodded and moved away from the sink, giving her room. "The last time I had venison, it was at a charity fundraiser for two hundred dollars a plate."

She laughed, tossing her head; her short red pony-tail skimmed over the back of her neck, drawing Ian's gaze. "Bet this is better—and I'm not even that good a cook."

—◦◦◦—

Cecily didn't enjoy cooking, though she wasn't a *bad* cook. She couldn't afford to be, living on her own. But either Ian was an overly kind guest or she really had done well, judging by the way he praised her simple stir-fry of venison and mushrooms.

Instead of coffee, she broke into her stash of tea. Now that her guest was really here, she was struggling to push aside her anxiety at the thought of having him in her house, and she needed something calming. Coffee kept her alert and sharp. Tea was meant to be savored.

Ian didn't try to make small talk, which she appreciated. Just hearing him breathe was a constant reminder that someone else was here with her, in her territory—someone she needed to watch out for and protect. But the quiet was comfortable, and she slowly relaxed. For a little while, she was even able to let her mind drift to her writing. She was worried about falling behind schedule.

Once their mugs were empty, she gathered the dishes and carried them to the sink. "Let me help," he offered, following her too closely. She imagined she could feel the warmth of his body driving the cool air away, and she found herself craving more in a way that she hadn't for years. Tall and slender, with his artfully long hair and glasses, Ian was nothing like the military men Cecily had served with, and the differences intrigued her.

She caught herself and sidestepped, saying, "That's okay. Go get settled in. Make whatever room you need in the dresser and closet."

Ian didn't leave immediately. Instead, she felt his eyes on her, though he was far enough away that she could relax. She started the water and set the dishes to soak.

"Will you let me make breakfast tomorrow?" he finally asked.

Startled, she looked back to see if he was serious. "You cook?"

He smirked and brushed the hair out of his eyes. "I rarely have the chance, with my schedule, but yes, I cook. I can even do dishes, if you give me some time to remember how," he added, a grin flashing to life.

She couldn't help but return the smile. "All right. You got it," she agreed. He nodded, satisfied, and disappeared through the archway.

Cecily exhaled and started to scrub the dishes, letting her thoughts drift as her hands worked. This might not be so bad after all, if Ian could find some way to entertain himself. He was polite and had a fair sense of humor, it seemed. But his looks... As she'd suspected, the long, bulky overcoat had been hiding a body that looked strong and sleek, with shoulders that were broad but not bulky. Not like his brother, Preston, who was strictly the pumps-iron-for-fun type. She'd had enough of that in the Marines.

He came back into the kitchen as she was stacking

the last of the dishes to dry. "Do you mind if I shower?" he asked.

She closed her eyes against the brief mental image of his light hair slicked back, hot water running over his body. Keeping her face turned, she picked up a towel to dry her hands and turned around to face him. "Go ahead. Try not to use all the hot water. It's only a forty-gallon heater."

He nodded. "Thanks for the warning," he said wryly, and left the room.

"Towels are under the sink!" she called after him as she went into the living room. She put on her coat, gloves, and hat, and then went out into the cold night, taking a deep breath to help clear her head. The temperature hovered just below freezing, and a few snowflakes were drifting down in a desultory way. She didn't think the snow would stick through the night, and it would definitely be gone by midday tomorrow.

Every night, Cecily walked the property to check on the fuel tanks, the hangar, and the cabin. Sometimes she went to watch the river, but not often. Growing up, she'd rarely seen more than a handful of stars at a time, thanks to a childhood spent in light-polluted cities. In the desert, she'd fallen in love with the infinite night sky, but that love had shattered just outside a blacked-out city. Now, she felt safer in the dark and shadows, as though the light of the Milky Way somehow stripped away her defenses, leaving her exposed and vulnerable.

It didn't escape her that Ian's steel-blue eyes felt like that starlight. Just thinking of them made her shiver in a way that might have been good and might have been bad but was definitely distracting. He was handsome and interesting and that voice—God, that *voice*—but she didn't let anyone in, and he seemed the type to pry and dig out all of her secrets.

Even after everything Cecily had experienced, she tried to be a good, fair person. She minimized her interactions with others because of the anger and pain lurking just beneath the calm surface of her mind. She could barely remember the young woman she'd been in her school days, when she never had trouble finding dates and had lived surrounded by friends and acquaintances.

She finished her walk-around in the hangar, where the sight of the quad reminded her that she'd need to double the emergency supplies kept in the saddlebags. It was ridiculous to think they'd have to bug out, but having an emergency plan in place helped keep her steady. Everything in her life was planned, except for the new twist that was Ian Fairchild.

A bit reluctantly, she went back inside and hung her outerwear by the front door, beside Ian's long coat. She touched the combed wool; it was thick and expensive, soft under her fingertips—another sign that he didn't belong here, with her.

The hot water heater in the central utility closet was gurgling. With a sigh, Cecily went to knock on the bathroom door. "You're almost out of hot water!" she warned loudly enough to be heard over the shower.

"Be right out!" Ian called back.

The water turned off a minute later, and she returned to the living room to light the fire. She'd learned early on that life was easier if she laid out a fire ahead of time. Now, all she had to do was put a match to the firelighter she made from dryer lint and paraffin and then wait a minute to make sure the fire caught.

Once the kindling was alight and flames were licking over the split logs, she sat down at her desk. She'd stopped typing in the middle of her last sheet. Now, she ran a finger over the typed lines, feeling the physical impression of the letters on the paper without reading the words. She let the story spin out in her mind until she could hear the voices of her characters. She considered how the different plot threads twisted together, weaving into a pattern that would hopefully go unrecognized by the reader until the climax, when it all came together. She was only thirty pages in, and already the characters were coming to life in her head, adding little nuances of behavior that would help make them more real to the reader.

The bedroom door quietly opened. "Cecily?" When she looked up, Ian smiled. The water had turned his blond hair to a warm brown. Without his glasses, his eyes looked softer. "Need anything from in here?"

She shook her head and smiled back at him. Even layered in pajamas and a bathrobe, he was still shivering. Before she could think about offering to do something about the shivering, she advised, "Go to bed. You'll be warmer under the blankets."

He laughed and nodded. "Good night." He closed the door with a soft click. A moment later, Cecily heard the bed creak.

Cecily's bed was big enough for two. She was prone to nightmares and liked having the room to thrash without falling. It'd be hell for her to sleep on the hard, narrow couch, but she couldn't let herself think about sharing the bed. Ian was a stranger—a guest. He didn't need to deal with her nightmares on top of everything else.

Closing her eyes, she pushed thoughts of Ian in her bed out of her mind and focused her attention on the next scene. When she found the perfect place to begin, she set her hands on the raised keys and began to type, finding refuge in a world of her own creation.

Chapter 3

October 22

IAN OPENED HIS EYES TO WARM SHADOWS AND UNFA-
miliar walls lit only by the faint glow of banked coals.
The window might as well have been painted black, the
darkness beyond was so thick. For a few minutes that
stretched into timelessness he simply lay there, allowing
his senses to report on the newness of the situation. The
air itself tasted ashy and alive, free of the car exhaust
that tainted the air around his Manhattan apartment. His
back ached, but not more than usual. The firm mattress
was a blessing.

For now, the novelty of the situation was enough to
distract him, though Cecily had been accurate in her
assessment of him as a city boy. He loved Manhattan—
the feeling of being surrounded by life at all hours of
the day or night, the chaotic rush of people and business, even the contrast of Central Park's greenery
surrounded by glass skyscrapers and old limestone
apartment buildings.

Here, the thought of the thick forest of trees that
had already lost their leaves and deep green pines, all
weighed down under thick, wet snow, made him shiver
and want to bury himself in the blankets, but he was
awake now. His back hurt, and he knew the ibuprofen
wouldn't help, but he wanted it anyway.

He wanted to be home in Manhattan, in his apartment or his office, rebuilding his life.

What a damned mess.

But if he had to be trapped in the middle of nowhere, at least he had attractive company. He closed his eyes, thinking of what little he already knew about Cecily Knight. She was nothing like the women he met back home. They were all so polished, so contrived, so focused on power or business or social status. For any one of them, meeting him at the airport would have meant makeup and a manicure and a carefully chosen wardrobe. In contrast, Cecily had put on comfortably worn clothes and a .45, and hadn't even fussed with brushing her hair despite the mess caused by her headset. She took the simplicity of no cosmetics and a plain haircut and turned it into a statement of quiet confidence that was far more enticing than anything dreamed up in a Parisian atelier.

Last night, she'd mentioned that she didn't sleep much. Now, he wanted to see her, if she was awake. He got out of bed, stuck his feet into his slippers, and wrapped up in his bathrobe. He put on his glasses out of habit, thinking that he'd sneak quietly out through the living room to the kitchen. He hadn't seen a coffeepot, but he'd find something hot to drink, even if it was more tea. His thoughts were drawn to the bottle of whiskey he'd seen on a high shelf by the fridge, though he wasn't quite ready to take that risk. The ibuprofen would have to be enough.

When he stepped out into the living room, Cecily rose from the couch so abruptly that his heart skipped. She stood there for a moment, silhouetted against the low fire in the hearth across the room, before she nodded and relaxed her stance. Her hair was loose around her face, falling in soft waves to her chin.

"Something wrong?" she asked alertly.

Interesting phrasing. Not "good morning," if this even qualified as morning. Her first thought had gone to trouble or danger. He shook his head. "No. Mind if I make coffee?"

She exhaled, some of the tension bleeding out of her posture. "Beans are in the pantry, second shelf down, green canister. Grinder is mounted on the inside—" She cut off with a sigh and reached up to pull back her hair. "Hell, I'll do it."

"I'm sorry. I didn't mean to wake you."

"I'm up anyway." She pulled her hair back and slid an elastic band from her wrist to the short ponytail. Then she bent down and picked up her holstered gun, which she'd put on the coffee table. He resisted the urge to ask why she went armed in her own home, especially if she left the doors unlocked. He kept silent, though, and just watched as she fastened the belt around her untucked shirt, sliding the holster over her right hip. She still wore her blue jeans and boots.

"Is the bed okay?" she asked, leading the way to the kitchen.

"It's fine. Better than the couch was for you, I'd guess."

Cecily crouched down by the old-fashioned black iron stove. "It's fine," she repeated, feeding two split logs into the belly of the stove. "I've fallen asleep on the couch before."

"I appreciate it," Ian said honestly.

She stood, picked up the kettle, and brought it to

the sink to fill. He considered sitting down, but moving around helped with the pain in his back. Instead, he walked to the back door and looked out into the darkness, watching out of the corner of his eye as she put the full kettle on top of the stove.

Why do you live like this?

The question was on the tip of his tongue, but he held back. If he really did end up staying here for a few months, he had more than enough time to satisfy his curiosity. Besides, he suspected that prying too hard would cause her to shut down even more. There were no soft edges to Cecily Knight, but she wasn't abrasive. Instead, there was a sort of quiet strength about her, one Ian couldn't help but admire.

She opened the pantry door, briefly hiding from his view. Then she looked out, saying, "Come over here. Let me show you how to use the grinder."

He walked away from the archway where he'd been leaning. Earlier, he'd barely glanced into the pantry. Now, he took note of the plastic tubs on the floor and the shelves stocked with cans and sealed jars. He stepped closer to estimate how much food she'd stored away, but he was distracted by the smell of wood smoke that teased at his nose. She'd moved the couch closer to the fireplace, and the smoke had curled around her hair and clothes, infusing her with a natural scent that suited her better than any perfume could. He turned, admiring her profile, wondering if he'd be able to taste the smoke if he kissed her.

She looked at him, and for one moment, he saw his interest mirrored in her eyes. He shifted his weight to step closer, and abruptly she tensed. She turned her attention back to the closet and inched away from him, pushing the door all the way open. "Beans are in the green canister," she said, pointing to one of the shelves. "Raw beans are in that canvas bag down there. I roast once or twice a week—Thanks." She took the green ceramic canister from him and opened the lid.

"It smells wonderful," he said, carefully keeping his distance, though the aroma of fresh-roasted coffee called to him. The last thing either of them needed was for him to make a pass, her to rebuff him, and both of them to spend the next few weeks awkwardly avoiding one another.

She smiled, the expression genuine and relaxed, and measured a scoop of coffee beans into a worn metal box mounted to the inside of the pantry door. It had a crank handle on the side. "Dry goods grinder," she said, seeing his interest. "It can be used for anything—wheat, spices, whatever—but I mostly use it for coffee." Steadily, she worked the crank. Inside, gears meshed and coffee beans crunched.

"You must have given a great deal of thought to living off the grid like this." He leaned against the far side of the pantry, watching her.

"Well, I hired a consulting firm for most of it. Civil engineering isn't my specialty; my degree is in electrical engineering."

Ian glanced up at the unused light fixture in the middle of the kitchen, wondering what had happened to drive her so far away from her field of interest.

"I can handle basic maintenance," she continued, "but for anything else—the fuel lines, for example—I call in a specialist." She stopped grinding and slid a drawer out of the bottom of the grinder.

"I'd imagine you'd have to be self-sufficient to live here."

She left the pantry and carried the drawer across to the counter, where she took a small copper pot out of a cabinet. "You could say that," she agreed, dumping the coffee grounds into the pot. "Did you want to see the specs?"

"Specs?" He stepped back as she returned to the pantry and replaced the drawer in the grinder.

"For the house."

Surprised by the offer, he nodded. "I'd like that, yes."

"Watch the water. When it boils, fill the pot," she said and left the kitchen.

The house plans were in the safe, along with two hunting rifles, two shotguns, three handguns, and a sniper rifle that Cecily could possibly explain away as a bear-defense weapon. She wasn't arming for a war; for her, shooting was both a hobby and a necessity, since she supplemented her grocery runs by hunting.

She opened the safe and knelt down in front of it. Two drawers held boxes of ammunition; the third was where she kept the fireproof file box. She opened the box and rifled through the files—insurance papers, identification and passport, military service record, school transcripts, medical records, property deed—until she reached the folded-up blueprints and engineering reports.

Despite her need for solitude, her urge to show off was natural. She was proud of what she'd accomplished here. There had been a few hiccups, especially that first winter, but she'd mastered the art of not just surviving but living comfortably in conditions that would drive most people mad. The desire to share her accomplishments was only natural, even for her. Maybe *especially* for her; she'd always been an overachiever.

She also wasn't a recluse by nature, but by circumstance. As she locked everything back away, she shivered, remembering how she'd nearly shot Ian as an intruder—an *enemy*—before her sleep-fogged mind identified him as a houseguest. Preston Fairchild was the only reason Cecily was alive. She wasn't about to repay that debt by killing his younger brother.

She brought the paperwork into the kitchen and flipped on the light over the dining table. The paperwork rustled softly as he picked up the stack, sorting through the folded blueprints, statements of work, and purchase orders. Once he reached the engineering specifications, he tapped the papers on the table to straighten the edges and began reading.

The glasses softened the sculpted angles of his face, she thought absently, watching him read. The cold brought a slight flush to pale cheeks.

When the kettle whistled, she realized she was staring and quickly went to the stove. She poured boiling water into the pot of coffee grounds and looked out into the dark night while it steeped. Occasionally, she gave the contents a stir with a spoon. After two minutes, she strained the coffee through a mesh filter into a thermal carafe and set the pot of wet grounds aside to dry.

She brought the carafe and two mugs to the table. "Sugar?"

"Please. And milk," he said with only a nod of thanks.

"Sorry, I only have powdered milk or creamer." She

fetched the plastic container of sugar from the cupboard. She had a larger bin of it in the closet, sealed against ants and damp.

"That's all right, then," he said. She could hear the wince in his voice.

"It's not very practical to keep milk out here." The defensive words slipped out before she could stop herself. She brought him the sugar and a spoon. "The fresh meat makes up for it."

"True." He smiled at her, the expression lighting up his eyes. "In case I didn't say it enough earlier, dinner was wonderful."

She smiled back at him, captivated by the warmth in his cool blue eyes. When he wasn't smiling, he was gorgeous, yes, but in a distant, aloof way. Surprised at how relaxed she felt, she said, "Thanks."

They fell into a companionable silence broken only by the sound of Ian turning pages and the clink of his teaspoon after he refilled his coffee mug. Cecily sipped her coffee and tried to think about her writing, but she was lazily distracted. She kept glancing at his face, the way his hair fell to brush against high cheekbones. He had long, graceful hands, and she absently thought that if he ever took up sign language, it would look like poetry in motion.

By the time dawn's light turned the outside world from black to a pale, foggy white, she felt almost human again. She'd had nearly five hours of sleep, which wasn't too bad for her. Ian looked over at the window and stood, grimacing as he flexed his shoulders. He took a rattling plastic bottle out of the pocket of his bathrobe and swallowed two tablets.

She got up, also feeling a bit stiff from sitting on the hard wooden chair for so long, and went to the refrigerator. The supplies she'd picked up in Pinelake a few days ago were mostly dry goods meant to keep a single person through the winter. She'd picked up cheese and had plenty of mushrooms, but only four eggs left. Those she got from her downriver neighbor in exchange for bags of chicken feed Cecily picked up whenever she had cargo space.

Behind her, she heard Ian's chair scrape against the wood floor. "I believe it's my turn to cook," he offered.

She looked back at him, pleased that he'd remembered last night's offer. "Go for it," she invited. "I'll start some more coffee."

"Don't get your hopes up. It's been a long time since I've had the leisure to cook. I may be out of practice."

She laughed over the sound of water running into the kettle. "So, was there anything you wanted to see?" she asked, playing the role of host.

"Is there anything *to* see?"

She shrugged. "River and forest, mostly, if you like that sort of thing. I need to take the quad and go visit Mags. You can come along, if you'd like."

"Mags?"

"Marguerite Lavolier. Lives downriver, about ten miles away. It's not a bad ride, on the quad. I have a bag of feed to bring her. She'll have fresh eggs for us, maybe some chicken, if any of them are ready for slaughter."

"Slaughter—" He cut off with a tense laugh.

Cecily grinned back at him. "No real supermarkets out here, remember? If you want meat, you've got to get it yourself."

—m—

Faced with the choice between isolation in the remote house and going *anywhere*, Ian decided on the latter. Cecily was good company, even if she didn't seem particularly interested in him. But as he stared at the clothes his PA had packed, he wondered if he'd even be able to go out at all in this weather.

Well, he wasn't going to wear any of the suits. He had two pairs of jeans—one black and somewhat dressy, one blue and comfortable. He tossed the blue pair on the bed and left the black ones in the empty dresser drawer he'd found. Other than T-shirts meant for sleep, his PA had packed only button-downs; plain white was the closest thing he had to informal.

Clearly he was going to need to go shopping, assuming there were any stores within a hundred miles. He wasn't holding out much hope for Pinelake, judging by what Cecily had implied. Surely he'd be able to shop online and have his purchases shipped here. She had to have some way to receive mail and packages.

This whole wilderness retreat was starting to feel like a mistake. Granted, there was no chance that reporters would find him. And he was honest enough with himself to admit that New York *would* be a temptation. Sometimes, he was too clever for his own good. As a criminal lawyer, he knew exactly how to get his hands on all sorts of illicit goods; prescription painkillers would be child's play.

So, he'd stay. He'd find a way to make this work. He would beat this addiction, and then he'd go back home, find a way to deal with the press, and rebuild his practice—his whole damned life.

Cecily emerged from the bathroom without warning, clad only in a towel wrapped around her body. Wet, her hair was a dark auburn that brushed her shoulders in a mass of gentle waves. Unable to resist, Ian looked farther down to pale skin dotted with freckles. He felt his chest go cold, his throat tightening to trap his breath.

High on the right side of her chest, just to the side of her collarbone, was a deep pucker of scarring. Years of looking at evidence photos helped him recognize it as a bullet wound. It was surrounded by thin jagged lines that looked too messy to be the result of proper surgery. There were more scars as well, disappearing beneath the edge of the towel.

Almost immediately, she turned her back and went to the closet in the corner. "Sorry," she muttered over the sound of wire hangers being shoved out of the way.

Ian told himself to leave and allow her to get dressed in privacy, but he couldn't move. The bullet wound was mirrored on her back, a starry web of white lines radiating out from a dull red center, showing the exit path of the bullet. *Shot in combat*, he thought. It was the only thing that made sense. But why had it scarred so badly? Years ago, Preston had been shot—and Ian still struggled with the memory of that terrible phone call— but the wound had healed cleanly. So why hadn't hers? Hadn't she been evacuated to a hospital?

Suddenly uncomfortable, he turned away, taking his time to lay out his clothing. Behind him, he heard her approach, open a drawer, rifle through the contents, and then close it. She left for the living room without dressing, though she did close the bedroom door behind her.

Ian let out a breath and sat down on the edge of the

bed. He didn't just want to know what had happened to her; he *needed* to unravel the mystery. He'd have to be careful, though. She obviously treasured her privacy. But the more he knew about Cecily Knight, the more he *wanted* to know.

———∿∿∿———

Between the quad's loud engine and the rattling cargo trailer, conversation was impossible, which suited Cecily just fine. She'd been tempted to leave as soon as she was dressed, but abandoning Ian for the day would just make things more awkward between them. The shower had relaxed her, and she hadn't considered that Ian would be in the bedroom when she finished.

He'd stared at her scar—of course he had—but then had been polite enough to turn his back and make no comment. In turn, she'd managed not to make an ass of herself by running out of the room.

Besides, better to get the sight out of the way now and save him the embarrassment of making a move on her. She knew his type: rich, powerful, and important. Even if she was interested in him—and she wasn't interested in anyone—there was no place for someone like her in his life, even as a vacation fling.

Telling herself not to think about the past was no help. She was a damned idiot. She should have at least put on a T-shirt before going into the bedroom, but she was so used to living alone, she hadn't even thought about it. Now, he was guaranteed to ask what had happened, and she would avoid the conversation, and soon they wouldn't be speaking at all.

She knew she shouldn't be self-conscious about the

scar. She'd been wounded serving her country, and if things had turned out differently, she'd still be over there, risking her life for her beliefs. Even in her earliest memories, she'd wanted to be a Marine, and she'd chosen her specialization to get as close to the front lines as possible.

No one had seen the scar since she'd left the hospital. No one had come close enough to even try. Isolation protected her from the past. Living as she did forced her to concentrate on the present and on planning for the future.

She felt no calmer by the time Mags's house was in sight. The sleek modern building was built at the top of a low hill, with huge glass walls that looked out over the river. Cecily had forgotten to radio ahead, but the quad's engine was loud enough to get Mags's attention. She appeared around the side of the house, parka unzipped to show a bright red Christmas sweater. She grinned and raised a gloved hand, waving.

Marguerite Lavolier was a few years younger than Cecily, a slender, dark-skinned brunette who was surprisingly well-suited for rural living. She was a riparian biologist who'd rented a vacation cabin in Pinelake a few years back to do a study on the ecology of the Pinelake River. She'd liked it so much that she had purchased land—she was from a wealthy New Orleans family, she'd once admitted—and had built a gorgeous modern house overlooking the river. Cecily thought she was the perfect neighbor, respecting her privacy and bartering fairly whenever they visited.

Cecily pulled the quad around the side of the house, just in sight of the outbuilding Mags used as a garage, chicken coop, and laboratory all in one. The chickens had the run of a large enclosed yard that she'd fenced in after her first year of trying to raise the chickens, a year that had been a disaster for everyone but the local predators.

"Isn't this a nice surprise!" Grinning, Mags jogged over to the quad.

Cecily dismounted awkwardly, needing to put some space between herself and Ian. He was moving slowly, sitting back on the passenger seat. Though he had wrapped one of Cecily's scarves around his face, his cheeks had gone red from the cold.

"Sorry I didn't call ahead," Cecily apologized. She gave Mags a kiss on one cheek as she stripped off her heavy gloves. She left the gloves on the seat of the quad and adjusted the handgun at her hip. The butt tended to dig into her ribs when she drove.

"It's no problem. Good timing, too. I was upriver yesterday, getting water samples." She smiled at Cecily, though her gaze kept darting to Ian. Her warm brown eyes were full of excitement and curiosity.

Obligingly, Cecily said, "Mags, this is Ian Fairchild. He's...staying with me for a few months. Ian, Dr. Marguerite Lavolier."

"Please, only my nana calls me Marguerite. Call me Mags," she invited, pulling off her glove to shake his hand.

He swung a leg over and rose, one hand braced on the seat as though trying to find his balance. Cecily felt a stab of guilt. The bumpy ride on the quad probably hadn't been the best idea for his back.

"Dr. Lavolier." He pulled off his glove and clasped Mags's hand, smiling with such charm that it stole

Cecily's breath. A quick peek showed Mags was just as vulnerable.

"Mags," she corrected, staring into his wintry blue eyes. "Are you a New Englander, Ian?"

"My family's actually from Virginia, but I've been in Manhattan for years. I can't quite place your accent," he admitted.

"I grew up in Wisconsin, did my undergrad at U of A, Phoenix, and then finished up in California, all while spending every summer with Nana down N'awlins way," she finished in a Southern drawl.

Ian laughed along with Mags. "And you complained every year to your friends when you couldn't spend the summers with them, but secretly, you loved it," he guessed.

The accent disappeared as Mags said, "Aren't you clever, for a city boy?"

Stomach churning, Cecily interrupted the banter by asking, "Usual place for the feed?" She started to unstrap the heavy canvas sack she'd bought in Pinelake. Beside it was a large cardboard box full of packing peanuts.

"Oh. Yes, please," Mags said.

Immediately, he turned back to Cecily, shoulders stiff. "I'm sorry. I'd offer to help, but..."

"Not a problem."

"I'll put up some coffee," Mags offered. "Come on, Ian. I'll show you the house." After giving Cecily one last look, he nodded to Mags and followed her toward the stone stairs cut into the hillside.

With a slight huff of exertion, she picked up the bag of seed and escaped, feeling a queasy mixture of irritation and relief. She could already see where this was going. Mags would be charming and intelligent, Ian would be interested, and by the end of the month he'd be staying in Mags's far more comfortable house.

After living alone for over six years, she should have been relieved at the thought of getting her privacy back. Instead, it felt as though the emptiness that had been growing inside her since the war had grown just a little bit bigger.

Under normal circumstances, Ian thought that if one were to be trapped in the middle of the wilderness, Dr. Marguerite Lavolier would be an ideal companion. She was educated, beautiful, and a charming, witty hostess. Proudly, she showed him around the first floor of her open-plan house and then ushered him into a comfortable, warm kitchen so she could make coffee.

Unlike Cecily's cabin, Marguerite's house had proper electricity; Ian had seen an electrical pole out front. The house also had a conventional heating system warming the kitchen without the need for a wood-burning stove.

"So, what are you doing out here, Ian? No offense, but you don't exactly seem dressed for Pinelake country," she said as she filled a glass carafe taken from a proper drip coffee machine. "Are you here for the fishing?"

He made a show of grimacing, hiding his laugh. "My brother's the fisherman in the family. We keep a boat in Miami. Cecily is an old friend of my brother's," he said, shaking three ibuprofen out of the bottle. He'd done well at taking only two at a time, but the bouncing, painful ride on the quad, only a day after he'd spent so many hours in airplanes, had pushed beyond even his endurance. "I was in a car accident last year. I'm still recovering."

Mags gave him a sharp-eyed look. "I thought you looked a bit stiff. Would you be more comfortable in the living room? The armchairs are much nicer than the kitchen chairs."

"If you don't mind, I just need to walk it off for a bit. But thank you," he said gratefully.

She nodded and went back to preparing the coffee. "So, what kind of car accident gets you shipped out so far into Canadian wilderness that we're not even on most maps?"

It was his turn to study her, surprised by the question that even Cecily hadn't asked. He walked to a sliding glass door that led out to a patio cantilevered off the hillside, overlooking the river.

"I'm a criminal defense attorney," he said, flexing his shoulders gingerly. "My last client was innocent— actually innocent." He glanced at her, and she nodded. "My team uncovered evidence of the real perpetrator, and he decided payback was in order. My car went off an overpass; the drop was meant to be fatal. They tried to make it look like an accident, but the police uncovered evidence that it was a hit."

Mags let out a low whistle over the sound of the coffeepot gurgling to life. "He's still after you, I take it."

His mouth twisted into a wry smile. "He's actually just started a twenty-year sentence." He took a deep breath and arched his back as he crossed the kitchen. His steps were a bit more graceful, now that his spine was starting to unknot itself.

"Then why come all the way out to the middle-of-nowhere, Canada?"

"To get away from Manhattan," Ian said with uncomfortable honesty. He had no excuse for being here—no story he could weave to explain away the extreme change in his lifestyle.

Mags went quiet for a moment, turning her attention to arranging cookies on a plate. A display of cross-stitched tea towels caught his eye. They were framed and mounted carefully behind glass, antiques that looked out of place in the sleek, modern house. He wondered if they were heirlooms.

"I'm trying to find a polite way to ask this, and I'm not coming up with anything," Mags finally said. She came up beside him and held out the plate of cookies.

"By all means, ask away," he invited. He picked up a cookie that smelled of ginger and spice and the white chocolate that coated half of it.

"What are you running from?"

A bite of the cookie bought him time, not to think of the words but to get up the courage to say them. "As soon as I was released from the hospital, I went right back to work. Fourteen-hour days, court cases... Painkillers were the only thing that got me through it all. I'm an addict," he finished, bracing against the look of condemnation—or, worse, pity—that he expected to see in her eyes.

But she was looking at him with a curious sort of interest, lips curved up in a gentle smile. "You don't know me. Why tell me all that?"

Ian shrugged, sending a twinge of pain down his back. "It's the truth."

One dark brow rose in a perfect arch. "You couldn't think of a believable story, could you?"

He laughed and shook his head. "Drew a blank."

"An honest lawyer?" she asked, her voice rich with amusement. "You're a guest in my home, so I won't tease you about your profession. But when I come up to Cecily's, you're fair game."

He grinned. "Says the woman wearing a Christmas sweater in October."

The door opened, admitting a blast of fresh, cold air and Cecily. She unzipped her down parka and tossed the hood back. Her ponytail was coming undone, framing her face with wavy locks of red hair that matched the color in her freckled cheeks, flushed from the cold. "No, don't get up," she told Ian.

"Everything all right?" he asked from the recliner where he'd been sitting for the last twenty minutes, browsing through Mags's collection of nature journals.

She nodded, looking past him. "Roof looks good." He turned the other way and saw Mags in the kitchen doorway.

"Thanks. I appreciate you going up there. I hate ladders," Mags added with an embarrassed smile. She crossed to the front door and took a heavy white parka from the closet. "Let me go pack up some eggs for you. You brought the box, right?"

"It's on the trailer."

"Perfect. Get yourself some coffee." With one last smile, Mags headed out.

He straightened the recliner and stood, feeling much better for the twenty or thirty minutes he'd rested his back. He followed Cecily into the kitchen. "The roof?"

She took a mug from the cabinet and poured herself a cup of coffee. "Her first year here, the garage roof leaked like mad from the weight of the snow. She lost an entire season's worth of river water samples."

"I'm sorry I can't be of any use," he said, frustrated. He rinsed his mug and put it in the sink.

"It's fine." She gave him a half smile and avoided his eyes.

Wondering at her mood, he asked, "So, this house isn't off the electrical grid. Why are you?"

"No point in running a line up to the cabin. I do well enough." She blew on the coffee and then took a sip.

He nodded and moved to look out the window. The view here was beautiful; he could see the appeal of living so far from civilization, despite how much he missed the city.

The house covered the top of a low hill. At night, the lights would shine through the huge plate-glass windows. In contrast, Cecily's little cabin was almost invisible in the trees, set far from the picturesque river. Had she refused to put in an electrical line because someone could track her to her home? He doubted she was afraid of someone—of anything at all, actually— but she was still carrying her handgun even here, at her friend's house.

"So, I think I'm going to head back. Were you staying?" she asked casually. Too casually.

"Here?" He walked away from the window, confused. "I think I can make it back, though feel free not to hit *every* bump on the way home."

Her brows shot up, hazel eyes going wide with confusion of her own. "Oh. No, I—" He glimpsed the way her cheeks darkened before she turned to the sink to rinse out her mug. "Right. Sorry. Oh, damn. The chickens."

He'd missed a turn in the conversation. "Chickens?"

"I'll see if she has any she wants me to slaughter," she explained and walked quickly out of the kitchen, zipping her parka.

Shaking his head, Ian followed more slowly. Had he been walking so stiffly that she didn't think he'd make it back to the cabin? He hoped not, or it would be hell to convince her to take him out another day. Even if he was surprisingly comfortable at the rustic cabin, he didn't want to be trapped there, with no outings to break up the monotony of the days.

As he put on his coat, though, another thought occurred to him: *Marguerite*. He closed his eyes and thought back to how he'd instinctively flirted with her, how she'd responded—and how quickly Cecily had left.

Was she jealous?

The thought had definite appeal. He'd been trying not to think of Cecily that way. She hadn't shown any overt sign of interest, and he was painfully aware that he was intruding on her solitary life. The last thing she needed was her unwanted guest rudely making advances on her. That would make an already awkward situation untenable.

He bundled up as best he could and went out into the cold. He took the stairs slowly, listening to the river rushing by, until his thoughts were abruptly scattered by a loud *thunk*. Worried, he moved as quickly as he dared. As he reached the bottom of the stairs, he heard another *thud*, and he rushed around the hillside to see Cecily standing by a barn, a bloody cleaver in hand. Nearby, Mags was holding two fluffy white chickens by their feet.

He stopped, heart pounding, and sighed in relief through the scarf around his face. He felt like an idiot. He hadn't actually considered how the chickens would get from Marguerite's barn to Cecily's dinner table without *someone* actually killing them. Some genius he was.

He walked forward at a more reasonable pace, watching the neat, businesslike way she handled the next chicken. One quick chop took its head, and she put it aside with the two others she'd butchered.

After she handed Cecily the fourth one, Mags confessed, "I feel awful. I can't do this. I don't mind fish so much, but the chickens are too…"

"Dad took my brother and sister hunting every year," he said uncomfortably. He'd never even seen anyone clean a fish, unless he counted sushi chefs. "Preston still goes. Does some sport fishing, too, down out of Miami."

"I have to use my hunting licenses before the end of the year," Cecily said, expertly slaughtering the last chicken. She glanced at Mags, asking, "Could you help me bag?"

"Sure, honey." Mags left Ian's side and went to a wood bench where several other headless chickens were hanging by their feet.

He turned to look at the river, watching the water rush by. He took the ibuprofen from his coat pocket and swallowed two dry in preparation for the ride back home.

Once Cecily and Mags had stuffed six of the chickens into plastic bags, they all returned to the quad. Ian followed more slowly, giving them time to strap the bags down behind the cardboard box that Cecily had brought from the cabin.

"If you need anything, I'm going to town in a few days, if the weather holds," she was saying to Mags.

"I should be all right, thanks. Dinner next Sunday?"

"What day's today?"

"Monday," Mags and Ian both answered. Mags shot him a quick grin.

"Right," Cecily said, cheeks coloring slightly. "Sunday it is. I'll see if I can get some fresh fish."

"Thanks." Mags smiled and leaned in to give Cecily a kiss on the cheek. Then she turned and wrapped a hand around the back of Ian's neck to pull him down for a similar kiss. "You take care of her—and yourself."

"If anything, it's the other way around," he answered, glancing at Cecily. Thanks to her sunglasses, he could read nothing of her expression. She turned away, picked up her gloves, and got onto the quad.

He climbed on behind her, resting his gloved hands on her hips. The feel of her strong, slender body, even with the padding of her heavy parka, was enough to distract him from the ache in his back. Her body fitted beautifully between his legs, and he thought of how much more pleasant this would be in summer, with nothing more than blue jeans between their bodies. He caught himself gripping her tightly and eased up before he could make her uncomfortable. She twisted to give him a curious look.

"Ready when you are," he told her casually.

She met his eyes for a second or two. Then she nodded and started the engine. "Keep an eye on the cargo, will you? That chicken's our dinner tonight. No sense having it fly off the trailer and feed the wolves."

Back home, Cecily lost herself in all the physical work required to maintain the house the way she did, enjoying the stretch in her shoulders as she built a fire out back and cleaned and butchered the chickens. She started most days with exercise—once a Marine, always a Marine—but today had been a break in her routine. Tomorrow, she'd get back to her usual morning run.

Ian was on the back porch, wrapped in his inadequate overcoat, waiting for her when she returned with the chickens, now cleaned, quartered, and bagged. "Need help carrying anything?" he offered.

Wary of hurting him further, she handed over the two lightest bags with a nod of thanks. "How are you holding up?" she asked as politely as she could. He hadn't brought up his injury, but anyone could see he'd been in pain from the trip downriver and back.

"I'm fine." He smiled and held the kitchen door open for her. "You don't have Internet access here, do you? I'd like to check my email."

Cecily hesitated; she wanted to get the chickens packed away, but ten minutes wouldn't hurt. "Let me wash my hands," she said, dumping her bags on the counter.

"Thanks. I was thinking... Well, I need better clothes, if I don't want to freeze to death," he said, leaning against the counter by the sink.

She looked over at him, taking in the casual-chic look

of his pristine white button-down shirt and blue jeans that hugged his legs. It would be criminal to hide that body under warm, bulky clothes, but he'd never make it through winter like that. Realizing she was staring, she pulled her eyes away and turned on the water so she could scrub her hands. "The general store in Pinelake might have something, but if not, we'll either have to fly somewhere more populated or have something shipped."

"Shipping is fine. I take it there's a post office somewhere nearby? Or does FedEx do supply drops here?" he teased, his low baritone making her shiver.

Her laugh was a little tense. "Pinelake has a post office. I'll get you the address for shipping," she offered, drying her hands quickly. Then she went into the living room, hung her parka, and sat down at the desk.

She had to move the typewriter to clear space. "Did you want to use your computer?"

"If you don't mind." When she nodded, he went to the bedroom, returning a moment later with his laptop bag.

Once he had the laptop on the desk, she showed him how to set everything up. A wall switch controlled power to the satellite dish and modem. She plugged the modem into Ian's sleek silver computer—about a quarter the thickness of her five-year-old laptop—and explained, "I mostly use it for email. Sorry, it's fairly slow."

"I'll keep that in mind."

She quickly wrote down her mailing address in Pinelake. "You can ship whatever you want to this address," she said, handing him the notepad. "It usually takes an extra day or two to get packages here. Think you can last until Thursday or Friday?"

"Only if no one else asks me if I like fishing," he

answered with a quick grin as he started to type. "One more suggestion of fishing, and I can't be held responsible for my actions."

Cecily laughed. "So much for our plans tomorrow," she said and went back to the kitchen to put the chickens away and start dinner.

―⁘―

Compared to Ian's high-speed connection back home the satellite was abysmally slow, but it was a lifeline to the outside world all the same. It took three minutes to sync his email, even though he'd synced it just yesterday. Mondays were always hellish at the office, though, so the backlog was no surprise.

He ordered his new clothes quickly, focusing on warmth rather than style. It wasn't as if he was going out to dinner every night. Not that he would mind taking Cecily out for a proper dinner. She wasn't emaciated and willowy, like so many women he dealt with. With her strong body and scrubbed-clean complexion and wavy red hair, though, she'd cut quite a figure in any crowd. He couldn't picture her in a dress, especially not the sort of ball gown meant for charity affairs, but a silk shirt and tight jeans and the right jewelry would definitely work for her.

The thought was more appealing than he'd expected. He considered the interested glances and the way Cecily had acted jealous of Mags's attention toward him, and then thought about the bleak months ahead.

Not so bleak, though, if he handled this properly. He couldn't count on Pinelake to have a properly stocked pharmacy and didn't want to be caught unprepared. He doubted that Cecily, living in isolation, was on the pill. Besides, he thought as he navigated to an online pharmacy, he needed more ibuprofen.

Once the orders were placed, he glanced back toward the kitchen. Cecily was still busy preparing dinner, so Ian turned his attention to the real reason he wanted Internet access. As a lawyer, Ian had learned all the tricks of background searches—credit reports, property and tax records, and computer-assisted legal research companies, to start. But he didn't want to use the bandwidth for a proper check, so he logged into Preston's corporate server and searched for "Knight, C."

He wasn't surprised when the search returned more than a dozen files. His remote access was only sufficient for him to open three; the others were all government and military files that required biometric authentication at headquarters or an authorized Samaritan laptop. The first file was a debriefing form that was blank other than the officer's name: Captain C. Knight. The second was a heavily redacted copy of a U.S. Marine Corps after action report. He skimmed it, but all he could pick out were references to a combat engineer platoon. The third file was a video, strangely enough. Curious, Ian set the video to download—the idea of streaming a video over this connection made him cringe—and turned his attention to the papers on the desk while he waited.

Apparently, Cecily was writing a novel—a *children's* novel, judging by the short sentences and the frequent mention of dragons, elves, and magical swords. He read a few paragraphs at random and found himself caught up in the story. But at the bottom of the pile, the tone of the writing shifted abruptly, going from fantasy to the grim reality of war without warning. He flipped back and forth, looking at the pages, and finally noticed that the notation at the bottom of each page changed. The fantasy pages were marked *CK*, but these new pages had *X* at the bottom. So she was working on two books at once—two extremely different books.

"Rice or potatoes?"

Startled, Ian looked back and saw her in the kitchen archway. His eyes immediately went to the pistol holstered at her left hip. "Either."

She let out an amused huff. "You're an awfully easy houseguest," she said and went back into the kitchen.

He stared after her, wondering if she was flirting or simply in a good mood. She'd been tense around Mags—a tension he had read as possible jealousy—but now she seemed relaxed and comfortable. She'd certainly been staring at him earlier; she hadn't bristled when he'd returned the admiration, either, though he'd tried to be subtle about it.

The laptop beeped with a download complete notification. Ian turned the chair back around and muted the volume. He didn't want to call attention to the video until he knew exactly what it was. Then he double-clicked it to launch his video player.

After a few seconds of black, the footage turned grainy, showing a poorly illuminated, unfamiliar green and white flag. The curved writing looked Arabic. Ian leaned forward, hiding the laptop screen from the kitchen, just in case Cecily tried to sneak up on him again.

The flag disappeared, replaced by a shot of several insurgents in motley brown camouflage, their faces masked behind checkered black and white scarves. They stood behind a line of three uniformed soldiers, all of them hooded and on their knees, hands behind their backs. His heart skipped as his mind leaped ahead to a conclusion that he wanted to deny.

The insurgents shouted and gestured with their guns. Then another man stepped into the scene, pointing back at the three bound prisoners. His mouth moved under the scarf that hid everything but his eyes. He didn't need the volume to understand that he was delivering an ultimatum: comply or the prisoners would die.

Then the man stepped aside and gestured. In unison, three of the other soldiers reached down to pull the hoods from their prisoners, revealing the bloody bruised faces of two men and one all-too-familiar woman: Cecily Knight.

Chapter 4

October 25

FOR THE NEXT THREE DAYS, IAN TRIED TO PUSH THE video out of his mind, to deny it even existed, but it was too wrapped up in the mystery of Cecily Knight's current life. It was fundamental to her, a shattered bridge between who she was now and whoever she might have been in the past.

Standing outside, wrapped up in his coat and the black jeans he'd worn the previous day, he looked up at an alien night sky full of stars and thought about Cecily. Polite, mild-tempered, isolated. Utterly skilled at surviving and even thriving in a solitary environment that would drive most people mad—Ian included, if not for the mystery of unraveling exactly who she was. And, more importantly, how she'd survived.

Late that first night, he'd run down his laptop's battery watching the video. It was just over two minutes long, and her face was only visible for under a minute, but Ian had studied her as thoroughly as he'd studied any piece of evidence for one of his cases. Comparing Cecily's posture and behavior in the video to his all-too-precise memory of the scar on her shoulder, he assumed she'd been denied proper medical treatment. In the video, he'd seen signs of other wounds—blood in her hair and low on the right side of her uniform.

He couldn't identify the terrorists' country of origin or their political or religious affiliation by accent alone. Even searching for the flag had turned into a dead end. The group might have been new or broken off an established organization. Maybe taking three soldiers hostage had been their opening foray, one that Preston's company had shut down before the terrorists had ever really gotten started.

He had no doubt that *this* was how Preston had come to know of Cecily Knight. This video was what had put her name on Preston's desk. And she had made it clear that Ian was here now as a favor to Preston.

What favor could be so great that a woman like Cecily—a woman who treasured her privacy and isolation—would accept a houseguest not for a few days but for a few *months*? Nothing short of a life saved.

Preston must have sent his security troops in to rescue the hostages, including Cecily.

But why wasn't she broken? Why wasn't she tearing herself apart from the inside, after all she'd endured? Living here in the wild, without a support system in place, she shouldn't have survived a year, especially not in a house full of guns. At the very least, she should have fallen prey to alcohol or tranquilizers, but so far he had yet to find more than a single bottle of whiskey, mostly untouched, and no drugs stronger than aspirin.

He paced through the yard, looking up at the sky, but the stars held no answers. There were tens of thousands of them, far more than he'd ever seen in the Virginia countryside where he'd grown up. The sky was washed with shades of pale blue and silver where the stars blended their light into radiant bands. He found himself drawn to it each night after dinner and coffee.

He listened as the rhythmic clatter of her typing, attenuated by the thick window, stopped. A moment later, the door creaked open. "Everything all right?" she asked, right on schedule. Twenty minutes in the cold, and she automatically grew concerned for him, but she never actually came out from under the shelter of the porch.

Only when she did her before-bed walk-around did she actually leave the doorstep to circle around the house. Ian had watched her moving through the darkness with certain, quiet footsteps as she checked the perimeter of the house, the shed where she kept the vehicles, and the fuel tanks some distance away. Not once on those checks did she look at the stars, though. Had she become blasé living here? How could she be so indifferent to a sight so remarkable and compelling that it even captivated him?

For the past two nights, Ian had let the query draw him back inside. Now, though, he stood his ground and kept looking up at the sky. "It's beautiful here."

Instead of taking the bait, she stayed by the door. "It is," she agreed.

He glanced back, noting how she seemed to stand to attention. Her shoulders were held stiffly squared, her chin upright. Her hands still hung casually at her sides, but the right was curled, fingertips just touching the holster she always wore or kept close at hand.

"Do you know the constellations?" Ian asked. The logical response would be for her to come out beside him so she could accurately point out groupings of stars.

"Got a book here somewhere. I'll find it," she said, disappearing back inside. So much for luring her out.

"Damn," Ian muttered and turned to follow.

For as long as Cecily could remember, she'd had an active imagination. She'd grown up on Tolkien's stories, from *The Hobbit* to the esoteric *Silmarillion* and almost-unknown *Smith of Wootton Major*. She'd read all of Madeleine L'Engle's Time Quintet, not just *A Wrinkle in Time*, and everything by Anne McCaffrey and Ursula K. Le Guin. Her most memorable birthday gift was the compiled Lord of the Rings saga, a single leather-bound volume with gold leaf and pages of foldout maps that were long since lost, having spent years taped to her bedroom walls.

Now, though, the images in her head had gone stagnant and dark, the musical Elvish language degenerating into harsh Arabic tones, clipped and bloody. She pressed her hands against her eyes, elbows braced to either side of her typewriter, and tried to see through the sandstorm to the tall blue-green forest with its golden wood tree houses in the world she'd created. She was off her timeline. She should have had a first draft finished already. Soon, the emails from her agent would start coming.

Finally, she ripped the sheet out of the typewriter and tipped it toward the oil lantern. She only had to read a few lines before she sighed in frustration and threw it into the discard basket below the desk. So much for story focus.

Of course, there was the *other* story, the one her agent didn't know about, the one she'd started not with the intent of sharing but to exorcise her demons one word at a time. That one came all too easily to her, as though the more her world of childhood fantasy slipped away, the more the nightmare took its place. But she wasn't ready. Not yet. One page a month, maybe two—that was the most she could handle.

She thought about Ian's beautiful blue eyes and how he'd reacted to the sight of her scars.

Before she even realized she was moving, she was up out of her chair and crossing to the bedroom. He looked up abruptly but didn't follow. He had a book in his lap, one of the books taken from the bookshelves that lined almost every available wall of the cabin.

She entered the eight-digit combination to the gun safe and swung open the door. The tiny halogen light mounted in the top of the safe came on, casting a harsh white glow over oiled metal and matte black composite and softer wood stocks. She got out the .22, an old, lovingly tended Remington, and slung it over her shoulder. The ammunition was dirt cheap and stocked in quantity in Pinelake, which made it perfect for target shooting.

Rather than going back into the living room, she cut through the bathroom, not ready to answer any questions he might ask. She put on the patched, threadbare jacket that she kept in the kitchen. She didn't bother with gloves, though she knew her fingers would go stiff, then burn with the cold, and finally go numb if she stayed out long enough.

It was a couple of hours until midnight, and there wasn't a cloud in the sky. Cecily walked out back, keeping her head down, and went to the airstrip. It made a convenient target range for everything but the sniper rifle. At the far end of the runway, she'd hung scrap metal plates from tree branches. She put the box of ammunition down on the edge of the gravel and crouched, not looking up at the sky as she dropped the magazine into her palm. It only held ten shots, which would force her to take a breath every few seconds while she reloaded.

When she pressed the first bullet into the magazine, her hands shook.

Her internal dissonance had to be caused by having Ian there in the house, a living, breathing presence where before there had only been silence. It didn't help that he was fucking gorgeous, with those eyes and that voice and that strange sense of calm intensity. He didn't fill the air with meaningless conversation; he was content to sit in silence, but he always watched whatever she was doing, wherever she went.

Even now, she kept an ear out for the creak of the back door. She wondered how long it would take between the first shot and when she heard the squeak of hinges. Probably only a few seconds.

She pushed the magazine home and rose, snugging the rifle to her right shoulder. The old wound still ached, especially in the cold; she wouldn't be able to fire too many rounds from a higher-power rifle, but the .22 she could fire all night.

The scope wasn't very powerful, but that didn't matter. She could barely see her target area, much less an actual target, so she looked in the right direction and brought the rifle up into her line of sight, waiting a few seconds while she tried to distinguish anything. It was pointless—without moonlight, even the infinite stars overhead weren't enough to light up her target—so she eased her finger against the trigger, changing pressure in slight increments until she heard the sharp report of the firing pin striking. A .22 sounded more like silverware dropped on a tile floor than the *boom* of a higher-caliber round, and the recoil was too slight for her to detect.

She squeezed off two more rounds before she heard the back door slam open, wood striking wood more loudly than the echo of the fourth round. That one hit a target, judging by the faint, distant *ting* she heard from the far end of the runway.

"Cecily?" Ian shouted.

"Clear!" she called back, raising the rifle's muzzle. Then, realizing he might not understand, she added, "It's safe. I'm on the runway to your left."

As she listened to his boots crunch across the late-autumn grass, blades made brittle by the cold, she crouched down, balanced on the balls of her feet, and dropped out the magazine. She felt for the box of ammunition and loaded four rounds to replace the ones she'd fired. Her fingers were already stiff, fighting the spring pressure, but her head felt clearer. When she wasn't firing at a living target—and when no one was shooting back at her—she found shooting to be relaxing.

"Are you all right? Did something happen?" he asked as he stopped beside her. In the starlight, he was a tall silhouette wrapped in a dramatic coat. She could just make out the pale face above the dark wool but couldn't pick out the details of his fine bone structure or beautiful eyes.

Just as well. She didn't need to torture herself with what she couldn't have.

"It's fine. I have some targets at the far end," she said, gesturing down the runway.

He turned to look into the darkness. "Can you even see them?" he asked skeptically.

"Not even a little." She looked up at him and impulsively asked, "Want to give it a try?"

His laugh was sudden and unguarded and did more to lift her spirits than the target shooting had. "I'm not the soldier in the family."

"It's a .22, not a grenade launcher." Cecily turned, holding the rifle out. "Ever fired one of these?"

"Once or twice," he answered with forced casualness.

"Uh-huh. Safety's behind the trigger." She set the weapon in his hands, covering them with her own, directing his fingers to each part of the weapon by feel. His skin was warm under her cold fingers, but he didn't pull away. "You've got ten shots. The bolt will work automatically. On the last shot, it'll stay open." Gently, she pressed the rifle up and circled around behind Ian's right shoulder. The wool coat was soft under her hands. "Snug it up in the hollow of your shoulder, but don't worry about recoil. You won't feel it."

"Easy enough," he murmured.

"Oh, did you want me to find safety glasses or ear protection?" she offered. She had some in the gun safe for when she went hunting.

"No need."

"All right. You're clear to fire, as long as you stay aimed down the runway. I own the property, and anyone on it is trespassing."

"I'll help hide the bodies," he offered lightly, shifting his stance. That was all the warning Cecily needed to step back, and a moment later she heard him fire the first round. As the echo died out, he brought his head back up. "There's really no point in aiming, is there?"

"Want me to dig out the night-vision gear?" she offered.

Ian laughed, a warm sound that slithered through her, coiling itself contentedly in her chest. "Another time."

—◆◆◆—

Cecily's abrupt departure hadn't caught Ian by surprise. Her typing had become more and more erratic as the hours passed, until the pauses between words stretched out into nearly a full minute each. The first surprise had been when he'd listened to her open the gun safe, and he actually wondered if he'd need to stop a suicide until he dismissed the thought as foolish. She wasn't depressed—*distressed*, yes, and angry, but not depressed. For someone who lived in the most boring back-end of nowhere, she was incredibly strong.

As soon as she'd left, Ian had checked the page Cecily had discarded from her typewriter. It was more of the same fantasy writing but lacked the vivid imagery of the other pages. He went back to his book, dismissing her behavior as a symptom of a bad night, until he'd heard the first gunshot.

Adrenaline slammed into his veins. He snatched up his coat and ran to her without even thinking, caught up in the fear that he'd assessed the situation wrongly. He had the terrible mental image of Cecily lying dead in the yard, starlight turning her blood to shadowy, liquid black, and he'd never been so glad to be wrong.

Her impromptu lesson in marksmanship was

unnecessary but seemed to amuse her, so he didn't bother to correct her assumptions that he was a novice. Instead, he enjoyed having her close beside him, cold hands guiding his fingers over the weapon. When he'd fired the first shot, Cecily stayed close, though she'd carefully moved out of the path of the ejected cartridges. When all ten rounds were spent, she showed him the release button and caught the magazine as it fell free.

She crouched beside him, shoulder-to-knee, and began reloading the magazine. "We can do this in daylight, if you'd actually like to see what you're hitting," she offered.

Supporting the rifle with his left hand, he found it natural and comfortable to drop his right hand to brush against her hair, thinking this wasn't so bad after all. "It's not fishing, so yes."

"I'll also show you how to butcher whatever you hit, so you might want to rethink that," she threatened with a laugh.

Surprised, he went tense, silently scolding his rusty, unused mind for not having anticipated this facet of Cecily's lifestyle. Of course she hunted. She was living across the continent from the nearest grocery store. Just days earlier, Ian had watched her butcher live chickens.

Cecily rose, resting a hand on his arm. "Or not," she said uncertainly. "It's fine. It's nothing—I mean, you don't—"

"No," Ian interrupted just as uncertainly, wondering how he'd so unexpectedly ended up in this new territory. Preston and Amelia had been the hunters in the family, along with their father.

A few seconds later, she said, "Well, whatever you're

comfortable with." She gave Ian's arm a brief squeeze and then ran her hand down to find his. She pressed the loaded magazine to his palm. "Did you want to keep shooting? It's freezing out."

Actually, he did—but while he was wearing his overcoat, she was wearing the jacket she threw on when she had to run out to grab more firewood, a battered windbreaker that would do little to keep out the cold. Her fingers were like ice against his palm.

"Let's go inside," he said instead.

Her fingers twitched against his hand as she reclaimed the magazine. "All right. One minute," she said, easing the rifle from his grasp.

She stepped ahead of Ian, raised the weapon, and fired all ten rounds with a quick, precise rhythm, filling the air with the sharp smell of gun smoke. Then she slung the rifle over her shoulder, bent to pick up the ammunition box at her feet, and said, "I'm going to make coffee, if you want some. Or are you going to bed?"

"I probably should," he admitted as they started toward the house. "It's late—not that the time matters very much here." He glanced at her in the faint light bleeding through the kitchen window and wondered if he should suggest she try to sleep. It seemed like she lived on catnaps of two or three hours, which couldn't be healthy, and for a moment he was tempted to suggest that they share the bed, even just to give her the warmth and safety of someone beside her.

He knew himself, though; he'd been attracted to her since the moment he saw her standing against that little airplane of hers. The last thing he wanted to do was to act on that temptation and make an already-awkward winter even more uncomfortable.

So instead, after they hung up their coats and built up the fires, he wished her good night and went into the bedroom alone. He undressed, wrapped up in her blankets, and lay in the firelit darkness, listening to her moving quietly around the kitchen, and wondered if there was anything he could do to help.

Chapter 5

October 26

A BLAST OF COLD WIND CARRIED CECILY INTO THE kitchen, cheeks reddened, eyes bright. She grinned at Ian, who'd been at the stove for fifteen minutes, making breakfast. His hair was still damp from his shower. "Morning," she said breathlessly, going right to the stove.

"Morning to you." He tried not to stare, but her unguarded happiness had him captivated. In the five nights he had been at the cabin, he hadn't seen her sleep more than three hours at a time until last night. Perhaps going shooting really had helped her to relax. "You went out early."

"Jogging." She grinned at his incredulous expression. "I'll be stuck doing calisthenics before too long. I don't mind running in a little snow, but it'll be measured in feet soon. Then it's all push-ups and sit-ups."

"Maybe I'll join you. I've got a list of exercises I'm supposed to do for my back."

"Which you haven't been doing since you got here," she scolded, shaking her head, though she couldn't hide a tiny smile. "Right. We'll start that tomorrow."

Surprised at the reprieve, he asked, "Do we have plans for today?"

"There's going to be another snowstorm later today or tonight," she said over the sound of frying bacon. "Think your order's made it to the post office yet?"

"I should hope so."

"We'll fly in today," Cecily decided. "Mark will keep the Pinelake runway clear, if it's not too bad, but if it sticks tonight and continues through tomorrow, we'll have to take the snowmobile and overnight in town."

Ian considered the gravel runway behind Cecily's house and the sheer difficulty of keeping it free of snow. "What about on this end?" he asked as he slid the bacon onto a plate.

She shrugged and came over to watch him crack eggs into the pan of bacon grease. "We'll be fine here. The snow at Pinelake is always worse because of the open air. If it gets that bad at Pinelake, I'll just leave the plane there until the weather clears, and we'll take the long way back here."

"Why?" Ian asked before he could stop himself. "Why do you live like this?"

A hint of tension appeared in Cecily's shoulders as she left his side and went to the pantry. "I like the quiet," she said in an absolutely neutral tone. With her back turned, Ian couldn't watch her facial expression, but he sensed that she was lying.

He could understand that Cecily enjoyed the physical work required to maintain a primitive lifestyle. Just watching her chop wood had made Ian's back ache in sympathy. He tried to help out where he could, mostly with cooking, but there was no way he could handle any heavier chores—not that his help was needed.

And yet, while Cecily was obviously practiced at some aspects of her lifestyle, in others, she was terribly unprepared for living in isolation. While wandering the grounds on his second day there, Ian had found a weed-choked, dead garden. Somewhat embarrassed, she had explained that she'd tried to grow her own vegetables for three years before deciding that she had no talent at gardening. Instead, she stocked canned vegetables and bartered with Mags, whose garden was small but significantly more successful.

But the reality was that Cecily really was a social creature, as she proved not two hours later in the so-called "village" of Pinelake. Everyone there liked her, and she seemed genuinely friendly in return. Ian had dealt with recluses in the past. He'd watched them attempt to function when forced into a social situation, with varying degrees of success, and Cecily bore none of the same traits. In fact, her only behavior that was at all unusual was a soldier's sense of awareness. As they walked through town, Ian watched her mark the location of every person or vehicle or animal on the street, saw the way she noted windows and doors, observed how she glanced to the side as they passed each corner.

She reminded him of Preston, actually.

―⁓―

Between Ian and the clothes he'd purchased, Cecily had only a few kilos of leeway for supplies. Before they'd even left the house, she'd decided there was no point in being practical about restocking. She wouldn't have the available weight allowance for the plane to carry even one bulk sack of rice. So while Ian tried on his new clothes in the bathroom at the general store, Cecily browsed the aisles and tried to remember the last time she'd indulged in any sort of luxury purchase. Her memory came up empty. For years, she'd focused on survival and challenging herself to live with less, not more.

She thought about Ian, who came from Manhattan, and about having Mags over for dinner on Sunday night. She considered a bottle of wine, but she didn't know good wine from bad. Besides, Pinelake's stock of alcohol tended toward the cheap and plentiful, a temptation she'd managed to ignore on all levels, though she did keep a single bottle of whiskey at the cabin. Ingestible alcohol was too useful not to have on hand in emergencies.

Instead, she wandered over to the baking aisle, thinking of her disastrous attempts at making desserts or casseroles. She'd finally concluded that it was impossible to actually bake anything using the woodstove with its variable temperatures and random cool spots. But she could improvise, she thought, eyeing the supply of crackers. Graham crackers and the last two bags of marshmallows were a good start, and there was more than enough chocolate stocked by the cash register. She picked up a bag of milk as well, recalling Ian's opinion about powdered creamer.

After she paid, everything went into the small rucksack she'd brought with her, and she went outside to check the weather. The snow was just light enough that it'd be safe to land back home, she guessed.

Ian joined her a few minutes later. He still wore his long, sweeping overcoat, though he'd changed his slacks for blue jeans and his shoes for heavy-treaded hiking boots. Over one arm, he carried a down parka with a fur-edged hood, and he had a blue and black rucksack slung over the other shoulder.

Cecily grinned. "Going to tell your brother you've

gone native?" she asked, heading out into the street. She turned toward the airfield, looking forward to being back home.

Ian took the phone out of his coat pocket. He went to turn it on but then hesitated. "I won't get a signal here, will I?"

She gestured for him to put the phone away. "No, but he wanted me to call him next time I was in town. Figured you might want to talk to him."

Ian's huff was amused. "He wants you to report on me."

She couldn't help but ask, "Do you two get along all right?"

"Very well, actually—well enough that he knows how difficult I can be," he admitted with a wry smile.

Thinking of some of the soldiers she'd dealt with in the past, Cecily said, "You're easy enough to handle."

"In that case, I should try harder."

———

"How're you doing?" Preston asked, his voice made thin and crackly by the quality of the connection.

A knot of tension in Ian's chest eased at the sound of his brother's voice. They didn't see each other very often, due to work, but they spoke frequently, and he hadn't realized just how much he'd missed Preston.

"Very remote," he said, glancing around the mismatched little office. Pinelake Airfield was run out of the trailer where the airfield manager lived. Ian felt a pang of nostalgia, remembering the early days of Samaritan International Security, when Preston had run the business out of a warehouse in Virginia.

"How's your back?"

"Hurts like hell, but that's to be expected. And yes, before you ask, I'm only taking ibuprofen."

Preston sighed. "Sorry. You know—"

"I know," Ian interrupted.

"How's Knight doing? You're not being a pain in the ass, are you?"

Ian smiled. "She's not exactly prepared for having a houseguest, you know. Did you even ask where she lives?"

The pause told Ian everything he needed to know. "We didn't have many choices if you weren't going to stay at the clinic."

"She lives in a one-bedroom cabin half the size of Dad's old hunting lodge."

"Oh. Well, shit," Preston said guiltily. "She never said anything."

"She wouldn't." Ian glanced at the doorway and thought about the thin trailer walls. He wanted to ask Preston for details about what had happened to Cecily, but he couldn't risk her overhearing. Instead, he said, "It's all fine. She's sleeping on the couch. But we owe her for this, Preston."

Preston exhaled thoughtfully. "I'll try and figure out a way to make it up to her, but…it's complicated."

"So it seems," Ian hinted.

Refusing to take the bait, Preston said, "Give her my regards, will you?"

"Of course. I've got sporadic Internet, so email me. Otherwise, there's no phone at the cabin, so I'll call you when we next fly to town."

"Fly?"

Ian rolled his eyes. "There's no road to her cabin. She

has to use a plane or a quad to get to civilization, and let's not talk about what the quad did to my back. Did you at all research where you were sending me?"

"Damn. I'm sorry, Ian."

"It's fine. Don't worry about it. It's…nice," Ian said, and it was only partially a lie. The quiet was a good change from his usual hectic routine, but it all too easily crossed the line into *too* quiet.

Then he recalled his brief look through the general store, which served not only as a grocery and supply store but also as a pawnbroker's. There'd been an old, scratched-up guitar hanging on the wall, gathering dust. Ian hadn't played in years, but at the moment, he had nothing better to do.

"Look, I'm going to run. Email me and let me know civilization still exists, will you?" Ian asked more cheerfully.

"You got it. Take care of yourself."

"You, too." Ian hung up and went out into what passed for a lounge.

Cecily and Mark were sitting at a small table, chatting. When she looked up and smiled at Ian, he was momentarily struck by how pretty she really was. Her self-confidence showed in her eyes and her smile—a self-confidence that came not from political power, money, or social connections, as with most of the women he knew back in Manhattan, but from being a survivor.

"Ready to go?" she asked, standing up.

Ian returned her smile, hoping that she liked music—and that he recalled his old skill. "Actually, can we run back to the store? If you think we have room in the plane, there's something I'd like to buy."

Back at the cabin, Ian followed Cecily into the kitchen, carrying a battered guitar wrapped in a quilt. "I'll drop this in the living room, and then I can start on dinner, if you'd like," he offered.

Cecily nodded, thinking she could get used to sharing cooking duties. "That'd be great, thanks. I'll go get the plane settled."

From the living room, Ian called, "Mind if I use the Internet? I need to refresh my memory on how to acclimate the guitar to the cabin. I know you have to let it rest when you transport it—new humidity and temperature— but I don't remember what to do with the strings."

"Go ahead." She hurried back out to the plane, surprised at how comfortable she'd become, having Ian here. He did his part around the house and didn't get in her way. And, she admitted to herself as she climbed into the pilot's seat, he was definitely nice to look at.

She steered the plane up to the hangar and got out to open the door. The snow had died off again, leaving the night sky obscured with thick, low-hanging clouds that were a comfort. The clear, infinite night sky reminded her too much of the desert—of a forced march at gunpoint through the pitch-black streets of a ruined city, heading deep into enemy territory.

She opened the hangar, absently thinking she'd need to clean and grease the rails for the doors; she was falling behind on her chores. Maybe tomorrow, she thought as she got back into the plane. Then she changed her mind. Tomorrow, she'd take Ian out for a proper shooting lesson. If nothing else, she wanted him competent with firearms. The last thing she needed was a city boy shooting himself because he'd decided to play with the gun she always carried.

Once she stowed the plane in the hangar, she did her final check quickly, wanting to get back inside. She hurried across the yard, boots crunching in the snow, and stopped to pick up some firewood. In the kitchen, she dropped the wood on the rack by the stove and asked, "No problems with it? Sometimes the connection gets sketchy when the weather turns."

"It's fine, thanks."

Nodding to herself, she picked up the grocery bags and went to put everything away. She tossed one bag of marshmallows onto the counter and put the second bag in the pantry.

"Marshmallows?" Ian asked from the living room archway.

She looked back around the pantry door and grinned at his puzzled expression. "Mags is coming for dinner Sunday night. I can't bake worth a damn in this stove, but anyone can make s'mores."

Startled, Ian laughed. He intercepted her when she brought a box of graham crackers to the counter. "God, I haven't had s'mores in…must be fifteen years or more."

"Good memories for you, I hope." She fished a few bars of chocolate out of the bag and set most of them down on the counter by the marshmallows. One, she offered to Ian.

His engaging smile softened as he took the chocolate bar. "What's this for?"

"For being such a good sport about living like this.

For a city boy," she teased, trying to encourage that smile to stay.

He laughed, but instead of his usual bright, sharp laugh, the sound was low and soft. "You're the one who's been a good sport about having me for a house-guest," he said, his blue eyes fixed to hers. In the dim light of the lamp over the sink, his eyes were very dark. Captivating. "How can I make it up to you?"

For a few endless seconds, Cecily forgot all about her reservations, caught up in the unexpected pleasure of a game she hadn't played for years. Ian was gorgeous and intelligent and kind and, against all odds, apparently *interested*.

But when Ian's free hand brushed against her right hip, too close to her gun, she twisted away violently enough that she bumped into the stove, rattling the kettle—not because she didn't want that touch, but because she *did*.

Her tension should've been Ian's cue to back off, but he didn't. He stepped closer, looking down at Cecily with almost predatory interest. "You don't think I'll hurt you," he said speculatively, and though the phrasing was ominous, it didn't come out as a threat. He studied her face as he spoke softly, curiously. "You're not in a relationship."

"Not looking for one," Cecily said, forcing herself to breathe steadily. The stove was hot at her back, so she sidestepped, breathing easier when she was out in the open space near the back door.

"Neither am I," Ian pointed out reasonably.

Before he could make an offer that would possibly be too tempting for Cecily to resist, she interrupted, "Good.

Settled, then. If you wouldn't mind starting dinner, I want a quick shower."

Uncertainty flickered across Ian's expression. He didn't take the single step that would bring him close again. "All right. I'm—"

"Thanks," she cut in again and retreated to get a change of clothes. She couldn't bear to have him apologize for offering her something she really did want but wouldn't allow herself to take.

Once she was in the bedroom, she let herself lean against the wall by the closet. Exhaling sharply, she closed her eyes and tried not to think about the way Ian's voice had made her shiver. Maybe if they both let this drop, they could go back to the comfortable, distant, *safe* friendship they'd developed. She wasn't ready for a relationship with anyone—especially not a high-profile Manhattan lawyer who'd go home in a couple of months, while Cecily tried to go back to the way things had been before she'd ever heard his name.

Chapter 6

October 27

AS IAN FOLLOWED CECILY INTO THE TREES THE NEXT morning, he couldn't help but glance at the shotgun slung over her shoulder. They weren't skeet shooting, and a shotgun wasn't a weapon for casual target practice, so why did she have it with her now? Of course, he also didn't know why they were going out into the woods for a lesson in shooting, rather than using the makeshift firing range on the airstrip out back. Perhaps her heavier weaponry was in case of bear attack.

The thought made his skin crawl. He'd rather face down a hundred of Manhattan's worst criminals than meet a single bear in the wild. It was all well and good for Cecily to be so competent and comfortable out here in the silent forest, but what the hell was he doing here?

He looked over at Cecily, appreciating the way the cold brought color to her cheeks. With the sun mostly hidden, he was able to wear his regular glasses, rather than his sunglasses. The wisps of hair showing from under her dark knitted cap were a bright contrast, and he found himself regretting her choice of wearing dark sunglasses that hid her eyes.

"Where are we going?" he asked softly. The cloudy forest seemed to encourage quiet conversation.

"Thought I'd show you some of the property." She

flashed him a quick smile that seemed genuine, though he had difficulty reading the nuances of her expression. "I promise, no fishing," she added with a laugh.

Last night had been tense and awkward. Ian had cooked dinner, and Cecily had made coffee. Instead of eating at the table, they'd taken their plates and mugs into the living room, where Cecily lost herself in her writing. Finally, he'd gone to bed—frustratingly alone—and had stared up into the darkness, listening as her typing finally achieved a quick, steady rhythm that lulled him into a doze.

At some point, Cecily must have slept, though she'd been awake and cooking breakfast when the dreary gray light of dawn came through the windows and woke him. She walked with easy, casual confidence, showing none of the wariness she'd demonstrated in Pinelake. To her, the unknown predators in the forest were no threat, Ian thought. Rather, she perceived *people* as a threat, though he had yet to tease out precisely why.

The rucksack Ian wore over his new parka was a heavy, unfamiliar weight. Cecily had insisted they both carry emergency supplies, though she'd also warned him not to stray too far from her side.

Not that Ian planned on letting her get away from him that easily. After last night, he was *more* interested in her, not less, but she seemed to have gone the opposite way. She was friendly and courteous, but she'd reverted to the polite, quiet distance of their first days together.

That thought naturally made him recall the life he'd left behind in Manhattan, and he stopped, feeling the cold air nip at his skin and bite at his throat as he breathed. His eyes went to Cecily's back as he realized he'd be going back alone.

To his surprise, he found he didn't want that. Oh, he desperately wanted to get back to Manhattan. He'd already been away for far too long. He needed the comfort and intellectual challenge of his old life more deeply than he craved painkillers to ease the ache in his back.

He closed his eyes, immersing himself in the sense-memory of the smell and sound and sight of a thousand windows looking out into the Manhattan night, every one of them hiding the possibility of mystery and intrigue, danger and pleasure, and he realized at that moment that he didn't just want to go back. He wanted Cecily to go back with him. He wanted to see how she, after years of self-imposed isolation, would react to his city.

Forget the tourist destinations and arts and culture. Ian would take her to the hidden city underneath the public veneer. He'd show her the buildings lost in time and the forgotten streets and unknown restaurants. They'd dine at the tiny cafes with no menus, where no one spoke English, and they'd watch the street performers and visit the hidden parks where nature flourished in the shadow of old brownstones. He'd take her into his world of nightclubs and private parties—and *that* was an image that nearly overloaded his imagination, Cecily not in some little black dress but in tight designer jeans and a silk shirt, maybe in deep forest green to complement her hair.

Cecily's sigh scattered the distracting thoughts. He opened his eyes, glad that he'd bought a parka that hung well past his hips, hiding the evidence of his unintended arousal. He saw her standing a careful eight feet away. Her gloved hands were shoved into her pockets.

"Look, I know this must be...uncomfortable," she said apologetically. She was turned to face him, but he had the impression that her gaze was averted, hidden behind the sunglasses. "Why don't we just go back? I can take you to Mags's house on the quad. The snow's not too deep. It's safe enough."

So much for a manufactured excuse to bridge the distance between them. Now he physically crossed that distance, watching the way Cecily tensed, not to attack or defend but to back away. But she didn't actually move, which was encouraging, and he didn't stop until he was only a foot away, close enough that their winter-fogged breath mingled in a pale cloud between them.

"Much as I look forward to returning to Manhattan, I have no interest in doing so now. And I have no desire to spend any significant time with your neighbor," he said, letting his voice pitch low and smooth.

Cecily shifted her weight, and Ian caught her sleeve, silently cursing the bulky jackets and gloves that separated them both. At the touch, she went still, saying, "Ian—"

"Cecily," he interrupted quietly. He wanted to pull away her sunglasses, but he sensed that she needed that little artificial shield. If Ian pushed too hard, she would shut down completely, and he might never get another chance at her. Even this might be too much, but Ian had to try.

Lightly holding her sleeve, he raised his free hand and used his teeth to tug off the glove. Her head turned sharply to watch the path of the glove as Ian tossed it aside. Cold air bit at his fingers, but he didn't care. He set his fingertips to her face, for an instant feeling the icy skin of her jaw before she flinched away.

"Cecily," Ian repeated quietly, soothingly, and touched again. This time, she didn't pull back. She parted her lips and inhaled quietly. The motion drew his gaze down, and he saw no reason at all not to chase that breath.

Tight with tension, her lips tasted of cold and snow. Subtle, burning points of contact connected them skin-to-skin—Ian's fingertips on her face, his thumb on the thinner flesh over her cheekbone, their lips touching lightly. The kiss was barely more than the air they shared for one breath, two. Her exhale shuddered against his mouth.

Encouraged, he licked at Cecily's cold, chapped lips, gently pressing with his fingertips. She shifted, her lips parting just enough for his tongue to flick across her teeth. Her inhale was sharper now, and her hand pressed against his side, not to pull him close or push him away but to simply touch. Her mouth opened further, and the brush of her tongue—just the tip—crackled through him like lightning.

Then Cecily did move, shifting a half step closer and standing taller, swiping her tongue across his before it pushed into his mouth, bringing with it heat and nerve-snapping tension and fierce desire. Their noses bumped, nostrils flared as they both tried to breathe without losing their connection. Ian's hand on her sleeve turned into a fist as her hand slid to his back, and it was maddening that he couldn't feel her body through the ridiculous layers of down-stuffed Gore-Tex and wool and far too much clothing.

It was Cecily who finally broke the kiss. Her hand fell from his body, and she stepped back with a deep breath as though to steady herself. She licked her lips, an action he mirrored, wanting to capture the lingering taste of her mouth before the cold stole it away. He felt her absence like a bone-deep ache that made him shiver. The tension was returning to her posture, though, just enough to warn him to tread carefully or risk chasing her away.

For a moment, they stood in the silent, snowy forest, breathing out of rhythm but equally deeply. He wondered if the cold felt like fire in Cecily's lungs the way it did in his own. He wondered if her body tingled painfully at the absence of touch or if she could still feel the impression of his lips against her own.

Cecily broke the silence as well, boots crunching through the light snow and into the fallen leaves beneath. She bent to retrieve his cast-off glove, her free hand automatically dropping to steady the shotgun at her side.

"Idiot. Do you want frostbite? Put that back on," she said as she offered the glove to him, a strange affection in her voice. He couldn't see her eyes, but he imagined the way they were bright with humor.

Ian took the glove with a laugh and put it on as he fell in beside Cecily, both of them walking again. Neither of them mentioned the kiss, and there was no attempt to hold hands or touch, but the distance between them had disappeared, which was good enough for now.

Kissing Ian Fairchild—kissing *anyone*, in fact—was a spectacularly bad idea. Without even trying, Cecily could think of fifteen or twenty reasons not to have a repeat, much as she wanted one.

It was just a kiss. No big deal. At least, at one point in Cecily's life, it wouldn't have been. Back in school, she'd never had any trouble dating. Even in the Corps, she'd managed to find company—not with her own troops, of course, but at various bases or while she was back in the States on leave. But now, she knew better. She liked him too much to give him up as a friend.

But she wanted it. Desperately. After all these years, she thought she'd trained herself out of craving intimacy and closeness, whether it was the rush of sex or the sweet laziness of cuddling with a loved one. She'd convinced herself that she didn't need that anymore, and she'd been so successful that she'd grown cocky. That was the only explanation. False confidence had made her vulnerable, and now he had slipped past her guard and under her skin, and there was no way in hell that she'd be able to say no.

As it turned out, he already knew how to shoot (though not as well as he kissed, a treacherous corner of Cecily's mind supplied), so she was able to give him a couple of tips to improve his aim and then lean back against a tree, watching him and trying not to overthink the situation.

Once Ian seemed to get bored with target shooting, she challenged him to lead the way back, thinking it best if he started learning his way around the forest in case he got lost. To Cecily's surprise, he didn't try to backtrack. Instead, he looked thoughtfully into the distance for a moment before he started walking. She followed, trying not to give any hints, lazily keeping an eye on their surroundings. Bears weren't usually a problem at this season, but an encounter with wolves or coyotes could be disquieting. She also kept an eye out for game animals, especially rabbits, so she kept some of her attention on the low brush near small clearings.

She was pleased to see that he didn't hesitate, though she couldn't help but wonder how a city boy knew how to navigate the woods. Once they were in sight of the cabin, she gave in to her curiosity and asked, "All right, how'd you do it?"

Ian turned and nodded at the position of the sun, barely more than a bright spot in the thick cloud cover. "Position of the sun, contour of the ground, sound of the river. I rarely get lost, especially not in an open area without many obstacles to my path." Then, grinning, he added, "Except in Boston. The streets there are laid out like someone dumped spaghetti onto a map."

Cecily laughed. "I'm impressed. You said yourself you're not the outdoorsy type."

"Neither are you."

The truth of that hit a little too close to home. For Cecily, camping had always been a fun diversion or part of a mission, not something she'd ever thought to turn into a lifestyle. More sharply than she should have, she said, "You *have* noticed where I live, right? I've been here for…six years now? Almost seven." A bit of bleak amazement crept into her thoughts at that. On December 31, it would be seven years.

Seven years, and she hadn't expected to live out even one. Hell, sometimes she thought she'd chosen to move out to the wilds to save someone the trouble of cleaning up her body after she finally got sick of the nightmares.

Seven years of surviving—not really living—weighed
heavily against a lifetime built in small, happy pieces,
from childhood to school to the terrible exhilaration of
war. She struggled against the weight pressing down
on her chest, the hot tension knotting up her throat, the
pressure behind her eyes, until her mind lost the battle
against her body and she was able to take a breath.

When she exhaled unsteadily, she realized he was still
watching her. "Sorry, planning the dinner menu for tomorrow," she lied clumsily. She'd never been a particularly good liar—not when honesty had served her well
through most of her years—and he didn't miss *anything*.

Now, his blue eyes sharpened, fixed intently on
Cecily's face as though he knew every thought slithering around in her fucked-up mind. Panic seized her
all over again, but this time, she channeled it into motion. She might have said something—*Let's get inside*,
perhaps, or something about the cold—but she had no
idea what. She pushed past him and headed with brisk
steps for the cabin's front door, forcing herself to think
only as far ahead as the next hour: build up the fires,
set up dinner, clean the guns. Everything else would
have to wait.

———∿∿∿———

Dinner was sausages made by the Tuckers, a family
of butchers and taxidermists in Pinelake. Last winter,
Cecily had shot a bear not too far away and had managed to get it to the quad and into town before the meat
could go rancid. The Tuckers had butchered it and
traded half the meat and the pelt for sausages, burgers,
steaks, and roasts enough to fill her deep freezer. She

served the sausages with beans that had been soaking since yesterday and pan-fried corn bread made with the morning's bacon drippings.

After Cecily washed the dishes, she dried out the skillet, listening as Ian finally pushed his chair away from the table. Usually, as soon as his plate was clear, he'd be in the living room to check his email. She had grown accustomed to bringing Ian his coffee at the desk. After email, they'd switch places, and she would get back to her writing.

This time, though, he had stayed at the table for coffee, and what had been a comfortable silence turned awkward as Cecily's imagination took flight, filling the quiet with expectations and prying curiosity.

She left the dry skillet on the counter and went to the pantry, watching him out of the corner of her eye. Instead of going into the living room, Ian followed her and asked, "Dessert?"

Cecily's breath caught. She'd never heard "dessert" laden with such innuendo—or maybe it was just her imagination, fueled by the heat of their kiss in the woods. It had been so long that she wasn't just rusty at flirtation; she couldn't even reliably tell when it was actually happening.

"Need to roast coffee," she managed to say. "We're running low."

"Must you, tonight?" He pulled the door open and stepped closer to Cecily, who was trying to remember which of the plastic tubs held green coffee beans. Once the water heater had regenerated, Ian had also showered and changed clothes. Now he smelled of soap, and the cool humidity had dried his hair in messy blond waves hanging down toward his right eye. All through dinner, her fingers had twitched from the desire to brush those locks away.

"We'll be out in three days if I don't roast more. Maybe two, the way you go through coffee," Cecily answered, resolutely not looking. She finally pried off one of the lids and glared at the rice inside. She replaced the lid with a loud snap.

"It can wait."

Realizing they were about to have *the talk*, Cecily took a breath to steady herself. She rose from her crouch and turned to find him standing much closer than she'd expected, only inches away. "Look, I—"

"Please, Cecily," he interrupted gently as his hands came up. Long fingers skimmed over her face, sliding back along her jaw to brush lightly, chillingly over her hair. "We've talked enough for tonight."

She stared at him—close, so close—and wanted to say something, but she knew that she'd come off sounding like a babbling idiot if she started to talk.

Ian took her silence for consent—which, in a way, it must have been, because when he leaned down to steal a kiss, Cecily couldn't find it in herself to protest. She leaned into it instead, hands sliding up to grasp his waist, holding him lightly but closely. The kiss was sweet, tasting of sugar and coffee, and full of his confident aggression, encouraging her to let go of her inhibitions.

Seven years of self-denial proved too much of a strain. The last of Cecily's reservations dissipated like fog, and she pulled him close to take control of the kiss. She reveled in the feel of a body pressed to hers, warm and hard and very real. His fingers twisted in her hair as he parted his lips further, allowing her to explore his mouth and nip at his lips.

Somewhere on the other side of the kiss Cecily knew things would be worse. For now, though, the kiss was enough—almost too much, in fact. She was starved for intimacy, for knowing that she had someone in her arms and that person wanted her just as much as she wanted him.

She broke the kiss to taste his skin, feeling the heat of his throat as she licked right over Ian's pulse. The answering exhale was just shaky enough to hint at a desire for more. Experimentally, Cecily bit, being overcareful because it had been so long and she didn't want to hurt him. A shiver passed through Ian, who shifted and got one foot between hers, pushing his hips forward against her body.

Heat arced between them, scorching away another layer of Cecily's fears and reservations. She stopped counting the reasons not to do this and started thinking instead about the sofa, which was close to the kitchen, versus the bed, which was much larger. She dropped her hands, feeling the back pockets of his jeans and tense muscle and tight curves, and she braced herself to pull his hips against her body.

With a muttered curse, he pushed Cecily back a step and twisted, crowding her back with another overwhelming, devastating kiss. Her shoulders pressed back against the wall beside the pantry, and he pulled her hair to tip her head back. He ran his tongue up her throat, the motion translating into a sinuous press of their bodies from knees to chests.

Ian's free hand braced on the wall beside Cecily's

shoulder, and her breath stuttered, catching like gears knocked out of alignment. She stopped breathing altogether. Suffocated and trapped, she felt panic rise up through her in a single heartbeat. She pushed, awkwardly at first, hands sliding over Ian's soft cashmere sweater before her instincts took over. Her second push was a solid shove to the sternum, a twist of her hips putting strength behind the blow that freed her.

She wrenched away from the wall, getting herself out into open space, and gasped in a breath as though she'd been drowning. Her heart was pounding, deafeningly loud, and she dragged in another breath, then another, until she could finally think.

Only then did she realize what she'd done. Thank God she hadn't actually hurt Ian. He was standing warily back, his eyes locked to Cecily's. He stood balanced and ready, as though prepared for her to come at him again. He hadn't run, though. He hadn't fled the cabin or tried to barricade himself in the bedroom. He hadn't fought back.

Cecily exhaled, confusion snapping through her as if her fraying thoughts were finally breaking under the tension. She realized her right hand was on her gun—thankfully she hadn't actually drawn it—but she couldn't pry her fingers away. She could still taste his kiss, and her throat had a single icy strip etched into the skin where the open air chilled the path he had licked.

Abruptly, she turned and rushed out of the house, needing to escape herself.

Chapter 7

October 27

IAN WATCHED CECILY STORM OUT OF THE HOUSE AND rubbed a hand soothingly over his chest where she had pushed him. She hadn't actually hit him, but the push had been hard enough to startle him off-balance and stagger his breathing. Because it hadn't felt like an attack, he had actually wondered, for a moment, if it was her way of escalating the intensity that crackled between them, and he hadn't responded in self-defense. And then, she'd left. Obviously, he had been wrong.

He closed his eyes, reviewing his memory in meticulous detail, wondering if he'd done something wrong. Body and mind, she'd most definitely been interested, until she suddenly *hadn't*. Both times they'd kissed, Cecily had waited for Ian to initiate, but she hadn't been passive. She hadn't mirrored his touches, and she'd followed her own desires. There'd been no hint of shyness or uncertainty after the first few seconds.

Then it had changed. When?

When Ian had pushed Cecily out of the pantry and up against the wall. For one moment, she'd responded, going relaxed and pliant under his hands, before everything had gone wrong. He closed his eyes, remembering her stillness in the moment before she'd pushed him away. Not just stillness, though. She'd gone from breathless and wide-eyed to tense and defensive, without a hint of the arousal that had been scorching through them both.

The speed of the change told Ian this wasn't some whim of Cecily's. Her assault, controlled as it was, hadn't been a conscious decision but a reflexive one.

The memory of her desire threatened to interrupt Ian's focus. Thinking to follow Cecily's example and go out into the bracing night air, he went into the living room and pulled on his coat. Remembering that she had gone outside without her jacket, he took it off the hook and went back to the kitchen, thinking to bring it to her so she'd be warm.

He reached for the back door, and the connections teasing at his thoughts finally snapped into place. When he had approached her at the pantry, she'd been momentarily defensive, only relaxing when he had stopped his advance. It had been Cecily who'd pulled Ian close with every sign of enthusiasm and arousal, and that responsiveness had encouraged him to crowd her up against the wall.

Trapping her.

Furious with himself, Ian pulled open the back door. Cecily was on the porch, not out in the yard. Her hands were braced against the railing, head bowed down. Her posture screamed her embarrassment, regret, and self-reproach.

"Don't be stupid, Cecily," he scolded. "There's only enough room for one idiot here tonight, and it's apparently my turn."

She flinched and started to lift her head, but then turned away. Carefully, Ian draped the coat over her back, feeling a twinge of regret. In retrospect, the little behavioral oddities and habits all added up to a conclusion that should have been obvious.

He stepped back, putting two feet of space between their bodies, eyes fixed on the faint illumination that spilled through the kitchen window. He looked out at the ruined garden and the gravel patch surrounding the barbecue and meat smoker, both improvised from steel oil drums.

Slowly, Cecily straightened and put on the jacket. Ian watched out of the corner of his eye as she zipped it to the collar but didn't tug it up to expose her handgun for quick access. She was cold but didn't feel threatened. A good sign, that.

"Thanks." The word was clipped.

Ian nodded. He considered stepping back to lean against the house, but that would put him behind her. Better to stay in her line of sight.

For a few long, freezing minutes, they both fell silent. Then, in a quick rush of words, Cecily asked, "Did I hurt you?"

He shook his head. "No. Which, if you consider it, is very impressive. You were very careful *not* to hurt me."

Cecily's exhale was too sharp to be anything but disbelief, not at Ian's words but at herself. "Good. Well, it's too late tonight—I prefer not to fly in the dark—but—"

"No," Ian interrupted. It didn't take a genius to see where this was going. "I'm not upset. I'm not angry, and I'm certainly not going back to Pinelake or to Marguerite's." He crossed behind Cecily with long, casual strides, trying to minimize the time he was out of her sight. The side railing creaked as he leaned back against it.

"You can't stay," she said as she turned to face Ian. Cecily's hands were in her coat pockets, and she pressed her arms against her sides as if to hold in body warmth, but her posture was balanced and relaxed.

Escape routes, Ian thought, hiding a grin at his successful assessment of what Cecily needed. If she took one step back, she'd be in line with both the kitchen door and the two creaky steps into the backyard. She wasn't claustrophobic—not with that little death trap of a plane—but she needed space. Space meant safety.

Then his mind lit up as things fell into place. It wasn't claustrophobia but something far more subtle: fear of being trapped *by a person*. When he had pinned Cecily to the wall—*that* was the trigger. It could well have happened if he had pulled her into a tight embrace or pushed her down onto the sofa.

And just like that, he knew how to prevent a repeat, at least of this specific incident.

"I'm not leaving," he said calmly.

"Why?" she demanded as she turned back to face him. "After what happened—"

"What happened," Ian interrupted again, "was perfectly understandable. I should have seen it before."

"What do you mean?"

"It's not important," Ian said calmly. He lifted his hands from the porch rail, holding them out toward her in a calculatedly inviting manner. The easiest way to ensure she was comfortable was to give her all the decisions. "Trust me, Cecily."

She glanced down at his hands and licked her lips. He didn't think her shiver had anything to do with the freezing night. "I feel like that should be my line, but I wouldn't ask it of you," she said quietly.

"You won't—" Ian cut off, realizing too late that using words like "panic" or "attack" would only reinforce Cecily's reticence. "You *can't* tell me you didn't enjoy the kiss."

Between the faint light radiating through the window and the chill that turned every inch of exposed skin ruddy, it was impossible to tell if Cecily was blushing, though Ian guessed that she was. Then her chin came up almost defiantly, and she admitted, "I did."

Ian smiled encouragingly. "And it's obvious that I did. So please."

"It's still not a good idea."

"I won't let you hurt me."

Cecily's smile vanished. She shoved her hands farther into her pockets, pulling her jacket taut against her tense shoulders. "You can't know that, Ian. I was a soldier for too long."

"Perhaps it's better phrased: I won't create a situation in which your instinctive response will be to defend yourself."

With a surprised flinch, she asked, "What?"

"Cecily." His exasperation was much less amused this time. "Either you can trust that I know what I'm doing here, or we can both freeze to death discussing it. I much prefer the option that *isn't* fatally boring."

Startled, she laughed. "Did you really just describe freezing to death as boring?"

"Yes. So *come here*," he insisted, twitching his fingers invitingly, both to get Cecily moving and to prove to himself that his fingers hadn't frozen solid.

Thankfully, she pulled her hands out of her pockets and accepted the invitation, closing the last step between them. Their fingers awkwardly intertwined. The contact did nothing to share body heat, but Ian was too caught up in Cecily's trust to care.

"We should go back inside," she said quietly, looking up at him. Their coats brushed together with a soft whisper of fabric.

"We will, in one minute." Ian leaned farther back, lowering himself a few inches to Cecily's height, and stretched out one leg. He brushed his fingers over her wrists, light and teasing. He would've been more comfortable spreading his legs to get her body pressed against his, but he wanted to avoid even the hint of keeping her trapped or surrounded. "First, I want another kiss."

Cecily's gaze flicked down to Ian's mouth. Her inhale was quick and light, as much a confirmation that he was on the right track as was the brush of her lips that followed a moment later. They were both cold and getting sniffly, but the heat of her mouth, as her lips parted, was more than enough reason for him to push winter out of his mind and focus instead on the feel of her teeth under his tongue. He encouraged her lips to part farther and shuddered pleasantly at the way she melted against him.

As the kiss grew heated and aggressive, Ian had to remind himself not to clench his hands around hers. He kept his touch light, feeling the steady, rapid beat of Cecily's pulse in her wrists, until she broke the kiss naturally. For a few seconds, she pressed her cheek to his, until their cold skin started to warm up.

"Inside?" she invited, with no sign of hesitation or anxiety in her voice.

Ian laughed, reveling in the way she shivered as his breath swept over her ear. "You'll have to be more specific, Cecily. Is that an invitation?"

Her inhale was a hiss of surprise that he ignored, biting back a laugh. Quietly, she muttered, "Fuck," under her breath.

Ian grinned. "Not out here." With some effort, he stood up straight. Cecily stepped back, giving him room to step away from the railing.

She smiled at him and said, "Right. I wouldn't want you fatally bored." She released one of his hands but kept the other, leading him into the warmth of the house.

———

It took five interminable minutes of careful touches and heated kisses for Ian to subtly steer Cecily through the kitchen and past the sofa, where she'd headed as though by instinct. The comfortable sofa in front of the fireplace was a good option, the type of romantic setting that would appeal to almost anyone, but the sofa had a back and arms, and he didn't want to chance her feeling trapped or cornered in any way. The only truly open option was outside, but freezing to death would accomplish nothing except feeding the local predators. The bedroom was the much better option.

As soon as Ian stepped backward through the bedroom door, he let go of Cecily's hand and pulled off his cashmere sweater. He tossed it aside and let her draw him close for another kiss, and for a few minutes he let himself be distracted by the feel of her mouth on his. The kiss turned into sharper bites along his jaw and throat, and her arms held him close. Then she let go, and her hands went to his shirt. When she opened the first three buttons, she moved down to taste the newly exposed skin.

There wasn't a hint of anxiety about Cecily now, and Ian's growing arousal spiked further, hotter, riding the high of successfully figuring her out.

At the fourth button, she paused, leaning her forehead against his sternum. She rose, avoiding his eyes, and said, "Shit. Ian, I—I wasn't exactly planning this."

Optimistically, he had anticipated this days ago, but he couldn't resist the opportunity to tease. Cecily was far too polite to have snooped in the shipping boxes that had come with his clothing delivery. "You're clean. Healthy."

"How do—"

"No medications. Not even vitamin supplements."

Cecily stared at him, lips curved up just slightly. She laughed and asked, "You noticed that? What, were you snooping through the medicine cabinet?"

"You don't have an actual medicine cabinet. But yes."

"I should be offended by the invasion of privacy, you know," she told him mock-sternly, grinning too much to be truly offended. "And how do you know I just haven't been tested?"

"You take good care of yourself. You're disgustingly healthy, in fact, for someone who actually kills and butchers half of what she eats and who lives a thousand miles from anything resembling civilization." He touched her chin, holding her still for another kiss. "And I'm healthy. The vampires at the hospital seemed to take particular joy in drawing blood daily, it seemed."

"All right," she conceded with another laugh, "but that doesn't change the fact that I don't do unprotected sex."

Ian leaned in to kiss her again. "Do you really think I hadn't anticipated this possibility?" he asked. He released her reluctantly and went to the closet, where he unzipped his suitcase to reveal the cardboard shipping box.

"Wait—anticipated what?" she asked as she walked up behind him. She looked down as he opened the cardboard, revealing multiple boxes of condoms shrink-wrapped together. "Dear God, are you preparing for the collapse of civilization or something?"

Ian looked up at her. "Is there anything *else* to do in the winter here?"

"If we actually use all of those, we'll probably be dead from exhaustion."

"At least we won't be bored." He ripped open the shrink-wrap and picked up one of the boxes.

Cecily laughed and left the closet to sit on the edge of the bed. She bent over, unlacing her boots. Ian pulled a strip of condoms out of the box and tossed them onto the bed. She glanced at them, kicked off one boot, and gave him a wry look. "Sure that's enough for tonight?"

Ian got rid of his shirt and let it fall as he walked forward to set his glasses on the nightstand. "Better too many than not enough." Instead of standing over Cecily, he sat down beside her, wishing he'd found an earlier opportunity to get rid of his boots. They were warm and offered decent traction in the snow, but had no business at all getting this close to the bed.

"Should I be insulted you decided we were going to…" Cecily laughed softly, brushing one hand up Ian's arm, lightly enough to make him shiver. "For some reason, the words 'have sex' seem incredibly inadequate."

"Why would you be insulted? You must know you're attractive," he said honestly as he bent to unzip his boots. "And judging by your self-confidence—when you're relaxed enough to express it—you know how to enjoy yourself. There's no reason I wouldn't want to at least hope."

Color rose in her cheeks, though her smile seemed pleased. "I'm not a car you can take out for a test drive," she mock-complained as she unbuckled her belt. She took it off enough to free her holstered gun, which she set on the nightstand.

He kicked his boots out of the way and tugged up his jeans enough to strip off his warm wool socks. "You were *interesting* from the moment I saw you," Ian told her quietly as he tossed the socks after his boots. He turned and touched Cecily's face to draw her closer. He pitched his voice low and intimate and said, "Yes, I took a chance that you might not be attracted."

"Not fucking likely," she murmured, drawn in to lick at his lips. He laughed into the kiss. Her nose was still cold against his. He moved back and lay down on his side, propped up on one elbow. She followed him down, distant enough that she could comfortably let her eyes rove over his bared chest. "You're too thin," she said quietly, pressing a finger to his body to trace the line of one rib. "I'm not interesting, Ian."

"Of course you're not interesting to *you*," he answered logically, fighting to keep his voice steady as the touch skimmed the edge between enticing and ticklish.

Cecily shook her head, flattening her hand around the

curve of his ribs. "So you…what? Set out to seduce me? That's a little coldly logical, don't you think?"

Irritation prickled through Ian, adding sharpness to his voice as he asked, "Do you want to spend all night talking?"

Cecily snapped, "I think we—" and then cut herself off, brows pulled down in a determined frown. "Fuck it. It's not even like I remember how this is supposed to work."

"'This'?"

"A…whatever 'this' is, between us." She wormed her way closer and slid her hand down to Ian's hip, fingers hooking possessively into the belt loop of his jeans. "What do you want to do?"

"How does 'whatever feels good' sound?"

Cecily exhaled, abrupt and unsteady. "Perfect."

———

Twice after getting out of the hospital, Cecily had allowed herself to get close to someone else. Both had been attractive and interested and willing to take things slow, but the quiet dinners and movie dates and gentle kisses had done nothing for her. There was no reason for her not to be interested in them…except that she hadn't been. They were what she should have wanted, but not what she actually did want—and what she did want, she didn't dare take. Intensity of any kind was too close to her triggers for her to risk striking out in self-defense, all for the selfish reward of sexual gratification.

Except for now, at least a little, because Ian, blunt as he was, seemed to understand. It wasn't the sort of sympathy that inevitably turned to pity; Cecily couldn't imagine him pitying anyone.

And now, here he was, sprawled on her bed, raising his hips to help her get rid of his jeans and underwear, pale skin and long legs and *everything* exposed to her sight and hands. And he watched her just as avidly, as though she were the most fascinating thing he'd ever seen. Without his glasses, his eyes seemed very dark, lashes shadowed against his face, which had resumed its pallor without winter's bite to add color to his cheeks.

Unprompted, after kicking off his clothes, Ian moved up the bed and twisted so he was no longer lying across it. When Cecily reached for the blanket, he huffed as if in annoyance but complied, contorting himself to go from on top of the blanket to underneath. Still fully dressed, she followed him, remembering at the last moment to snag the condoms and stash them close at hand.

She fought her way under the blanket and pushed Ian's legs apart so she could settle between them. Weight braced on her good left arm, she slipped her free hand over the inside of his thigh, smiling in the darkness as she listened to his breath catch. One of his hands came down to brush through her hair, but there was no twist or pull—only a gentle, almost tentative touch that wasn't enough but also wasn't too much.

Using her own hand as a guide, Cecily pressed a quick, dry kiss to Ian's leg, noting the lack of any reaction beyond a slight shift in position. Then she licked, tongue pressed hard against his skin, moving slowly and taking her time to taste and feel. His fingers clenched in her hair, a momentary reflex that he conquered almost immediately, leaving only the memory of a sting on her scalp.

She inched up the bed, biting back a soft sound at the way her jeans rubbed over nerves that had been dormant for too long. Being clothed like this seemed deliciously obscene, narrowing her focus not to her own desires but to Ian's. She trailed her tongue up the crease at the top of his thigh, and he brought up his legs and twitched his hips in response.

"Cecily," he complained, the sound muffled by the heavy blanket.

She laughed, intentionally turning her head to the side, knowing her breath would be warm on Ian's erection. "Something wrong?"

His answering growl made Cecily grin. "Just because we *have* all winter doesn't mean you need to *take*—" He cut off with a moan as she wrapped a hand around his cock and gently moved down, circling the base with her fingers.

Despite her earlier concerns, Cecily couldn't fault Ian's assertion that they were both most likely healthy. So she took a risk and swiped her tongue up the length of his cock and over the head, holding him steady as his hips bucked up again. The fingers in her hair went tight, and this time they didn't relax. The spark of intensity fanned her arousal from a slow burn to a blaze, and she couldn't stop herself from taking his cock in her mouth.

For a moment, she held still, pressing up with her tongue, feeling the hard flesh against the roof of her mouth. Enjoying the way Ian's breath caught, she carefully moved down, feeling his responses resonate in her own body. It had been far too long since she'd done this, but she'd once been good at it. She licked generously, extravagantly, pulling off to wet her lips before she went back down, each time taking Ian deeper into her mouth. His breathing went ragged, and another hot spike of arousal and satisfaction cut through Cecily, spurring her to fight her body's reflexive protest until soon she was gasping for breath and then holding it.

Ian's hand fisted hard, nearly tearing strands of hair free. "Too close," he warned, flailing to throw the blanket off.

Cecily scrambled up Ian's body, feeling as though seven years of celibacy had turned her into a damned teenager again.

"What do you want?" she asked, bracing her hands up over his shoulders. Now she wished she'd stripped off her clothes. She wanted to feel skin on skin, to let his body's warmth sear against her. His hands rested on her hips, thumbs pushing down over the crease of her thighs. "Tell me what you want."

Most other partners, as Cecily dimly remembered, would have made some polite request. Ian's patience had worn thin, though, and he snapped, "I already did," in a tone that was an intoxicating combination of harsh and commanding but also desperate and needy.

"Right." She nodded and tried to remember what she'd done with the condoms.

"Your jeans."

A knot of tension deep in Cecily's chest untwisted when Ian made no mention of her layers of shirts. Given that he had already seen one of her scars, it was ridiculous to feel self-conscious, but there was nothing logical about that part of her past or its impact on her psyche now. She twisted off his body and rolled onto her back, darting a wary glance at him to make certain he didn't take her position as an invitation to climb on top of her. He didn't; he rolled onto his side and propped up on one elbow, looking under the blanket as best he could.

She kicked her jeans and panties free, shoving them down toward the foot of the bed, under the blanket. Then she sat up and turned to face him as she pulled off the button-down flannel shirt she'd been wearing under her sweatshirt, leaving her only in a long tee.

Ian sat up and piled the pillows against the headboard. "Come here," he said, holding out a hand. He guided her to straddle him, and then caught her face between his hands to pull her into a deep kiss. As soon as she was settled in his lap, he pushed his hips forward, cock sliding against her, lighting up her nerves with such heat that her breath caught.

Struggling to keep her composure, she dug her fingers into his shoulders, thumbs rubbing over his collarbones. He was so different from the men she'd been with in the Marines, with only a few faint scars to break up the planes of his pale skin and sleek muscles. "You're too thin," she whispered, trying to distract herself from the feel of his cock.

"Too long in the hospital, recovering. Alone," he added, a hint of complaint edging into his tone. He let go of her hip to pick up the condoms. "Cecily."

She understood. She nodded and tore one free of the strip and then ripped the packet open. Feeling unusually shy, she looked down to roll it in place, loving the way he hissed in a breath at the contact. His hands slid up her back, over the T-shirt, and up into her disarrayed hair, freeing it from the low ponytail she usually wore. The strands slipped free to brush against her jaw, curling around her face. Ian combed his fingers through it and used his hold to guide her into another kiss as she rolled the condom all the way down. She brushed her fingers through the short curls of hair and smiled when his breath caught.

She raised up on her knees, realizing that she might be rushing things. "Can I—" she began.

"Anything," he interrupted. His hands moved to her shoulders and then skimmed down her sides, still over her T-shirt, until he touched her bare hips. "Whatever you want, Cecily."

Swallowing nervously, she nodded and took hold of his cock, gasping as it brushed over her clit. She couldn't quite hide a little whimper at the way heat coiled deep in her belly. God, she wanted him—*needed* him—inside her. Her eyes closed as she pushed down, clenching her teeth at the sharp stretch and burn.

His hands caught her hips, strong fingers digging in to hold her still. "Wait. Wait," he said tightly.

Startled, she froze, asking, "What's wrong?" Uncertainty quashed the tide of arousal more efficiently than a blizzard-cold gust of wind.

"Can I touch you?" he asked softly.

She nodded, breathless and tense, and let him ease her back down to straddle his thighs. He was watching her with burning eyes and not a hint of disapproval that she'd left the T-shirt on.

"You're beautiful," he said, touching her face. His fingertips were featherlight, and she closed her eyes, feeling him trace the line of her cheekbone. When she shivered, he laughed quietly, dragging his finger down to her lips. He pushed gently on her lower lip, and she ducked her head to kiss his fingertip, opening her eyes.

"Ian."

"Shh," he said, dropping his hand to her left shoulder. He slid his fingers down her sleeve to her bare arm, where he followed the curve of her muscles down to the soft, sensitive underside of her forearm.

She shivered again, her skin coming alive under his gentle touch. His fingertips moved across her palm and then over to her thigh, slipping over the curved, taut muscle to the inside of her knee. He watched the trail of his own fingers as though fascinated, moving without any haste. His gentle touch stole her breath, building a slow, hot ache deep in her core.

"Ian," she said again, softly, and he looked up to meet her eyes.

He sat forward to claim a kiss, mirroring the touch of their lips with a gentle swipe of his fingers over her clit, lighting sparks behind her eyes. He captured her gasp, flicking his tongue against hers, and moved his fingers in a slow, heated circle.

"Oh, God," she whispered, pushing her hips against Ian's hand. She buried her fingers in his long, soft hair and took control of the kiss. He caught her lip between his teeth in reprimand and then licked to soothe the sting. Breathless, she backed off to stare at him, wide-eyed.

"Let go, Cecily," Ian urged, his fingers pressing and sliding, moving in ways that made her breath catch and stutter. "I have you."

She let her hands fall from his hair and leaned back, resting her palms on his shins. The position arched her back, pushing her hips up against Ian's hand. Her head tipped back and she closed her eyes to better concentrate on his long, gifted fingers.

He accepted her unspoken invitation and indulged them both, exploring her with strong, certain touches. She bit back a sigh when he slid one finger inside her, turning his hand to swipe his thumb over her clit. His finger curled, stroking inside her, and she shivered as new heat coiled deep in her belly, adding to the flame already there.

He teased out every last cry and moan until she was gasping, and only then did he ease a second finger in beside the first. He curled his fingers and rubbed circles with his thumb, coaxing, "I've got you, Cecily."

She lasted only a few more seconds before the searing pressure in her reached a breaking point. One last twist of Ian's fingers made Cecily's world white out, a single pinpoint of pleasure shattering into flames that pulsed through her body, clenching down around his fingers. He kissed her and whispered her name, barely heard through the blood rushing in her ears.

When she could think and move again, she lifted her head to stare through a haze of pleasure into gorgeous blue eyes. Some last bit of reservation inside her broke. She twisted her fingers into Ian's hair and kissed him, rocking her hips forward into his cock. His gasp woke a rush of power in the back of her mind as she realized just how much he wanted her.

After nearly seven years of solitude, it was intoxicating to feel so desired.

This time, when she rose up on her knees, he didn't try to stop her. He looked down, watching hungrily as she lowered herself, taking the head of his cock into her body. "God, look at you," he whispered, dragging his gaze up to her face.

She ached with need, and she pushed too hard, too fast. Something must have shown on her face, because he caught at her hips to stop her, but she said, "No, Ian."

Whatever he wanted to say was lost in his groan as she finally settled all the way. She struggled to breathe against the tide of pleasure rising up inside her again, sooner than she'd expected. It had been so long—*so damned long*—since she'd felt anything like this.

"Oh, fuck. Cecily," he grated out, pulling her against him for a kiss as he tensed his abdomen. The sweep of his tongue and shift of his cock lit off sparks behind her eyes. Into their kiss, he said, "Not going to last."

"That's fine," she murmured, flexing her thighs. Seven years out of practice, but she was strong and Ian thought she was sexy, and God, she *wanted* this.

She moved, raising up on her knees with a delicious slide of friction and heat, and he let his head fall back against the headboard. His pulse beat strongly under his jaw. She ducked to nip at his throat as she rocked her hips back down and up again, setting up a slow, steady rhythm that had Ian breathless.

His hands locked around her hips, fingers digging in, and he thrust up into her as best he could. "Cecily. God, Cecily," he mumbled into her hair.

Her muscles burned with the effort, but she didn't let that stop her. Hands braced on Ian's shoulders, she moved faster, harder, letting him guide her rhythm until they were both gasping for breath.

With a shout, he thrust up into her and pulled her down to meet him, and she felt the hard pulse of his orgasm. The sensation was enough to push her over the edge, body clenching tight around his cock.

"God," he whispered as he moved his hands to Cecily's back. He pulled her against him with a lazy, sated kiss to her cheek.

I did this, she thought and let herself simply be held. But the chill in the room intruded all too quickly, and she pulled uncomfortably away. Ian gave her a quick, puzzled look but got out of bed. "I'm going to wash up," he said. He turned and leaned down on the bed to kiss her. His long, blond hair tickled her face. "Will you stay?"

Cecily's throat went tight at the invitation. She wanted to say yes—she almost did say yes—but she closed her eyes and found the strength to say, "No." Then, because she felt guilty, she added, "You'll sleep better without—"

Ian silenced her with another kiss. "It's fine." He pushed up off the bed and crossed to the bathroom, quietly closing the door. A moment later, Cecily heard the water start to run in the sink.

She got out of bed, wishing she could trust herself enough to stay, and not just because the bed was infinitely more comfortable than the sofa. She couldn't remember the last time she'd fallen asleep beside someone, and after what she and Ian had just shared, she knew she *should* stay.

All the more reason not to take that risk. She changed her clothes quickly, conscious that he could come back in at any moment, and checked the bed to see if she needed to change the sheets now or if it could wait until morning. Shivering at the chill in the room, she tossed her clothes in the laundry basket with Ian's, put another couple of split logs on the fire, and then left, closing the living room door to give him privacy.

She built up the fire in the living room and went to the couch, automatically reaching for the side table where she kept her gun before remembering she'd left it in the bedroom. The water in the bathroom was off, which meant Ian was probably in bed, possibly asleep, but Cecily knew she'd never be comfortable sleeping unarmed.

Quietly, she went to the bedroom door, only to have it open as she reached for it, startling her.

Ian was dressed in ridiculously impractical silk pajamas, lips curved up in a half smile as he extended his arm, offering Cecily her holstered gun.

"How did—" she began. She stopped herself and took the weapon. "Thanks."

He nodded. "If you change your mind, you're welcome to join me," he invited, leaving the door open as he went to the bed. With the fire banked for warmth, it was too dark for Cecily to clearly see more than the shift of the blanket as the mattress creaked.

She hesitated, wanting to stay, but not daring to try. Then she retreated back to the sofa. She put the .45 on the side table and wrapped up in her blanket. She stared at the fire for what felt like hours, conscious of the bedroom door still open in invitation, until exhaustion finally dragged her under.

Chapter 8

October 28

CECILY SHOULD HAVE KNOWN BETTER THAN TO EXPECT AN awkward morning-after. Despite the hard sofa, she slept deeply and well, rousing only when she heard the bathroom door creak. Even then, she came awake swiftly but without the jolt of adrenaline that usually had her reaching for a weapon before her eyes were even open.

A moment later, Ian came into sight, looking through the kitchen archway. "Coffee," he said, going right for his laptop. It wasn't an offer but a request.

Cecily watched him, wondering what he was thinking. There was definitely nothing awkward or uncomfortable in his body language, which was a relief. He seemed fine. He'd dressed as he had been since they'd gone to town to pick up his clothes: jeans, a button-down shirt, and a sweater, this one a finely knit deep maroon that was probably a wool/cashmere blend. Today, Cecily knew exactly what was under that clothing, and she couldn't help but stare as he crossed the wood floor with light, silent steps and no hint of pain in his back.

Ian sat down at the desk and flipped the switch that turned on power to the modem and satellite dish. "Is it your turn or mine to make breakfast?" he asked a bit more politely.

"I've got it," Cecily said, affectionate warmth spreading

through her chest. By the time she was in the bedroom, searching through what little remained of her clean clothing, she was grinning at the thought that Ian wanted a repeat encounter. At least, he'd said so last night. Or implied it. Her exact memories were a bit fuzzy on that point.

She kept grinning all through her morning wash. Remembering that Marguerite was coming over, she pulled her hair back into a ponytail that wasn't as short as she normally liked. Usually, she cut it once every couple of months, when it became unmanageable. Now, though, she thought about last night, the feeling of Ian's fingers twisted in her hair, sparking bright pinpoints through her scalp.

She'd leave it, she decided. After one last splash of water on her face, she went through to the kitchen to start breakfast. She crouched down to build up the fire so she could start coffee.

The desk chair's wheels rattled over the floor, and Ian came through the archway a moment later. He looked at her clothes and asked, "You're not going running this morning?"

Uncharacteristically shy, she shook her head. "I feel lazy this morning." With a bolder smile, she added, "It's your fault."

His sly grin sent hot tingles down through her body. He stalked toward her, challenging, "Tell me it wasn't more fun than jogging or calisthenics."

"It was all right," she mused, "though you don't get out of proper exercise tomorrow morning. Be glad Marguerite's coming over."

"Damn. That reminds me..." He rubbed his jaw,

watching her put two ham steaks into a frying pan. "Have you got any razors? I forgot to order some."

She looked over and couldn't help but smile a bit at the hint of gold stubble over his jaw. "You could skip it for a day or two."

"You *don't* want to see me try to grow a proper beard," he said with a laugh. "Anything—even some horrid pink razor?" he asked, walking up to look into the frying pan.

She let out a laugh and handed him the spatula. "Yes, because so much of what I own is pink," she challenged, thinking of her father's old things, stored in a box in the basement. "Stay here. Watch breakfast."

He looked at her curiously but didn't ask where she was going. He just went to get plates out of the cupboard, keeping one eye on the ham steaks.

At the bottom of the steep, narrow staircase, she turned on the light. She had her washing machine and an old gas dryer down here, along with her tools and a single trunk that had traveled with her from college to base housing to a Stateside storage locker while she'd been deployed. She wasn't one to keep mementos, except for the contents of the old trunk.

Her father's razor was old but stored carefully in oiled cloth to protect it from rust. It was nothing fancy—not a carved ivory heirloom—but she remembered being fascinated by it as a child. She used to sit and watch him shave every morning before he'd gone off to work. Later, when she came home on weekends during college, she used to shave him, sparing him the indignity of shaky hands or the electric razor he hated. The hospice had sent it to her with his effects; the package had been waiting for her at the base when she'd been flown home on emergency compassionate leave.

Now, she opened the trunk to get the box with her dad's old razor and the rest of his shaving kit. After last night, she was surprisingly comfortable with the idea of lending the heirlooms to Ian, though he'd been a stranger less than two weeks ago.

———

Ian was getting better at cooking on cast iron, though none of the pancakes were precisely round and one was markedly frayed at the edges from when he'd tried to skimp on oil. Still, Cecily was kind enough not to mention it, and she even complimented him on having finally gotten the coffee strong enough without letting it turn bitter.

"So, any ideas, or am I attempting to grow a beard for the first time since I was seventeen?" Ian asked as he helped Cecily bring the dishes to the sink.

She nodded in the direction of the cardboard box she'd brought up from the basement. "Found my dad's old shaving kit. Will that do?"

Ian was intrigued; she hadn't mentioned her family at all. He went to the box and opened it, expecting to find an old-fashioned metal safety razor and maybe an ancient, rusting red and white can of Barbasol. Instead, at the top of the box, he found a second thin cardboard box, the ends tearing. Inside was a piece of oiled cloth wrapped around an old straight razor, blade gleaming.

"The strop should be under there," Cecily said as she started running the water in the sink. "You can use the bar soap in the bathroom. It should lather up just fine."

"Wonderful," Ian said uncertainly. He considered pretending that he actually knew what he was doing, but he'd never so much as touched a straight razor in his life. He glanced over at Cecily and said, somewhat embarrassed, "This is a little awkward, but I have no idea how to avoid cutting off anything important with a straight razor."

"Oh." Cecily glanced over at him, pushing a strand of hair out of her face with the back of her wrist. "If you want, I can...help."

Ian held back his instinctive refusal. He didn't like anyone near him with sharp objects. "You *have* used a straight razor before?"

"Of course," she answered as if it should be obvious. She dried her hands and took the razor out of his hands. "If you finish the dishes, I'll make sure it's sharp enough."

"Comforting," Ian muttered and took her place at the sink. He rolled up his sleeves and picked up the scrub brush.

Cecily grinned at him and took the box to the kitchen table, where she started to unpack the contents. "I used to do this for my dad, after he had a stroke." She moved one of the chairs over to the stove, and then crossed the room to flip the light switch on. "Would you set a small pot of water to warm? I don't want to run the water heater empty."

Ian found her smallest pot, filled it, and put it on the stove. He wanted to ask for details about her father, but they were still essentially strangers, even after last night. God, she'd been beautiful and brave, allowing him to coax her body to heights of pleasure that had seemed to catch her by surprise. He couldn't wait for another chance to see what else she hid under her reserved, quietly competent facade.

He finished up the dishes, listening as she moved through the kitchen and bathroom. She stacked a couple of hand towels on the counter, checked the water, and then moved the pot off the stove. "Almost ready," she told him.

He turned to watch her hang a broad strop from the pantry doorknob. It was leather with a canvas backing. He watched, confused, as she started to run the straight razor back and forth over the canvas side with a soft whisper of sound.

At Ian's curious look, she explained, "I'm just making certain it still has an edge. Have a seat."

"You don't have to do this," he told her as he sat down by the warm stove.

"It's no trouble."

He took a deep breath and told himself that she wouldn't be offering if she didn't know exactly what she was doing. She was self-confident enough to admit when she was out of her depth. He could trust her.

After a few more passes of the razor, this time over the leather side of the strop, she crossed back to the counter. She put down the razor so she could soak a towel in the pot of warm water. "Lean back. Or would you rather get the desk chair from the living room? That can't be comfortable."

"It's fine," he assured her, slouching down. He folded his hands in his lap and tipped his head back, waiting.

―――――

Cecily wrung out the towel, darting quick glances at Ian. He'd been tense when she'd first offered to shave him, but now he was relaxed and calm. The weight of his trust settled on her, giving her a moment's pause.

Determined to be careful, she draped the towel over his jaw and said, "Let that sit." She covered the towel gently with her palms, both to warm her fingers and to press the cloth against Ian's throat. She couldn't resist brushing her thumbs over his high cheekbones, aware of how odd it was that they hadn't even kissed this morning, after last night's intimacy.

Not that she could bring herself to kiss him now. Instead, she removed the towel, soaked it again, wrung it out, and replaced it. She felt as if she should say something, though she didn't know what. Then again, neither of them needed the silence filled with meaningless conversation and small talk, something Cecily appreciated. So she left the towel in place and poured some warm water into the tin cup of soap. She had to work the badger-bristle brush for a minute or two to finally get a lather.

She turned back to Ian and took the towel off his face. She draped it over the sink, and then touched his warm, damp cheek, feeling the stubble, turned a richer golden brown from the water. She told herself that the touch was just to ensure that his beard was soft enough to properly shave, but she knew that was just an excuse.

Ian smiled slightly, a bare uplifting of the corners of his mouth, and opened his eyes to look at her. "So far, so good," he murmured.

She smiled in response and looked down as she gave the brush one last swipe over the soap. "We're just getting started," she answered and began to brush the lather into his beard, hiding skin turned ruddy from the heat under a layer of whitish foam. Ian shivered under the touch, hands shifting restlessly on his thighs, and Cecily paused for a moment, arrested by the image of using the brush, dry and soft, over his entire body.

Finally, she put the brush aside and touched Ian's hair in warning. She opened the razor, saying, "Stay relaxed," as she set the blade at the edge of the foam high on his cheek. Smoothly, she drew it down, marking the subtle catch of the blade on the hairs. His breathing turned shallow but stayed slow, encouraging Cecily to continue. After she wiped the excess foam on a towel, she made a second stroke, just forward of the first.

Confident that Ian wasn't going to flinch and end up needing stitches, Cecily continued, losing herself in the concentration to keep from causing even the slightest injury or irritation. He was entirely pliant under her fingers, allowing her to tip his head or press a finger to his lips to hold the skin taut. The only time his breath actually hitched was when she touched his chin and pulled the razor down the underside of his jaw, but even then his hands stayed relaxed on his legs.

When Cecily finished, Ian went to sit forward. She touched his shoulder, and he froze. "Something wrong?" he asked, lifting a hand as if to check for blood.

"I'm not done."

"But—"

"Trust me," she said, remembering when he'd said those same words to her last night.

Ian met her eyes, and she knew he was remembering. He licked his lips and leaned back again, tension in his posture. It took a moment for Cecily to realize he really had no idea what she was doing.

She moved the towel from the sink to the pot of warm water. Then she touched Ian's face, stepping to the side of the chair to better meet his eyes.

"For a perfect shave, you do this two or three times," she explained, stroking her thumb down the line of Ian's jaw and then back up. The stubble was imperceptible compared to a safety razor or electric, but it was still there.

Ian smiled, tension melting away. "It's good enough. It's just dinner with Marguerite."

There was no reason to hesitate—no reason not to pick up the threads of last night's intimacy. So Cecily leaned down and pressed her lips to the path her thumb had just traced, and she listened to the way his breath stuttered. "She doesn't get to feel the difference. I want to do this, Ian."

"How the hell am I supposed to say no to that?" Ian asked breathily.

Cecily smiled.

—◆◆◆—

Every six weeks, like clockwork, Ian's personal assistant scheduled him for a visit to the salon she'd chosen. He'd been something of a local celebrity in Manhattan, and he'd had an image to maintain. But he'd never had anyone shave him—not when he could take care of his beard in five minutes with an electric razor or ten with a disposable.

Not content to shave him twice—once with the grain of his beard, once across it—Cecily insisted on three separate shaves, the last one against the grain over skin so smooth that the blade barely whispered.

After the third pass, Cecily carefully ran the wet cloth over Ian's face, leaning in close to study his skin. Her eyes were practically glowing with satisfaction, and the subtle smile tugging at the corner of her mouth made it worth all the fuss and effort and the ache that had settled in his back.

"Perfect," Cecily said, tossing the cloth aside. She set her fingertips to Ian's face and traced little circles over every inch that she'd shaved, making him shiver. Her fingertips were callused but illegally talented, and he found himself entirely content to sit in the damned uncomfortable wooden chair all day if it meant she would keep touching him.

A distant part of his mind wondered what had brought this on. Cecily didn't strike Ian as the intimate type. She hadn't wanted to sleep in his arms and hadn't offered a morning kiss, leaving him to wonder if last night had been a one-night anomaly. Now, though, he found himself rethinking that. Whatever brought on this moment of gentleness, he could get used to it.

Then, realizing his idle fantasies had strayed into dangerous territory, he muttered, "Thank you," and got up out of the chair, letting the burn in his back and neck distract him. He was in no position to think about things like "relationship" or "long-term" or anything at all beyond the end of winter, when the last of the aching emptiness of his addiction was under control. And then he'd go back to Manhattan and Cecily would stay here.

Best to look at this as a vacation, Ian reminded himself. Vacations ended, leaving fond memories to cling to when everyday life became too boring or stressful.

He avoided looking back at Cecily and instead went

into the bathroom to rinse away the last of the shaving foam. She kept a glass jar of moisturizer on the bathroom shelf, a natural blend made locally in Pinelake, or so she'd said. Ian opened the jar and used a finger to scoop out the thick lotion. He rubbed it between his palms and smoothed it over his face and neck, remembering the touch of her gentle, strong hands on his skin.

The door opened. "Ian, there's lotion—" Cecily cut off and met his eyes in the mirror, mouth quirking up in a faint smile. "You found it."

"Thank you," he said, and he didn't mean the moisturizer. "I never put in this much effort."

She pushed the door open the rest of the way and stepped closer. "You should."

He studied her in the mirror; firelight suited her better than electric. It brought out rich red-gold highlights in her hair and gave warmth to her pale, freckled skin. He permitted himself to stare, thinking of how Manhattan's electric night would turn her hair to deep mahogany, how she would glow under the bright Miami sunlight, how the midnight-blue ocean would bring out the rich green of her eyes.

She took another step as though drawn forward, lips parted, and it was as natural as breathing for him to turn and lift a hand to her soft cheek, tipping her face up to meet his kiss. The light touch of her lips was tentative and fragile, but he resisted the impulse to pull her close. He wanted this to be on her terms.

Chapter 9

October 28

IAN LAY ON THE SOFA, STARING UP AT THE BEAMS SUP-
porting the attic floor, idly running his fingers over his
jaw. Cecily's hands had been absolutely steady as she
held the razor. He thought back to the video and the
bloodstains on her uniform, and he pictured the scar on
her shoulder. He felt queasy thinking of how long she
had been held captive before her rescue.

Cecily had gone out fishing for tonight's dinner, an
activity Ian had no desire to share. To fend off the boredom that threatened, he rolled off the sofa and went to
the desk. He'd already checked his email, so he left the
power off and turned his attention instead to the typed
pages on the corner. She had made no effort to hide
them, so he didn't hesitate to pick up the stack, turn it
over, and start reading.

The fantasy novel was elegantly written but transparent, the plot devoid of complexities that would
alienate young readers. (Ian distinctly recalled his frustration with such simplistic plots in the early days of
school, when he'd been more interested in sports than
completing his homework, because school had been
tedious and unchallenging.)

At the bottom of the stack was the second book,
darker and more ominous in tone than the fantasy

novel. The story—less a proper manuscript and more
a very detailed summary with bullet point outlines and
notes—was set during the Cold War. The main character
was a U.S. Air Force pilot, not a Marine, but there were
similarities nonetheless. The pilot was shot down in
contested airspace north of Japan, captured, and handed
over to the KGB for interrogation. A few early pages,
labeled *REV2*, detailed a parallel plotline about a special
ops team being mobilized to rescue the main character
and had notes about a possible KGB traitor who would
help with the escape, but nothing had been done with
those story arcs.

Ian restored the pages to the stack and abandoned the
desk to think. He set up and tuned his guitar absently,
wondering if Cecily's writing was a good thing or not.
It was clear that her past experiences had left deep scars
on her psyche as well as her body, but writing seemed
just as pointless as group therapy. If she'd really been
trying to write this story for years and had only made it
to thirty-odd pages, clearly this form of therapy wasn't
working for her.

He lost himself in playing and thinking about Cecily
until he took a deep breath, and his nose caught a distinctly wet, fishy odor. He opened his eyes and saw that
she had returned at some point during his distracted
playing but had been too polite to interrupt.

"That was beautiful," she said from her seat at the desk.

Ian smiled and looked her over, noting the dark spots
of mud on her jeans and two fresh scratches on her right
hand. "You were successful."

"We won't starve," Cecily agreed, grinning. She rose,
looking even shorter in her socks; apparently she'd left

her waterproof boots elsewhere. "I'm going to have a shower. I didn't want the water heater rattling to interrupt your playing."

"I can scrub your back, if you'd like," Ian proposed, letting his voice go deep and inviting. He knew Cecily would refuse; what he didn't know was *how*.

She tensed, but not as much as she might have, if she were actually upset by the offer. "Thanks, but even I don't want to be in there with me at the moment," she said with a quick smile, wrinkling her nose.

As Cecily went into the bedroom, Ian sat back down and picked up his guitar. He idly ran his fingers over the strings, thinking. She had liked the idea enough to consider it, despite her deep-seated need to hide her scars. Slow steps, he decided, setting himself the private goal of seeing the full extent of her body by the end of the week—by her invitation.

———

The engine rumble of Marguerite's quad shattered the silence that filled the cabin, rousing Cecily from her doze. Ian was in the bedroom, probably locked away with a book or napping, so Cecily took it upon herself to go out front and greet her.

Mags pulled off her helmet and dismounted, grinning cheerfully. "Hi! Not too early, am I?" she asked, unhooking the bungee cords holding a bag to the back of the quad's seat.

"Not at all." Cecily jogged out into the cold and took the bag with one hand, giving Mags a hug with her free arm. "How was the trip?"

"Be careful. I saw this"—Mags tugged off a glove

with her teeth and stuck her bare hand into the pocket of her jeans, pulling out a thin bundle of cinnamon-brown fur—"on that stand of pines by the river, the one where I spotted the beavers that one time."

Cecily nodded, remembering the spot from photographs. "Black bear or grizzly?" she asked worriedly. Either one might have brown fur, contrary to the name, but their behavioral patterns were very different.

"I couldn't tell," Mags admitted.

"Want me to ride back with you tonight?" Cecily offered. No matter how enticing Ian's company was— assuming he was still interested—she didn't like the idea of taking chances with Marguerite's safety.

Mags gave a shy smile and shrugged, leading the way up the front steps to the cabin. Cecily knew Mags wanted to play brave and refuse, but she was sensible enough to instead say, "Maybe." They both knew Cecily was a much better shot than Mags.

Ian was out of the bedroom, now dressed in one of his suits from last week and a charming smile. "Good to see you again, Marguerite," he said, offering his hand.

"Oh, hi," she answered, clasping his hand as her cheeks went pink. She looked down at herself as she shrugged out of her parka, revealing a fleece sweatshirt and jeans. "Look at you. I feel all underdressed now," she told Ian.

Cecily put an arm around Marguerite's shoulders and stage-whispered, "I lied and told him we were going to a fancy dinner in Edmonton, just so he'd dress up." Mags laughed, and Ian's smile turned genuine, which Cecily counted as two small victories.

"Well, we can pretend," Mags said, gesturing to the bag

in Cecily's hands. She bent down to take off her boots. "I made a salad with the last of the fresh vegetables."

"I'll start dinner," Cecily said. She glanced at Ian's guitar, uncertain if he'd take offense at a request to play for Marguerite. He'd never precisely offered to play for Cecily; he'd just done it.

Before Cecily could think of what to say, Ian turned and strode away from them to go open the guitar case. "Do you like the classics, Marguerite?"

Her expression turned pleased. "Yes. You play? Really?" She circled around the couch and sat, looking adoringly up at Ian. Cecily couldn't blame her.

"I do." Ian must have been planning this, because he didn't bother to tune the strings. He just ducked under the guitar strap. Grinning, Cecily leaned against the kitchen archway, watching as he touched the strings, playing a flourish of notes that sounded almost like classical Spanish guitar, until he broke into a familiar song.

"I know that one!" Cecily exclaimed, recognizing the first notes of "Limelight" by Rush. Then she snapped her mouth shut, giving Ian a silent, apologetic smile. He ignored the interruption and kept playing, though she saw the subtle tension in his body as he tried not to laugh aloud.

Relieved that the afternoon had started out so well, Cecily took the salad into the kitchen and got started on dinner, listening as Ian played through the highlights of Rush, The Smiths, and The Cure, finishing with Queen by the time the pan-fried trout was ready.

⁓

Growing up, Ian had developed a reputation for being terrible company at the dinner table. He hated family dinners with awful food and even worse conversation. As the eldest of the three siblings, Preston had taken his role seriously and learned to deal with the adults at a young age. Ian had gone the other way, after learning that sulking and mouthing off would get him exiled from the table. All he needed to do was to strategically time his bad behavior to happen after he'd eaten enough to satisfy his hunger—and reconnoitering the kitchen to see what the night's dessert was.

Somewhere along the line, though, they'd switched roles. Preston had adopted Ian's abrasive, aggressive demeanor, and Ian had learned how to smoothly join and even control a conversation. It had surprised more than one relative or family friend who only visited occasionally, though it shouldn't have. Ian was a Fairchild; he hadn't been raised by wolves, after all.

Once Ian had joined Manhattan society, he'd learned that charm was as much a weapon as it was a lure. Now, he had no qualms at all about enchanting both women. All through dinner, he engaged Marguerite in conversation and subtly drew Cecily back any time she grew too quiet.

The close quarters helped. The table in the kitchen was built for two, and Cecily brought the desk chair in from the living room for herself. Their proximity meant that they were all bumping feet and knees under the table, so Ian had the perfect excuse to press his leg against hers. The touch seemed to soothe her.

It also helped that Marguerite wasn't tediously boring. Granted, compared to Ian's clients and business associates, she was easy to read, without a hint of deception in her personality. She also proved to be intelligent, especially when Ian asked questions about her field of expertise. He didn't know a damned thing about the ecosystems of northern wilderness rivers, but he'd been a fairly good science student and could figure out what questions to ask.

The trout proved to be surprisingly good. When they finished the last few scraps, Cecily asked, "Coffee and dessert?"

"Dessert?" Marguerite gave her a surprised smile. "Did you two figure out how to use the oven for baking?"

Ian waved a hand in Cecily's direction. "This is all Cecily's idea."

"Wonderful disclaimer there, thanks," Cecily drawled, rolling her chair back from the table. She flashed Ian a quick grin. "For that, you get to clear the table while I set up the living room."

"I'll help," Marguerite offered at once, despite being a guest. Then again, Cecily had done the washing-up at Marguerite's house, so perhaps this was customary between them.

Having someone to assist with the washing and drying cut the time substantially, but Ian missed his dishwasher—and his maid service—all the same. When they finished most of the dishes, he suggested, "Why don't you make coffee while I finish the pans?"

"Okay. No soap," Marguerite warned as she went to the pantry.

Ian laughed and poured a bit of coarse salt into the cast iron skillet. "I learned that the hard way," he admitted, scrubbing the salt in the seasoned pan to loosen up any burnt-on bits of trout. Cecily had stopped him from pouring soap into the pan and explained that soap would destroy the seasoning. He cleaned and dried the pan, and then went out to the living room.

Cecily was sitting on the floor by the hearth, surrounded by bags and boxes and partially unwrapped chocolate bars. She beckoned for Ian to join her and ripped open the first plastic bag. "You have roasted marshmallows, haven't you?"

"Intentionally or because I lit something else on fire?" he asked a bit evasively as he sat beside Cecily, careful not to crowd her. His back twinged, and he took the bottle of ibuprofen out of his jacket pocket.

She glanced at the bottle, a little frown creasing her brow. Then she looked up at Ian suspiciously and said, "There's a story there."

"It wasn't *my* dorm," he protested innocently. He shook out two ibuprofen, quickly pocketed the bottle, and then swallowed the pills.

Cecily grinned. "Now I have to hear it, some time. But first, here." She took a marshmallow from the bag and impaled it on a long metal skewer. "Hold this in the fire. Not too close—you want it melted and a little crispy, but not solid black, unless that's what you like."

"This is more like science than cooking," he said, thinking that this was definitely more appealing than his teenage nights of shivering around an insufficient campfire, watching marshmallows fall off crooked sticks.

Cecily shifted unnecessarily closer and reached for one of the chocolate bars. "Feel free to experiment," she said quietly, and judging by her inviting smile, she was no longer talking about dessert.

Ian met her eyes and hid a triumphant grin when he

saw nothing but interest there—no wariness or reticence at all. He lifted a hand to Cecily's face, tracing his thumb over the path where he'd set a line of kisses last night, and her eyes closed in obvious memory. He pressed a finger over the pulse in her throat, marking the rapid acceleration with satisfaction.

"If you have any suggestions on where you'd like me to start…" Ian hinted quietly, leaning closer to replace the finger on her pulse with his lips.

Cecily's hand slid over his leg, fingers tightening. "Ian," she protested tightly. "Marguerite's right—"

"Making coffee," he interrupted, though Cecily's protest didn't go silent until Ian nipped her throat, making her gasp. "But there's no need to rush," he lied, leaning closer so he could brush his lips over her ear. "We have time for any experiments you'd like to try."

Cecily's soft curse was lost under a delicate cough from the kitchen, followed by Marguerite saying, "Uh, fire."

Cecily jerked away from Ian, face flushed with embarrassment. Then she laughed a bit raggedly and gestured to the fireplace, where the marshmallow had reached critical temperature and was now blazing.

Ian laughed and tried to sound at least a little serious as he said, "It's nouvelle cuisine. Marshmallows flambées." Before he could say anything more, the marshmallow finally lost all structural integrity, liquefied, and splashed into the flames.

Smiling, Cecily leaned over and took the skewer out of his hand. She gave him a soft kiss on the cheek and said, "Let's stick with s'mores."

—ᴡᴡ—

From a practical standpoint, s'mores had been a successful choice for dessert—the perfect solution for the limitations imposed by Cecily's absolute lack of ability to use a wood-burning oven for anything but lighting things on fire. In fact, she was already planning on going back to Pinelake at least once more before the snow got too heavy in hopes that the store had restocked, just so she could buy out every marshmallow and chocolate bar. She looked forward to watching Ian lick his fingers clean every damned night.

But as the sky darkened and Marguerite hinted at leaving, Cecily's protective side reared its head. Leaving them to talk, Cecily snuck off to the bedroom, where she unbuckled her belt and removed her holstered .45. She'd need to change to a weapon with more firepower, just in case they did meet up with a bear. She knelt down and unlocked the safe.

Ian stepped through the doorway. "Something going on?"

"Taking Marguerite back. She found signs of a bear on the way up here. It's probably safe, but I'd rather not take any chances." She looked back, letting her eyes rove over Ian's body. God, he was gorgeous in his suit—and out of it. She'd been looking forward to undoing every single button, one at a time. "You should stay here."

"Don't be ridiculous," Ian countered. He closed the bedroom door and shrugged out of his jacket, then tossed it onto the foot of the bed.

"It's safer," Cecily insisted, turning back to the selection of guns. She had a Kimber 8400 classic bolt-action rifle for big game hunting. Loaded with 160 grain .270 Winchester rounds, it would be sufficient to take down a bear. She loaded three rounds and pocketed another three. Then she set the rifle on the bed, muzzle safely facing away from Ian.

When she glanced up at him just in time to see him step out of his slacks, she couldn't help but stare. He wore nothing but black silk boxers that made Cecily want to forget about everything but petting him, contrasting the feel of silk with skin.

"You're too damned distracting," she accused, finally forcing herself to turn back around.

Ian's laugh was low and knowing, and it took all of Cecily's self-control to ignore it. She took out the old .44 Magnum revolver and gave it a quick check, even though she knew all of her weapons in the safe were clean and ready to go. She hated the Magnum's recoil but had fired it enough to be confident that she could hit a close-up target, which was all that mattered tonight. She wasn't hunting a bear; she was just trying to keep everyone safe.

"Really, Ian, you can stay. I know the quad hurts your back," she said as she found a box of bullets for the Magnum.

"I'm not an invalid," he snapped with abrupt heat in his voice.

Startled, she looked up to see him frowning down at her, wearing only blue jeans. She couldn't help but let her eyes roam over sleek, tight muscles. "I know," she said truthfully. "But you're always taking those pills—"

"They're over-the-counter." He turned his back, showing faint, careful surgical scars, such a contrast to the ragged, unattractive marks of war on Cecily's body. She turned her attention back to the safe, not wanting to

have this conversation. He was constantly taking ibuprofen, and over-the-counter or not it couldn't be healthy.
But it also wasn't her business. Instead, she concentrated
on loading high-power bullets into the Magnum before
she slipped it into a holster. She stood up to thread it into
her belt; the weight difference was immediately apparent. She drew it a couple of times to remind her muscles
of the change from her usual .45.

"Marguerite could stay here tonight," Ian said gently.
It sounded like a peace offering or an apology, and Cecily
seized on it, wanting to get past the awkward moment.

"We'll be fine," she said, looking over at him. While
her back had been turned, he'd put on a hoodie, hopefully over thermals and not just a T-shirt. She picked up
the rifle.

"I take it this isn't excessive?" he asked, eyeing the
firearms.

"Anything less will get it angry. As I said, it's probably safe, but best not to take chances." She headed for
the bedroom door.

Ian intercepted her with a smile, hands catching her
around the waist. "Are you always this protective?"

She looked up at him and nodded honestly. "For as
long as I can remember," she admitted. "I'm sorry—"

"Don't," he interrupted and leaned down to brush his
lips across hers, a light touch that made her lips tingle.
"I think it's wonderful. She's lucky to have a friend
like you."

Cecily felt her cheeks go hot. She looked down and
shrugged, embarrassed.

Then Ian touched her chin to tip her face back up.
When their eyes met, he said quietly, "And so am I."

Chapter 10

October 28

"WELL, THAT WAS A COMPLETE WASTE OF THREE hours," Ian said acidly as he dismounted gracelessly from the quad Cecily pulled right up to the front of the cabin.

"You didn't have to come," she growled back, fumbling the key out of the ignition. She left the quad where it was, too cold and irritated to give a damn about stowing it safely away. She'd deal with it tomorrow, assuming the storm didn't bury it, in which case she'd just shovel the damned thing out in the spring and scrap it.

Ian actually had the audacity to accuse, "There was no bear." He banged the cabin door open and went right for the fireplace.

As if Cecily could make a bear appear on demand? She followed Ian inside, stamping snow off her boots. The cabin was almost as freezing as the outside air. As always, she had banked the fires on the way out. She left the rifle by the door—it would need to be dried and oiled before she put it away.

She went to the hearth, saying, "I'll do that."

"I have it!" he snapped back. "I know how to build a damned fire!"

Cecily resisted the urge to smack the back of his head and remind him that he was the one who'd wanted to spend three hours on the back of a bouncing quad in the freezing-cold snow. Instead, she dragged herself to the kitchen. The woodstove heated more efficiently than the fireplaces, so the kitchen would warm up quickly, and she wanted to get a hot drink into both of them. A few years ago, she'd picked up a box of herbal tea meant to fight insomnia. It tasted like shit and had done nothing to help with her sleeping problems (which were far from ordinary insomnia), but it might calm Ian's temper.

As soon as she had the fire built and the kettle heating, she went into the bathroom and started the shower. "Ian! Get in here!" she shouted. Because the pipe from the water heater was only a couple of yards long, the bathroom almost immediately began filling with steam. She breathed deeply, letting it burn through the ice clogging her lungs.

Stubbornly remaining in the living room, he shouted, "I'm perfectly capable of—"

"I know!" Cecily interrupted sharply, leaning against the sink. She pressed her hands to her eyes, thinking this was a fine time for Ian to become a complete asshole. *Lawyers*. "Just get in here."

He stormed in a moment later, tall and furious, sharp eyes glaring, pale cheeks flagged with color. It would have been imposing if not for the snow-damp hair that hung in his eyes, waterlogged from light gold to brown. His glare softened into suspicion when he glanced at the tiny shower stall.

"Get in there before you actually do die and I'm stuck with your corpse for the winter," Cecily told him. "Pinelake doesn't have a mortician."

Ian frowned as though puzzled. "You should shower first. Your shoulder's too stiff for over-the-counter pain-killers to help much."

Startled by the consideration, Cecily resisted the urge to touch the old scar. It *was* aching, but she thought she'd hid it well. "I'm fine," she lied, gesturing toward the shower. "Just don't use up all the hot water."

"You need it more than I do."

"Which is why you should get your ass in there and stop wasting it. God, are you *always* this stubborn?" Cecily muttered, trying to push past Ian so she could go build up the bedroom fire.

He caught her arm, making her tense warily, but all he did was study her face intently. Slowly, Ian's fingers uncurled, releasing her. He turned away, apparently satisfied with whatever he saw.

"The Tuckers."

Baffled, Cecily asked, "What?"

"Taxidermists. Almost the same skill set as morticians."

She stared at the pale line of skin at the back of Ian's neck. Droplets of melting snow were slithering down his nape, disappearing into the collar of his shirt. The last of her irritation vanished under the desire to taste those drops as his words finally registered in her brain.

She snorted out a laugh and forced herself to turn away. "There's a gruesome thought."

"Impractical, too. Though you're welcome to keep my skull. Didn't they do that sort of thing in the Victorian era?"

Cecily laughed. "Gruesome, but romantic," she said, charmed despite herself.

Ian's laugh sounded pleasantly surprised.

Ian pulled his knees to his chest and wrapped himself in the blanket taken from Cecily's bed. He should have felt ridiculous in all his unwieldy layers of clothes, including three pairs of socks, but he still felt cold, and that *never* happened to him. Before the surgery and addiction, he'd been able to ignore cold or fatigue or hunger or any other discomfort his body imposed on him. Now, he'd apparently lost the knack. Despite the hot shower and the fire and the way he'd pushed the sofa right up to the hearth, he was still freezing.

And the cold had apparently reduced his inhibitions to nothing. What the hell was he thinking, suggesting something so grisly, so *serial killer* as he had?

But Cecily's response was equally as puzzling. She'd *laughed*. She hadn't reacted with disgust or disdain or even a hint of fear at what was, in retrospect, a blatantly sociopathic statement. Then again, police, like soldiers, tended to develop certain defense mechanisms, gallows humor being the most common. She should have adapted her behavior back to civilian standards when she'd reintegrated, but she hadn't. Ian was glad of that. "Normal" was even more boring than nearly freezing to death—as he knew all too well, having experienced both.

Cecily's showers normally lasted just under four minutes. This one took six, and it was another five before she came out to the living room.

"Still cold?" she asked.

Ian nodded, turning to look at Cecily. "I hate Canada." Instead of taking offense, she smiled at him. "I assume you didn't make coffee or tea. Which would you prefer?"

"Tea," he said a bit plaintively.

Cecily left him to his misery, returning a few minutes later with tea that smelled like decomposing plant matter. "We're now out of milk," she said as she climbed over the arm of the sofa and sat down opposite Ian. Leaning over, she set both cups of tea on the hearth and tugged her fleece blanket off the back of the sofa so she could wrap up warmly. Like him, she was dressed in layers, though perhaps not so extremely.

After a few minutes of staring at the fire, Cecily said, "I'm sorry. I should have been more clear about going out in this kind of weather."

Ian huffed in irritation. "You didn't even anticipate it. You were no more prepared than I was."

"Well, no," Cecily said, frowning, "but it's more than just wearing snow—"

"Or *did you*?" Ian asked as new connections sparked deep in his brain. "You take precautions, but minimally. Your whole lifestyle is centered around *personal risk*. You brought a rifle and backup handgun to deal with the possibility of a bear attack—to keep Marguerite safe—but you didn't bother to dress for what you surely recognized as the possibility of a snowstorm. And now you're apologizing to me because your risk didn't involve only you."

Taken aback, Cecily went silent. Her face, usually so open and expressive, became a blank mask.

Ian twisted on the sofa, tucking one leg under the other, and leaned forward, studying Cecily's face. Firelight and shadow changed the shape of her cheeks and eyes and jaw, darkening her green eyes to a shade closer to emerald.

"Tell me something," he said quietly. His thoughts were soaring now the way they did in court, when he picked apart his opponent's argument point by point. He was high on the exhilaration of watching the pieces of a mystery come together, giving him another facet of the puzzle that was Cecily Knight. But this time, his high was tempered with the realization of a truth she was probably hiding from herself.

"What?" Cecily asked tightly, still staring at the fire.

"If you had been alone, would you have carried your usual handgun instead?"

The last day of December. Seven years ago. Cecily could still remember that first day, the first year, how often she'd forgotten something critical. Food supplies. Firewood. Clean, warm socks. She'd risked injury and nearly died a hundred times that winter, and every time, she'd faced her trial with a stoic sense of calm. She'd never thought about it or psychoanalyzed it, because she'd been too busy trying not to get herself killed.

She didn't want to think about what Ian was saying. She didn't want to follow his thoughts to their ultimate conclusion. She wasn't a complete idiot; she could see where this was all leading.

"I'm not suicidal, if that's what you're implying," she said, as coldly as she could manage, and she threw in a glare for good measure. Then she picked up her mug, cupping her hands around the warmth, though she didn't take a sip.

Rather than looking properly apologetic, Ian smirked. "No. You just face ever-escalating risks and don't care if the price of failure is your life."

"Stop." Cecily snapped out the command and turned away, unable to meet his eyes. "Just stop it, Ian. I'm not being cross-examined by you. You have no right to go digging around in how I think."

"Someone has to. Seven years, Cecily. *Seven years*," Ian said relentlessly. "You're still hiding in the middle of nowhere, turning meaningless danger into a game and challenging death to win because you know that one day, it must."

"So?" The word came out as a shout. Cecily put her mug down on the stone hearth so she wouldn't give in to the temptation to throw it. Anger raged through her, burning along her veins in an irrational blaze that she had to control.

She breathed deeply, eyes closed, and listened to her heart pounding in her ears. Refusing to think about Ian's words, she focused instead on her body: the crude support of the old sofa cushion over the hard wooden frame, the contrast between the cold air at the back of her neck and the fire's warmth on her face and fingers, the smell of the smoke and the clean snap of wood.

Slowly, she calmed down. Ian had been speaking, but Cecily hadn't heard a single word. She took another breath, falling through the last, lingering anger to the other side, where everything inside her was cold and deathly still. "Are you staying up?"

Ian's frown turned puzzled. "Yes."

"Fine." Cecily untangled herself from the blanket and rose, climbing back over the arm of the sofa. She

threw the blanket over her shoulder and went into the
bedroom, closing the door to keep in the heat. It took
two minutes to bank the fire for warmth and darkness.
She put the gun on her nightstand, took off her belt and
holster, and dropped them on the floor beside the bed.
Then she climbed onto the mattress and dragged the
blanket over herself. She didn't want the damned herbal
tea anyway.

Ian leaned back, staring at the wall over the fireplace.
At first, he couldn't decipher Cecily's reaction. He was
correct about her motives—of course he was—and he
was accustomed to hostile reactions, usually from witnesses. But Cecily had gone from anger to hostility to…
something else, something he couldn't readily identify.
And then she'd left, going to the bed where he had been
sleeping for the past week. Was that an invitation or
simply a practical reaction to Ian remaining on the sofa?

He rearranged the blanket more comfortably and
looked down at the fire, mentally replaying every word
and nuance of their conversation. On the surface, her
actions seemed reasonable, but not when scrutinized.
Tonight, the easy solution would have been to invite
Marguerite to stay at the cabin. Then they could have es-
corted her home tomorrow, in daylight. Instead, Cecily
had risked an accident and the weather, as well as a
potential encounter with a bear. If she were genuinely
interested in *avoiding* the risk, she simply would have
stayed at home.

Ian closed his eyes, thinking of the criminal world
of Manhattan, of how he often had to venture into the

city's underbelly to ferret out truths about his clients, both guilty and innocent. That was part of his appeal as a lawyer; he still did much of his own investigative work, which was how he'd ended up getting attacked and injured in the first place.

A normal girlfriend would tell Ian he was insane for living the life he did. But Cecily was hardly "normal." Now, he just had to figure out if he had a chance of convincing her to go from friend to girlfriend.

———

Even before Cecily was fully awake, she rolled off the bed, dropped to one knee, and braced the surprisingly heavy weapon on the mattress, muzzle aimed directly at the open door. Her trigger finger trembled as she was caught between the conflicting urges to identify her target first or shoot blindly, and for painfully long seconds she had no idea where she was. The darkness and fire and smell of smoke disoriented her more than her sudden awakening did.

"I'd rather you not shoot me."

Silky baritone, full of dry wit. Cecily exhaled and dropped her face to the bed as her fingers relaxed, letting the gun rest safely on the blankets. "Fuck," she muttered, trembling with the jolt of adrenaline coursing through her veins. She didn't think she could stand, so she sat down on the floor, resting her right arm on the bed. "Are you trying to get yourself killed?"

"You didn't shoot," Ian said, as if the end result was all that mattered. Cecily heard him cross the room and felt the other side of the mattress dip under his weight. Fabric rustled loudly—one of the blankets. Air moved in a soft breeze against her arm and face as Ian shook out the blanket.

"Right. Want the bed back?" she asked, leaning on the mattress for balance as she stood.

"Stay."

"No." Cecily moved her gun out from under the second blanket, hands still shaking.

"Cecily, *stay*."

"Which part of 'no' did you miss?"

Ian sighed dramatically. "You're not going to hurt me, and I'm not going to hurt you."

She gritted her teeth. "I don't sleep near other people." She stripped her blanket off the bed—or tried to. Ian was holding the other end.

"Stay," he repeated. This time, he added, "Please."

Forced to either give up or put down the gun and get into a schoolyard fight over a blanket, Cecily let go and stepped back from the bed. The cool bedroom air had her starting to shiver already. "I'm sorry, Ian, but I'm really not interested in sex right now," she said bluntly. Silently, she berated herself for not keeping extra blankets on hand. She had a sleeping bag rolled up in the basement, but she had no energy to go down there and get it.

Ian laughed in amusement. "I turn down most clients because their cases are too boring. Police cases, too. I did cold cases as a hobby during law school."

"What the hell are you talking about?" Cecily asked, giving her blanket an experimental tug. Either Ian was still holding it or he'd rolled on top of it. Of all the times to revert to being a five-year-old, apparently he had to pick *now*.

"My work, Cecily," Ian said as if that should be obvious. "When I was new, I had to take the boring cases—DUI, assault, theft... Things any half-competent law clerk could do."

Cecily shoved the gun into the back of her jeans, pinning it temporarily in her waistband. It was ridiculously unsafe, but at the moment, she didn't care. "So?" she asked, folding her arms as if she could trap her body heat.

"I defended an accused serial killer three years ago. Only five victims, so the police didn't have much to work on. Circumstantial evidence. The killer electrocuted them. Did a good job making it look accidental, too."

Cecily went cold, flashes of memory—of the war—shattering her composure. She sat down, landing on the edge of the bed by sheer luck. Her arms tensed, pressing against her body, fists clenching against her ribs.

"The detective investigating the last death needed a conviction. As it turned out, the killer had stolen uniforms from my client's service truck two years before, and that's where their DNA evidence came from."

Faced with the choice of listening to Ian's odd story or venturing into her own nightmares, Cecily clung desperately to his voice. She told herself to breathe, steady and deep, and tried not to count her too-rapid heartbeats. She didn't feel cold anymore, but that was an illusion. She knew she should get under a blanket. She just didn't want to move.

"The real killer wasn't in some run-down tenement or abandoned warehouse. Movies are hardly an accurate representation of reality," Ian scoffed. "He lived with his wife in an apartment in midtown. Worked at a bank. When the police wouldn't listen to my evidence, I went to his apartment and confronted him."

Slowly, the foolishness of Ian's actions worked its way through the jagged thoughts scraping at Cecily's brain. "That's incredibly stupid. You went alone, I take it?"

"The idiot detective had no interest in accompanying me, so yes." He huffed as if irritated. "My mistake was dismissing the wife. She stabbed me with a fork."

"*What?*" Cecily twisted around to stare at Ian in the darkness. The motion tightened the waistband of her jeans, forcing the gun to dig uncomfortably against her spine.

Propping himself up on one elbow to face Cecily, Ian shrugged. "It happens. After I disarmed her, I called in a detective who wasn't so obsessed with fame as to blind himself to reality, and that's one less serial killer on the streets."

"Were they working together?"

"No. She was apparently afraid of losing her husband's pension if he went to prison."

Cecily couldn't help but laugh. It was terrible, because Ian was talking about a serial killer and an insanely devoted (and greedy) wife and an incident in which he'd ended up stabbed, but once the laughter started, she couldn't stop.

"So tell me," Ian continued, reaching out to touch Cecily's hip, "why should I let you go back to the couch?"

"What does that have to do—"

Ian shifted closer, sliding his hand down to curve over Cecily's thigh. "You won't hurt me."

"It's not…" Cecily hesitated, shaking her head. "It's not just that, Ian. You saw how I woke up. It's dangerous. It's not—"

"Don't say 'normal,'" Ian interrupted quietly. He sat up so he could move closer, pushing the blankets aside. "If I wanted normal, I would have followed my family's very successful, very boring traditions instead of going into criminal law."

Cecily closed her eyes and raked a hand through her hair. She supposed she should take offense at the thought that the only person who was actually stupid enough to want to spend an entire night with her, nightmares and all, was most likely clinically insane, but "normal" held little appeal for her, too. Logically, she knew she should get up and leave the room, even if it meant shivering sleeplessly through the night until Ian relented and surrendered a blanket, but logic had nothing to do with the emptiness inside her. She'd never meant to be alone.

Ian moved even closer, drawing his hand up from Cecily's thigh to her abdomen, resting right over another patch of scar tissue that he hadn't yet seen. She flinched, but he made no effort to get under her shirt.

"You don't have to talk about your scars."

"Fuck." Cecily gasped, flinching violently this time. How the hell could he know what she was thinking? "Ian—"

"I already know."

Through clenched teeth, Cecily accused, "Your brother told—"

"Told me nothing," he interrupted. He closed the distance between them again and touched her face as if to hold her still. "I saw enough, Cecily. I know you."

"Ian—"

"And I'm still here."

Cecily closed her mouth, turning away from Ian, though the motion pressed her face against his palm. His hand was warm and steady, holding her without trapping her.

"That's just one more indication that you're probably crazy," she managed to say, her voice distant and faint.

"So?"

Cecily laughed and nodded tightly. She pulled the gun out of her waistband and put it on the nightstand, finally feeling the cold. Shivering, she pushed back into Ian, saying, "Back up. You're hogging the bed."

"We'll be warmer if we share blankets," he suggested.

Cecily hesitated. "Ian…"

In answer, he moved back, mattress shifting as he settled down on the far side of the bed. "Tomorrow night, then."

"I didn't picture you as an optimist."

"Realist," Ian corrected. "Go to sleep. You're awful company if you don't get at least four hours."

"Thanks," Cecily muttered, pulling her blanket up and trying to tell herself that Ian was right about sharing warmth. She curled up at the very edge of the bed and stared into the darkness, wondering if she'd be able to fall asleep listening to the sound of someone else's slow breathing.

———

Cecily moved in her sleep, sprawling over the bed one limb at a time until she seemed to achieve an impossible state by all laws of physics and anatomy, occupying far more of the mattress than a woman of her stature possibly could. Ian had awakened each time a hand or foot had invaded his side of the bed, determined that Cecily was restfully sleeping, and retreated until he was at the very edge of the king-sized mattress.

This time, though, when her movements woke him, he immediately identified the difference between those previous movements and a nightmare.

Without full disclosure of Cecily's past experiences, thoughts, and feelings, Ian couldn't be entirely certain that she suffered from post-traumatic stress disorder. The professionals couldn't agree if PTSD existed or if it should have a different name. They couldn't even agree on a course of treatment. Still, Ian had a vested interest in knowing as much as he could about it, given his family's tradition of military service. And because of that knowledge, he was prepared to handle the abrupt onset of her nightmare.

She didn't scream of thrash or even speak. Instead, she went quiet and tense, body moving in minute twitches, reminding Ian of watching the guard dogs dreaming in a pile on the kennel floor. He couldn't have been more than five when he'd asked Preston why the dogs' feet were moving, and Preston, twelve years old and pompous with unearned wisdom, had given some platitude about chasing rabbits. He'd been entirely unprepared for Ian's demands to explain the difference between dog and human consciousness and to explain how dogs could dream if they were "only animals."

Without a proper bedside light, Ian had to depend on his cell phone. He knew better than to try and wake her while still in arm's reach. He guessed that Cecily would perceive any attempt at stealth as a threat, so he moved off the bed quietly but naturally, picked up his cell phone from the nightstand (where it served as nothing more than a clock), and stepped back.

He powered the device up and turned it, playing the glow of the start-up screen over Cecily. The blankets covered her from the neck down, magnifying every little twitch of her hands and feet into wavelike motions of fabric. Behind her closed lids, her eyes were moving rapidly and her jaw was clenched. Her pulse and respiration were accelerated.

Definitely a nightmare.

Ian couldn't gauge if it was a particularly bad nightmare, but it was best not to take any chances—not for his own safety but for Cecily's peace of mind. Shivering in the cold, he moved to the foot of the bed and held his mobile in one hand, pointed upward to illuminate both himself and the rest of the room as best he could.

"Cecily," he said, his voice calm and pitched low but firm. He waited a few seconds before repeating her name two more times.

The fact that she didn't immediately awaken and grab for her weapon felt like an accomplishment. Subconsciously at least she might well have recognized Ian's voice and categorized him as safe.

Cautiously, he said, "Cecily, wake up," as he reached down to touch the top of her foot.

Immediately, her body coiled in on itself. She twisted and sat up. The blanket went flying as she reached out with both arms, a quick motion to assess her surroundings. Then she started to reach for the weapon on her side of the bed, but her hand never made it that far. She stopped as her fingers crossed the edge of the mattress; she stared up at Ian, panting to catch her breath.

"Ian?" she asked, her voice soft and very tight, almost a whisper.

In answer, he pressed and held the power button on his cell phone. "Go back to sleep," he said, determined to treat the situation as nothing out of the ordinary. He crawled up the bed, tossed the BlackBerry on the table, and then tried to sort out his blankets.

"What—" Cecily began, still sitting up. "Are you all right?"

"Fine, though I have no idea how someone your height can take up even more space than me," he accused, mostly to divert Cecily's mind from any lingering trace of the nightmare.

She didn't immediately answer. She moved gracelessly back down the bed and thrashed under her blankets to get herself sorted. Only when she was lying down, blankets pulled up over her body, did she roll onto her right side to face Ian. "I had a nightmare," she said.

Ian bit back his response: *Obviously*.

After a few silent seconds ticked by, Cecily asked, "Did I hurt you?"

"No."

Cecily's exhale was shaky. "That's good. I didn't... say anything, did I?"

Ian moved a bit closer, shifting his pillow. "No. You barely even moved."

He couldn't see Cecily's frown, but he could hear it in her tone of voice as she asked, "Then why did you wake me? Did I take up that much of the bed?"

Ian laughed softly. "Yes, but that's not why. Consensus

is that it's best to wake someone from a nightmare. Did it help?"

"Hell if I know. Night always seems to last forever. Even if I shake off the nightmares, it's like I'm still half-asleep." She moved then, reaching out to find Ian's arm with her fingertips. "Thanks."

He resisted the urge to take Cecily's hand and instead pressed into the touch, taking it as an unspoken invitation to move closer. "If this were group therapy, I'd be expected to ask you how you feel," he said, unable to hide the distaste in his voice.

"God. Don't," Cecily said, sounding equally repulsed. "If you want to stay awake, there are far better things we can do than *talk*. Or I can just go out into the living room and let you sleep."

"Sleep *is* a waste of time," Ian agreed, trailing his fingers along the underside of Cecily's forearm, though she was still wearing her long-sleeved shirt and jeans. She shivered and made a pleased little sound. Encouraged, Ian hinted, "You're wearing too much for anything but talk, though."

Cecily laughed. "Let me build up the fire. You deal with the mess we've made of the blankets."

Ian sighed and reached for his cell phone to turn it back on for light. "Cecily..." he began as an idea struck him.

"Hm?"

"When you told my brother I could stay with you this winter, did either of you specify *where*?"

"Well, no..." Cecily hesitated. "Did you want to leave?"

"How would you like to see Ibiza?" he asked, surprising her with the odd question.

She said nothing as she worked on building up the fire. Slowly, light filled that corner of the room, throwing long shadows everywhere. She rose, surrounded by an aura of red-gold light that brought out bright highlights in her night-dark hair. Her back was turned, arms crossed, hands rubbing over her biceps.

"Afraid you'll have to do that one on your own. I told him you could stay here, but you're not a prisoner. If you want to go—"

Startled by the change in her tone, Ian interrupted, "Cecily. I'm not going anywhere without you. If you'd rather stay, we'll stay. Going somewhere warmer would let us take off our clothes without worrying about freezing to death, that's all."

She took a deep breath and rolled her shoulders as though telling herself to relax. "Is that your way of saying sex with me is boring?" she asked, turning enough for Ian to see her profile. Though the words were delivered deadpan, he caught a hint of amusement—or at least a lack of anger—in her half-glimpsed expression.

He forced his sleepy, dull mind to work faster. "Freezing to death before we even get to the sex is definitely boring."

Cecily laughed and broke away from the fireplace, crossing to the bathroom. "Then sort out the blankets, lazy bastard," she said, her voice light and full of the humor she'd been hiding. "And go break into your stash. We have a lot of condoms to get through before spring."

The bathroom door shut firmly, and Ian laughed, satisfaction warming him more than the blankets. He knew better than to suggest they go anywhere crowded—and Ibiza was nothing if not crowded—but Cecily hadn't taken offense at his slip. Instead, she'd pushed past any sense of embarrassment and discomfort to make a far more clever joke of her own.

Cecily was resilient. That was how she'd survived for this long, even if she hadn't healed from the trauma of her experience. And that deep, solid foundation of inner strength was all Ian needed to help her recover.

Chapter 11

October 28

STANDING IN THE BATHROOM, CECILY SPLASHED WATER over her face and tried to push away the surreal feeling that had crept over her. Her nightmares were nothing new. Fragments of imagery clung to her day and night, and she never went twenty-four hours without waking in a cold sweat at least once. When Ian had stubbornly insisted on sharing the bed for sleep, she had expected this. Feared it. And now that it had happened...

Nothing.

Ian had safely pulled Cecily out of the nightmare. She didn't miss the fact that he had awakened her from the other side of the room, intentionally visible and recognizable in the light of his cell phone. And then he'd treated the whole incident as nothing remarkable. No awkward questions, no demands that she share her fears, no crushing insistence on cuddling or any physical contact at all, in fact. He hadn't even commented on her reaction to his travel invitation, though he had to know it wasn't *normal* for a grown woman to avoid other people the way Cecily did.

This could work, whispered the little voice in the back of her mind, the voice that had been silent for seven years.

Hope felt alien to her, but in a good way. She didn't

try to hide from it. Instead, she allowed herself to ac-knowledge that Ian might be just as strange as Cecily was, in his own way. And he might be just what she...if not needed, then at least *wanted*.

She went back into the bedroom and found Ian under both blankets, pillows stacked under his head. His bared arms were visible, hands tucked behind his neck, his posture lazy and casual. His pajamas were draped over the side of the bed. Deliberately, he'd placed a zigzag fan of condoms on the corner of the mattress, where Cecily wouldn't miss them.

"Not bored already, are you?" she asked as she pulled off her heavy sweatshirt.

Ian's eyes dropped to watch Cecily's fingers, and his lips curled up in a sly, satisfied smile. The subdued firelight brought out gold highlights in his hair, now that it had dried from the melting snow. He wasn't wearing his glasses, and his blue-gray eyes seemed darker. "Not anymore."

Cecily's heart started to pound at the look of obvious desire on Ian's face. She had to turn away. She hadn't been self-conscious about getting undressed in front of someone for years. High school locker rooms, univer-sity, the Marines... Any hint of body-shyness had been long since cured, except for the scars she'd gotten seven years ago.

She tossed the sweatshirt aside. Cold air slithered over her bare arms, and she told herself she was keeping the T-shirt on for warmth, not to hide. Sometimes, she could almost believe her own bullshit, though tonight wasn't one of those times.

"I take it you have some ideas, then?" she asked to hide her own embarrassment.

"A list of them," Ian confirmed.

Cecily grinned as another layer of tension melted away. He rid herself of her jeans as quickly as she could, stripped off her socks, and got under the blankets. She pushed them up so she could roll on top of Ian. "Where did you want to start?"

Moving slowly, he slid his hands out from under his neck and reached up to touch Cecily's face. He combed his fingers back through her hair, tugging lightly. "You shouldn't think about cutting this short," he said thoughtfully.

"Not exactly an answer," she said, trying to sound unaffected, but the gently rough touch stole her breath. The beginnings of panic slithered down her spine, but she pushed up onto all fours, and the freedom of movement helped keep her anxiety at bay. Trying to seem like the movement had been nothing more than a casual stretch, she lay back down, chest against Ian's, and waited for their shared body warmth to steal through her T-shirt.

Ian pulled Cecily up for a kiss, slow and undemanding. His hands never moved down to her hips or back or T-shirt but stayed tangled in her hair, and she let the kiss relax her into the possessive touch. She moved one hand to trace the line of his jaw with soft kisses.

"You're right, you know."

"Of course I am," she answered with a curious smile, continuing a lazy path up toward Ian's ear.

He laughed and said, "About the shaving. It's an interesting difference."

Cecily could feel his smirk against her cheek. "I'm always right," she teased and then nipped at Ian's earlobe. In response, his fingers twisted, and heat spiked down from her scalp, making her skin tingle. She shifted to get her legs over his, regretting the thin fabric of her underwear separating their bodies.

Deciding it was the perfect time to do something about that, she shifted her weight to free her left hand and clawed at the waistband. Ian made no effort to help. Instead, he took advantage of the distraction to bite more sharply at Cecily's throat, and the tingling in her body turned to fire. She fought to get the waistband over her hips, shoved the underwear down as far as she could, and kicked them off the rest of the way.

When she straddled Ian once more and rolled her hips, pleasure shot through her body like a lightning strike. He let out a soft gasp of his own. His hands relaxed, releasing Cecily's hair, and he shifted himself down on the pillows. "Move up," he said, reaching down to curl his hands over her thighs.

Momentarily confused, Cecily rose up on all fours, spreading her legs when Ian inched down even farther. Then he moved down, still lying on his back, and she forgot how to breathe as she realized what Ian was planning.

"Ian, you — *Oh, fuck*," she gasped, feeling his tongue sweep over her clit. One hand slid over the back of Cecily's left thigh, holding her in place.

"Stay still," Ian said, his voice gravelly and quiet. His hand moved farther up, fingers curving around Cecily's ass as he licked again.

She bit her lip to keep from cursing. The blanket's weight draped over her back was almost too much, but it was soft and familiar. She took deep breaths of cold air from the room mixed with the slight warmth trapped beneath the blankets. Her fingers dug into the sheets, and she pushed the pillow away. Breathing a bit more easily, she braced herself on her left hand and reached down with her right, searching for Ian in the darkness under the blanket.

"Cecily," he warned sharply. "Stay still."

She hesitated, very much aware of her body, positioned exactly how Ian had placed her, though she wasn't held down or trapped in any way. It was different and tense, but not quite enough to push her over the edge into fear. She took a deep breath and forced herself to think about complying and waited to see if the fucked-up darkness in her mind would wreck everything.

Finally, she decided she could do this. She *wanted* to do this, or at least to try.

Slowly, she pulled her hand back and dug her fingers into the sheet, balancing her weight on all fours again.

Ian didn't say anything, which was fine with Cecily. This wasn't something she was prepared to think about, much less to discuss—not that she could have tried, once he went back to his meticulous attentions. This time, as he pressed his tongue to her clit, rubbing in gentle circles, he teased a finger at her entrance.

She let out a soft moan and buried her face against her forearms. She couldn't remember the last time anyone had done anything like this, and by the time Ian slid a finger inside her, Cecily gave up even trying to think.

———

With every touch, Ian could track Cecily's thoughts. She was torn between allowing him to explore her body and wanting to leave, and her thighs were so tense that

she was trembling. Her abdomen was tight from trying to control her breathing. Between the mattress and
his best efforts to break down her self-control, she was
struggling to stay balanced on all fours. Her shoulder
probably still hurt, especially after the cold and stress of
driving the quad over rough terrain. But short of standing up in the middle of the room, this was the best way
to keep Cecily warm, give Ian access to her body, and
leave her free to escape if she felt the need.

That restriction was perhaps more difficult for him
than it was for her. He wanted nothing more than to
throw her down on her back and pin her to the mattress, leaving her body open for him to take whatever he
wanted, but not yet. Perhaps not ever, though he would
work diligently to help Cecily overcome her fears. The
thought of watching her struggle to endure not pain but
pleasure, of Ian pushing the boundaries of her desire
before granting her any relief, was intoxicating.

He started now, using one hand to keep her hips
steady while he tasted her. He worked a second finger
into her body, conscious that she was still tense and
tight, and Ian made every effort to help her relax. He
teased at her clit with gentle licks and then pressed his
tongue hard against her body, reading Cecily's breath
and movements to decipher what she liked and what she
wanted and what was too much.

It was almost unfair, really. Sex was less about specific technique and more about reading one's partner,
and above all else, Ian indulged solely because he lived
to uncover every hidden desire. Physical gratification
was a poor second to exposing someone's secrets.

When Cecily was gasping for breath, hips twitching

with her need for more, Ian backed off. He smiled when she cursed aloud.

"Don't move," he reminded her and fought his way out from under the blankets. Cecily seemed barely able to lift her head and give Ian a wide-eyed stare, too lost in her own pleasure to even form words.

All but purring with satisfaction, Ian rolled over onto his back and made a point of arranging the pillows comfortably under his head. He picked up one of the condoms and said, "Come here."

Cecily unfolded from her collapsed crouch and moved to lie against Ian. She kissed without hesitation, though he could still taste her body on his own lips, and another thrill passed through him at her honest, raw sensuality. Without breaking the kiss, she allowed him to guide her over his hips.

He rolled his hips up, permitting himself a single, lavish brush of his shaft against her slick heat. She groaned into the kiss, and it took all of Ian's self-control to break the electric contact.

"Lift up," he told her, looking up into her eyes. They were wide and dark, and he couldn't resist teasingly brushing his fingers over her clit again, making her moan.

"Ian," she complained, nearly begging.

He lifted his head and kissed her, the touch equally gentle and fleeting. "Tell me what you want."

Cecily's hesitation lasted a moment too long. "More," she said, evasively dropping her gaze. She tried to prevent further questions with a kiss.

Ian lifted his free hand to Cecily's hair, pulling sharply enough to break the kiss. She gasped, lips parted, and her eyes fell closed.

The tentative conclusions building in Ian's mind all coalesced into clarity. He was learning what she liked. He kept hold of Cecily's hair and pushed two fingers into her body, fast enough to hint at roughness and intensity and control, without actually hurting her.

Cecily cursed and bucked her hips down, body pressing hard against Ian's hand. Her eyes opened, meeting his gaze, and she pulled against the hand in her hair so she could kiss him, hard and demanding.

Every cell in Ian's body was screaming for him to forget self-control. He wanted nothing more than to bury himself in Cecily and stay there until they both forgot how to think, but she wasn't ready for that. Instead, he twisted the fingers in her hair until the kiss broke enough for him to insist, "I said, tell me what you want."

Cecily took a single breath. "You," she finally said breathlessly. "Inside me."

Staring up at her, Ian hid a smile as he realized Cecily, for all her swearing, was actually shy. Here was a boundary he could push easily.

He drew his fingers out enough to make her hiss with pleasure, and then pushed slowly back into her, curling his fingers to brush against the spot that made her gasp. Then, deliberately, he stilled his hand and said, "I *am* inside you."

"Ian." It was almost a plea.

In response, he pulled his hand back, pressing a thumb against her clit as he moved. "Be specific, Cecily," he whispered remorselessly as he pushed the tips of his fingers back into her heat once more.

The sound she made in response was closer to a whimper than a moan. "Fuck," she whispered.

"Not specific enough," Ian teased, flexing his wrist to move his fingers deeper, just up to the second knuckle. Cecily's body was tight and hot but she was ready, and that knowledge tested his ability to hold himself back.

"Bastard. Fuck me," she snapped, fingers digging into the sheets on either side of the pillows.

Satisfied for now, Ian let go of Cecily's hair and pushed his fingers a bit deeper. "Get the condom. Put it on me."

"*Lazy* bastard," she muttered and twisted to the side, lifting her hips.

Ian caught her body with his free hand, taking the risk of holding her gently in place, and distracted her with another twist of the fingers still buried inside her. "*Without* moving away," he ordered. "I'm not finished." To punctuate his words, he pressed gently against her clit once more.

Quietly groaning, Cecily fumbled the condom she'd picked up. It took her two tries to pick it back up off the bed. She braced up on her left hand and used her teeth to rip open the packet. Ian allowed himself a small smile as he deliberately interrupted her attempts to extract the condom. He twisted his fingers, sliding them in and out of her body, as she fumbled to get the condom properly lined up and rolled over his cock. By the time it was in place, Cecily was nearly trembling.

She let his hands guide her hips into place, and he gritted his teeth against the tight, hot pleasure of her body. "Slowly, Cecily," he said tensely. "I want to feel you."

Trembling, she exhaled in brusque frustration and leaned back down, hands braced on Ian's shoulders for balance. She eased down onto his length, thighs shaking with the effort to go slowly, until she was seated on his hips, leaving them both panting and breathless. His hand found her clit, and he rubbed teasingly, aware that this time she hadn't come.

Her hips bucked at the touch, and she started to move. He let her take control and concentrated instead on her pleasure rather than the tight heat of her body that threatened to push him too far, too fast. He wanted—*needed*—her to come first.

"Is this…?" she asked as she leaned forward a bit more, changing the angle. Obligingly, Ian tensed, shifting his cock to make her gasp as she pushed back down. "God. Is this okay?" she gasped out.

"It's perfect. Whatever you like," he said, trying to match the movement of his fingers to her body's rhythm. She moved just fast enough to burn through Ian's self-control like a slowly spreading fire. He wished he'd thought to turn on power to the bedroom so he could see her in proper light, but he wasn't about to interrupt this exquisite pleasure to find the switches or build up the fire.

As Cecily's body tensed, her movements grew faster, more uncoordinated. She dug her short, blunt fingernails into Ian's shoulders, and he responded by pressing her clit with the steady, hard rhythm he'd come to learn she enjoyed. She let out a little gasp, and her movements stuttered, becoming hesitant.

Barely another minute passed, punctuated by Cecily's little gasps and quiet moans. Then she ground down hard on Ian's cock, muscles clenching tight, and he thrust into her as best he could. She was so tight and hot and gorgeous in her uninhibited pleasure, head thrown back, eyes shut, that she pulled him over the edge with her.

———<small>~~~</small>———

Ian stood in the dark shower stall, leaning against the cold tile, hot water running down his chest as he fixed every detail of Cecily's reaction in his memory. Tonight's sex had answered some questions, but others had taken their place. What else did she like? What had she never tried? How far could he push before she'd push back?

He turned, closing his eyes as the hot water hit his cold back. One day, he'd get Cecily into a proper hotel, even if he had to kidnap her and drag her across international borders. Ibiza was too crowded, but there was always Switzerland. She wouldn't object to the weather—not after living here—and Ian could probably convince Preston to make all the arrangements.

New goal, then: Get Cecily out of the primitive hell that was Canada before year's end. He pictured her in a steaming hot tub, surrounded by snow, and his smile turned predatory.

The bathroom door opened, admitting a faint glow from the dying bedroom fire. Cecily entered and closed the door. "Almost done?"

Ian hid a sigh and made a mental note to rent a ski lodge that had a proper hot water tank or an on-demand system. "Yes." He pushed open the plexiglass door and went to step out, but Cecily was right there. Cold hands pressed against his chest for a moment, confusing him. He stepped back and heard the rustle of fabric.

Then Cecily stepped into the shower stall and pulled

the door closed. Wishing he'd thought to turn the lights
on, Ian held still, back pressed to the tile. There was no
way to avoid crowding her; even breathing took up too
much room.

Cecily rested her hands on Ian's hips and leaned
her forehead on his shoulder. Water hit the back of her
shoulders, splashing up onto his face in a cool mist. He
wanted to pull her close and wrap his arms around her
body, but he didn't dare. Even this might be too much.

So he stayed there, moving his hands just enough
to brush his fingers against her hips, touching without
holding. After a minute, Cecily turned her face enough
to press a kiss against his collarbone. Then she turned
and moved a few inches away—as far as she could go—
and said, "I banked the fire. You get to fix the blankets."

Ian allowed himself a smile, relieved that the close
quarters hadn't provoked a panic attack. "I suppose I can
do that," he said as he pushed open the shower door. He
got out and dried off quickly; there was hardly enough
room in the small bathroom for them to both dry off at
once, and he didn't want her worried that he'd see her
scars, as much as he wanted the chance. Cecily trusted
him, and he wouldn't betray that trust.

He left the warm bathroom and shivered while he put
on his pajamas, though he was tempted to sleep without any clothes in hopes of encouraging Cecily to stay
close. It was just too damned cold for that, which made
him mentally note that the ski lodge should have central
heating as well as fireplaces for ambiance. *Good* central
heating—maybe a radiant system in the floor, to start.

Cecily was finished with her shower by the time Ian
had the blankets sorted out. From the warmth of the bed,

he watched her emerge from the bathroom as she had that first morning, wearing only a towel. The banked fire showed no details at all, but he watched anyway, appreciating the way the reddish light changed the visual quality of her skin.

She went to the dresser and put on a T-shirt, underwear, and fleece pants. Ian didn't bother to hide his sigh of disappointment. Cecily heard him and laughed, getting quickly under her own blanket. As she lay down, she reached out with one hand to touch the gun on the table, making a minute adjustment to its position.

Then she rolled over to face Ian, burrowing down under her blanket. "Thank you," she said quietly.

He smiled at her and slipped a hand from under his blanket to Cecily's, finding her fingertips. He touched lightly, giving her every chance to pull back, but she didn't. Instead, she spread her fingers just enough to lace the tips with Ian's, joining their hands without either of them holding the other in place.

Chapter 12

October 29

IAN CAME AWAKE SLOWLY AND LAZILY TO DULL WHITE light intruding on his consciousness. He opened his eyes and blinked at Cecily, who lay beside him, watching him. Their pillows touched, but their bodies didn't, separated by a barrier of clothes and blankets.

"Sorry if I'm rusty," she said quietly. The window glowed with sunlight diffused through a blizzard of snow, casting new shadows over her face. She looked tired and serious, and he felt the immediate impulse to erase her grave expression and transmute it into a smile.

"Rusty?"

"At talking." She took a deep breath and rolled onto her back. She lifted her arms and folded her hands under her head. The cold bedroom air raised the hair on her forearms, a pale aura over her skin. "Twelve years ago, I was an officer in the Marines. Combat engineers. I left seven years ago. Something happened—" She shook her head, the motion barely visible. "My dad was from Canada. I came here to get away from people."

He clenched his fingers in the blanket to keep from reaching for her. He wanted to say something—*I know*—but he wouldn't immediately be able to rationalize his conclusions without mentioning the video.

"It's not that last night was…bad," she continued

uncertainly. Her brief laugh was soft and nervous. "Anything but that. But I don't—I can't do this, Ian." She turned her head to look sadly at him. "Trust me when I say you don't even want me to try."

"Trust has nothing to do with you being wrong." He moved closer and watched her arms tense, though she didn't try to move away. "As a blanket statement, 'I trust you' is almost always invalidated by reality. I trust you to safely fly that death trap of yours, but I don't 'trust' that you'll get us safely back on land every time. The factors are out of your control."

Her expression had slowly shifted from sad to puzzled. A hint of irritation creased her brow. "Do you ever actually listen to yourself speak?" She rolled onto her side, propping up on her right arm, and tossed her head to throw her hair out of her face. "I'm saying you shouldn't be involved with me, Ian. I'm not what you want, no matter what you think. I'm not even *safe*."

"How many others have gotten this close since you—" He cut off before he could reference the reason she had left the military. He blamed the near-slip on the unexpected, unwelcome surprise of this conversation happening without even a single cup of coffee, which would help them both be able to discuss this rationally. "Since you left the military?"

Evasively, she looked away. "None. Not for lack of trying—"

"Failures," he dismissed. "Did you enjoy last night?"

She met his eyes for an instant, color rising in her cheeks. "Well, of course."

"And the night before?"

"Ian, it's just a matter—"

"It's *not* just 'a matter of time,'" he interrupted sharply. "It's the fact that almost everyone else is too stupid to *understand* you—to recognize what you want and what you don't want and what you want but can't have, and to help you have it anyway."

She shook her head. "That makes no sense."

He let out a huff, wanting to roll on top of her and hold her down and try to make her understand, but that would only make matters worse. So instead he caught her by one arm and pulled as he rolled onto his back. Surprised and wary of hurting him, she didn't struggle, though she snapped, "Ian!"

Only when she was on top of him, blankets tangled around their legs, did he let her go. He looked up at her, saying, "I know how to make this *safe*, Cecily. You don't have to be worried. I know you won't be held down. If you feel trapped, your instinct is to fight free—"

She went pale. "God," she muttered as she pushed up on all fours, kicking at the blankets.

Before she could back up, he reached up to touch her face. "Stop. Cecily—"

"No. No, this is what your brother said you do in court. You fuck with people's minds."

Outwardly, he huffed in irritation, but secretly he smiled. She was still on top of him as though tethered there by the featherlight touch of his fingertips on her cheek. "Let me give you what you want," he offered. "What you thought you could never have again."

Slowly, she sat back on his thighs, looking down at the blanket. She closed her eyes and pushed a hand through her sleep-mussed hair. "Why?"

It was his turn to fall silent, his confidence faltering

as he realized there was no easy answer. At first, it had been simply an effort to alleviate boredom, but in slow, small steps, his motives had become less selfish. He'd looked at her as a challenge—a puzzle to solve, or someone who could be fixed—but at some point, he'd begun to care. She was intelligent and sexy, and she reacted to him in unpredictable ways, which no one, not even Preston, had ever done.

Finally, she shook her head and moved off him, throwing the blankets roughly aside. "Forget it. Forget I said anything. I told you—"

"Cecily." His mind snapped back into gear, and he caught her T-shirt just as she stood up beside the bed. When she looked back down at him, he said, "I'm staying, Cecily. You can't scare me away, and you won't hurt me."

"You don't *know* me," she said angrily, though again, she didn't pull away. He saw desperation in her eyes. She *wanted* to believe, but her past had taught her otherwise. Now, she needed time to think.

He let go of her shirt and twisted to sit up on the edge of the bed. "I do know you, Cecily. And because I know you, I trust you."

—⁓—

Cecily spent the day apart from Ian. While he had been showering, she'd opened the gun safe, closed it again, and left the property on the quad, despite the blizzard outside.

Ian tried to summon his usual calm detachment, but the effort was a miserable failure. He went through two pots of coffee, focusing on the fact that she was strong. She wouldn't get lost, even in the snow, and she wouldn't shoot herself. He had been very careful to avoid pushing her too far.

Finally, he went to his laptop and turned on the power to the satellite connection. He checked his email, hoping to find anything interesting enough to help lure her to Manhattan, but he had no idea what might work. He doubted she liked concerts, theater, or sports.

Frustrated, he played the guitar and drank more coffee and read more of her fantasy manuscript. Then he reread the other pages until the disturbing images they evoked in his mind grew too much to bear.

Hunger forced him into the kitchen, where he heated up leftovers. While he cooked and ate, he tried to figure out if the meat was venison, beef, bear, or something else. He couldn't tell, though he'd had all three during his childhood.

When she finally returned, entering the cabin on a gust of wind-driven snow, he snapped, "Where were you?"

She pushed back her fur-edged hood and pulled off a ski mask crusted white with snow and tiny shards of ice. "Hunting." Her voice sounded raspy and harsh. She stamped her foot and went right for the kitchen, fumbling to take off thick gloves. Over her shoulder, she carried the rifle she'd brought to Marguerite's last night.

"You were hunting a bear?" he demanded incredulously. "Alone?"

She threw her gloves down out on the kitchen counter and took a mug out of the dish rack. "Of course not. I have a mule deer tag—but no fucking luck," she added in a mutter as she used a towel to pick up the kettle. She gave it a shake and snapped, "You couldn't have kept this full?"

"You left! You said nothing about where you were going! You went out in a blizzard alone—"

"*I live alone!*" She slammed the kettle down onto the counter and turned, bracing her hands against the edge as she took a deep breath. "I'm cold, I'm hungry, and I'm tired, Ian."

He wanted to retreat. He wanted to shout at her for how stupid she'd been to take such unnecessary risks. This was why he kept people at arm's length.

"Go. Just…go into the living room or something," she said only a bit less angrily. "I'll get dinner started in a few minutes."

"I'll do it," he said, not realizing he'd spoken until the words were out.

She looked back over her shoulder. "What?"

"I'll do it!" he repeated. He crossed the kitchen and took the towel out of her hands, and then used it to pick up the kettle. "Go take a hot shower. I'll make dinner and tea. Or coffee."

"Tea's fine," she said, confused. "But—"

"Stop arguing and go!"

───※───

The water went from hot to warm, warning Cecily that she had less than five minutes to finish up, but she still felt the cold deep in her body. Only her right shoulder felt warm, and that was an agonizing flame, not a comfortable glow. She stood sideways to the shower spray, aiming the water directly at the bullet scar, and rested her forehead on her other arm, propped against the cold tile wall.

Ian's words twisted in her like knives. The unspoken

accusation had hit home. She should have asked him to come out with her. She'd *wanted* to, which was exactly why she hadn't. She didn't dare grow dependent on his presence. As it was, just having him in her bed was an addiction that she already felt hooked deep in her mind.

The bathroom door opened. She didn't have the energy to complain that he hadn't bothered to knock.

Then the light went out, and she looked up abruptly. "Huh?"

In answer, the shower door opened. "The water's turning cold," he said, his voice subdued. He slid a hand over her abdomen, startling her into flinching back. A moment later, the shower turned off, and she shivered at the absence of warmth.

"Where's my—" She cut off as her groping hand encountered rough fabric. Then he was right in front of her, wrapping her in a towel. Wondering if this was some sort of apology for losing his temper (and thinking that *she* was the one who should be apologizing to him, not the other way around), she said, "Ian, you don't have to."

His hands went still, lightly resting on her upper arms. "I want to."

She nodded before remembering that he wouldn't be able to see. "All right," she agreed quietly and shivered as he went back to drying her off.

Instead of taking the towel from her shoulders, he reached for his own towel to dry off her legs. Tentatively, she brushed her fingers through his long, soft hair. "I'm sorry. I shouldn't have snapped at you like that."

He rose, letting his towel fall. His hands returned to her arms, sliding up, but he stopped at her shoulder as if he knew how badly the bullet scar ached. "I don't *do* relationships, Cecily. I don't even have many real friends. I know hundreds of people in Manhattan, and only a handful are friends."

"Ian—"

"Don't say anything," he interrupted. "I'm not like other people. Neither are you. Everything you think you know about me—everything you think you should fear—is wrong."

"That's supposed to make me feel better?"

His hand lifted from her left arm. A moment later, soft fingertips brushed over her lips. "Trust me, Cecily. You trusted it last night. Did you regret it then?"

She couldn't bring herself to say no and she didn't dare lie—not to him. Instead, she asked, "Why did you turn off the light?"

His hand moved to press against her chest. "You want to hide your scars, though you don't have to."

Her heart thudded uncomfortably against her ribs. Was she that transparent, or was he really so perceptive? She was suddenly very glad for the darkness.

"It's getting cold," she said evasively, though truthfully.

He left his hand resting over her heart as he leaned down to kiss her. "Get dressed. The kitchen's warm and dinner's almost ready."

When he stepped back, it took all of her self-control not to go after him. As it was, she felt almost dizzy without his warm, steady presence close by. To distract herself, she asked, "What did you make?"

"Meat and mushroom rice. I would have made proper risotto, but I don't know what sort of rice you have in the bin."

"'Meat'? What kind?"

"I've no idea. It's not chicken, fish, or human."

"*Human?*" she asked, horrified.

"An accused cannibal tried to hire me to defend him two years ago."

It was awful to consider, but she couldn't quite hold back a choked laugh. She could all too easily picture him assessing the meat in the deep freezer and choosing dinner based not on a particular recipe but on the "not cannibalism" requirement.

Impulsively, she reached up and pulled him close for another kiss. "Thank you again."

—∿∿—

"You're not going outside tonight?" Ian asked when Cecily joined him on the sofa. She'd finished the dishes and they'd had their coffee, which meant it was time for her to do her usual check of the property. "The blizzard?"

"I spent enough time outside. We have firewood and water even if a pipe breaks. Everything else can wait until daylight," she confirmed, turning to sit sideways opposite Ian, rather than cuddling close beside him, as he would have preferred.

He had taken the guitar from its case and had been idly playing. He considered putting it back, but instead held it across his lap and began practicing his fingering. His fingers were less dexterous in the cold.

"So, you keep saying you know me," she said. "How?"

He couldn't hide his smirk. "It's more than that. Anyone who's not dead or comatose takes in far more information than most people realize. Right now, what are your senses telling you?"

For a moment, he was disappointed to see confusion on her face, and he braced against the bland report of "It's cold" and "The fire's lit." Then she said, "The fire's been lit all day, but the ashes haven't been shoveled, so the flame's not as hot as it could be. I probably need to clean out the soot, too."

"Good," he said, unable to hide his surprise. "Very good."

She grinned. "The wind's from the northwest, so hopefully it won't still be snowing come morning. I can just barely hear the water heater. It's running but not filling, so you can have a long shower. You get tetchy if you don't have two showers a day."

He laughed. "True. What else?"

"Um…" She looked around. "That's it. I mean, it's my house. It's not like any of it's unfamiliar."

He nodded, resting his hand on her warm wool sock for a moment. "Your right shoulder hurts. The damp and cold aggravates the scar where you were shot, but you went out this morning anyway," he said, feeling the subtle shift as she tensed.

"We could use the venison," she said with a tense shrug.

He looked pointedly toward her scarred shoulder. "You're sitting with your right side to the back of the couch. You keep shifting because your shoulder hurts when you put any weight on it, but you want to stay facing me, so you're enduring it for now."

Unconsciously, she lifted her right hand to rub at the site of the bullet wound. Then she caught herself and shrugged, lowering her hand again. "Okay. All true."

He pressed his fingers against her shin a bit more

firmly to ground her, rubbing in little circles. "You were shot while standing or kneeling over someone," he said more quietly, keeping his voice very steady and calm.

Her eyes widened, and she hitched in a quiet gasp before she stopped breathing altogether. Her lips parted, shaping the word *How?* though she said nothing.

"The angle between the entrance and exit wound is too sharp. The bullet most likely fractured your collarbone, rather than shattering it, and exited out the top of your trapezius muscle. There's a chance it nicked the upper part of your shoulder blade, but I doubt it."

"God," she whispered. She swallowed hard and licked her lips.

He considered remaining silent, but he knew that they needed to have this discussion at some point. Best to get it out of the way now, rather than leaving her to worry over it for days or even weeks.

"It was intentional," he said quietly. "The shot was disabling, not fatal."

"Intentional?"

"You were targeted. Most likely, you went to a civilian's aid. He was someone you didn't know, but he appeared wounded and in need, so you trusted him enough to lower your guard. As soon as you were in range, he shot you from a prone position."

Her skin had gone ashen. "How—How do you—"

"Something like ninety percent of people are right-handed. The shot was precisely placed to disable but not kill. An inch in any direction and it could have been fatal, especially without immediate medical treatment. So he was a crack shot, able to play at being harmless to lure you close, and capable of taking precise aim and shooting flawlessly."

"He did," she whispered. "He looked like a civilian. I thought…"

When she didn't continue, he filled the silence, saying, "It happened at night, somewhere outside a city."

"Fucking hell." She turned, pulling her foot free so she could turn and sit properly, feet on the floor. She rested her elbows on her knees and let her head hang down, taking deep breaths.

Tentatively, he moved toward her, though he sat back as soon as her shoulders tightened. "You went to help someone you perceived as a noncombatant, and you were attacked—"

"Noncombatant," she whispered tightly. She lifted her head, eyes closed, and drew in a harsh, deep breath. "I had my rifle slung. I didn't even see him aim. I saw him go down and I thought… He looked young. He wasn't carrying a gun—not that I could see. He was near my position, so I ran to help him."

He studied her profile, taking in a thousand little details, from the way the firelight muted her freckles to her steady hands. Carefully he said, "That's when you were captured."

She turned just enough to look at Ian. "Your brother—"

"Your scars," he corrected. "You weren't treated by a military surgeon or even a proper doctor."

She started to nod, but her self-control broke. She rose, pushing away from the sofa, and paced stiffly into the kitchen. He stayed where he was, knowing she needed to feel open space around her. He listened intently for the sound of the whiskey bottle or the metallic clatter of her sidearm, but all he heard was the sink running. After a few seconds—just long enough to fill a glass—she turned off the water.

"They wanted a hostage," she said, just loudly enough to be heard in the living room.

He rose, intentionally bumping against the sofa to make noise. He walked to the kitchen archway but stood on the other side, away from the sink where she was still standing, back to the room.

"One of their leaders had been captured," she said tonelessly. "They wanted a female hostage to trade. Better impact in the media. They ended up taking me and two of my troops."

He remained silent, though he moved into the kitchen, putting himself into her peripheral line of sight. She put down her glass of water and took two mugs from the dish rack. She set them on the counter and went to the pantry. She took an old, faded box of tea bags from the shelf and dropped it when she tried to open it. Her hands shook as she crouched down, balanced on the balls of her feet, and started scooping up the sachets of tea. Finally she got all but two back in the box and replaced the box on its shelf. She ripped them open as she walked back to the counter.

"How long did they have you?" he finally asked.

"Don't you know?" she snapped. Then she shook her head and said, "I'm sorry." She dropped one tea bag into each mug.

"It was at least three days," he said, unable to could stop himself. "Perhaps as long as six or seven."

"How do you know that?" she demanded. She'd picked up the towel she used to handle the kettle. Now, she threw it down and turned toward him, her face a mask of shock and anger. *"How do you know?"*

Silently berating himself—he always had to be clever, too clever for his own damned good—Ian considered his options. There was no room to lie convincingly, and he had a feeling she wouldn't accept anything but a full, complete answer, so he forced himself to look up and meet her angry gaze as he admitted, "I saw the video."

Chapter 13

CECILY BREATHED IN, TASTING SMOKE AND STEAM. SHE was cold, especially the lower half of her body, but her hands were warm. Everything around her was quiet, except for the crackle of flames and the familiar bubbling gurgle that she identified as a water heater.

Water heater. The cabin.

She opened her eyes and found herself staring at the wood floor of her kitchen, with its layers of scuff marks and polish and dried mud. Another inhale brought the distant sense of snow under the taste of wood smoke.

Her hands twitched, reflexively tightening around warm ceramic. She looked up and tried to sit up straight, only to have her back and right shoulder scream in protest.

"Fuck," she muttered, closing her eyes when she saw Ian sitting on the floor, off to one side. Her throat felt tight, and her eyes were stinging. She lifted the mug in her hands and took a sip. The tea was lukewarm and tasted stale and bitter.

"The floor is cold," he said quietly. "Should I get you a blanket?"

Embarrassed, she shook her head, wondering why the hell she'd blacked out. "I'm fine," she said, though it was a lie.

She shifted the mug to her left hand and tried to lift her

right to scrub at her face, but doing more than twitching her fingers sent shooting pains down from her shoulder. She stopped trying to move and tried to breathe through it.

She glanced at him, hating how difficult he was to read even at the best of times. Now, he looked at her calmly, impassively.

"Aspirin?" she requested, needing a moment of privacy to recover her composure as best she could.

Ian nodded and rose stiffly, as though he'd been sitting on the floor for some time. She looked to the window, but all she saw was the reflection of the oil lamp hanging over the sink. She put the mug down beside her hip and rubbed the damp tracks on her face.

After a minute, he returned with three aspirin. Lecturing him about dosages was pointless, and she was actually regretting not having anything stronger, so she just took all three, washing them down with the tea. When she went to put the mug back on the floor, he took it instead.

"Do you want to stay here?" he asked as if it was perfectly normal for adults to sit on the kitchen floor.

She shook her head. Thankfully, he didn't offer to help her up, though he stayed a bit too close as she got awkwardly to her feet. She couldn't feel her toes or tailbone. Exhaustion lay heavy in every muscle, making her want nothing more than sleep. She just knew that if she tried, she'd have nightmares.

She went to the bedroom anyway, knowing that somewhere in her fucked-up mind, she considered it the safest spot in the cabin. He followed, still silent, and went to the hearth to build up the fire, which left her free to go right for the bed. As was her habit, she drew her gun and set it on the nightstand, only then realizing that he had left her armed despite her loss of self-control.

The last thing she wanted to do was to discuss what had happened, but she'd already neglected his safety too much. She sat down on the edge of the bed and leaned forward, resting her elbows on her knees. "Ian."

"Hm?" he asked casually, focused on building up the fire.

She clasped her hands tightly together, trying to think of where to begin. The words were all there in her head—everything she needed to tell him, to make certain they were both safe if her self-control broke again—but she couldn't figure out where to start. For a writer, it was doubly frustrating to fumble through mental false starts and incoherent phrases all jumbled together.

When the fire was blazing, filling the room with warmth and light, he took the two steps to the edge of the bed. He sat, turning to face her. Despite Preston's warning that he could be short-tempered, he seemed the embodiment of patience, as if he would be content to sit all night in silence. Finally, she decided there was no point in trying to explain. Ian probably knew more about this than Cecily herself did.

"I don't want to hurt you," she said without looking at him. "If...*that* happens again, you can't leave me armed."

"I was safe."

Anger flickered to life, but she was too tired for it to actually take hold. "You weren't. Ian, when—"

"Cecily, I—No, sorry," he said, sounding unhappy. "It's best for you to say whatever you need."

She glared at him. "This isn't some mind game, Ian. I could have killed you!"

"No, you—Well, you *wouldn't*," he said. "Not without provocation."

"What the hell does that mean?" she demanded.

He took a breath and looked up at the ceiling. "Haven't you been paying attention *at all* for the past week? I know what provokes your self-defense reflexes, Cecily. I sat next to you for two hours, and I was *never in danger*."

"God," she whispered, looking away. Two hours. The sad part was that two hours was actually an improvement over some of her earlier episodes.

"You won't hurt me," he repeated confidently. "I sat beside you for two hours, Cecily. I touched you. I handed you a mug of tea. Twice. Neither of which you drank," he added in gentle accusation. "I promise, Cecily, you don't have to worry."

"You're wrong," she insisted. "You don't understand. *Anything* could trigger me. You can't predict—"

"I did."

Her thoughts, spiraling out of control, abruptly stalled. "What?"

"I did. I knew it was a possibility. No, not a possibility. When we started our discussion, I knew something like that was inevitable."

"Why didn't you stop it, then?"

He sighed. "I wanted to get it over with. Now you can stop trying to hide, so I can—"

"Is *that* what this was about?" she demanded in disbelief. "Me wearing a shirt to bed?"

He glared and deliberately continued, "So I can stop

hiding the fact that I know. I've known since I first saw
you, after your shower."

She turned away and took a few breaths, trying to rationalize what he was saying, but she was exhausted and
worn down and felt childishly resentful that he could
function so damned normally while she couldn't go
twenty-four hours without nightmares, asleep or awake.

"I see everything, Cecily. I put together the smallest minutiae, things most people never consciously ac-
knowledge, into a coherent picture that no one else can
see until I show it to them. It's how I'm such a damned
good lawyer."

She nodded, still refusing to look at him. On the
surface, it all made perfect sense. Deeper down, on
an emotional level, it was all kinds of fucked-up, but
she had the feeling that was nothing more than a fear-
based reaction.

"The video," she said, trying to stick to calm, cold
logic. "How?"

"The first day I had Internet access, I broke into my
brother's server and found your files. Most of it was
redacted, but there was enough left for me to form a
coherent picture. The rest, I figured out based on observing you."

He'd been sitting on this knowledge since last
Monday, then. More than a week. She let out a sharp,
bitter laugh. "And you still stayed? You still—" She cut
off awkwardly and gestured at the bed they'd shared just
that morning.

"With most people, the longer I know them, the more
boring and predictable they are," he said. "It seems to
work backward with you."

"Fuck," she whispered, shaking her head. Logic could only go so far against her emotional exhaustion. "I can't do this now."

"I'm staying," he said at once, as though prepared to defend his right to share the bed.

She just waved a hand at the far side of the bed. She rose enough to push away the blanket and got under its comforting weight, fully dressed. Without hesitation, he followed suit. She started on her back, but she gave in after only a few seconds and rolled over to face him.

"You really will sleep better under both blankets," he said quietly.

"You're burning two days' worth of firewood," she answered, even though he was right. She was still cold, and she could feel the weight of his knowing stare. She sighed and said, "Fine. Just don't crowd—"

"I know," he interrupted impatiently. He sat up and shook out his blanket over Cecily's. Then he got out of bed, put his glasses on the nightstand, and started to strip off his clothes.

Wondering if there had been a miscommunication, she said, "Ian, I'm not really in the mood..."

With a huff of frustration, he asked, "In the military, did you sleep clothed?"

"Of course... Wait, you're stripping for *contrast*?" she asked, a smile flickering to life for the first time since everything had gone wrong.

"You should as well." He dropped his shirt on the floor and looked back over his bare shoulder. "If I wanted you out of your clothes for sex, you'd know it. This is only to help you sleep."

She surrendered, though more because it was damned

uncomfortable to sleep in blue jeans than because his theory made any sort of sense. Then again, a whole battalion of therapists had accomplished virtually nothing. Ian had as good a chance as anyone else to accidentally stumble upon something to help her start to recover. And there was no sense hiding her scars, though she did keep her back turned when she took off her shirt. She made a point to get under the blankets as quickly as she could, hiding her scars from his sight.

Two minutes later, they were both back in bed, this time under layers of blankets. Already, the heat had worn away the sharp edges of her post-blackout nervousness. She lay on her side, absently rubbing at the scarred entry wound on her shoulder. Another night, she might have tried a hot water bottle to soothe the ache, but right now, she wasn't getting out of bed.

"Tomorrow, I'll give you a massage," he offered.

"Do you know how?"

"Of course," he said as though offended by the question. "It's a useful skill. People talk when they're relaxed."

She laughed and reached for his hand. "I hope that's not how you get your clients to open up to you."

"Well, no." He grinned, lifting her hand to kiss her fingertips. "But still, I'm very good at it."

"Modest, too."

Chapter 14

October 30

CECILY SHIFTED HER WEIGHT WITHOUT LIFTING HER feet, the movement silent despite the crust of half-inch-deep snow and fallen leaves that carpeted the forest. With every breath, the air in front of her fogged downward, deflected by the field glasses held to her eyes. She turned so slowly that Ian, watching for any sign of movement, almost didn't notice the subtle contraction and extension of muscles as she scanned the area and then went still again.

One corner of her mouth twitched upward in satisfaction. Slowly, she lowered the field glasses, taking care to catch the neck strap so it didn't swing free.

He was supposed to be helping to search for deer. He was positioned thirty yards away, with low-powered field glasses of his own but no rifle. She had started explaining Canadian hunting laws about giving him a rifle, only to admit that they were breaking those laws just by having him come out to help spot game. And then she had negated the explanation by saying, "No one's going to check, in any case. The two part-time rangers around here are both from Pinelake. They don't care, so long as the deer population stays stable."

Not that he particularly cared about deer. He watched Cecily instead, his mind filled with excitement as he took the measure of her patience. Early in his career, he had spent hours, even days, in alleys and abandoned apartment buildings or on rainy rooftops, observing potential witnesses. Stakeouts had been the worst part of his work. And while this deer hunt had lasted only hours so far, not days, she hadn't shown the slightest sign of being bored. With anyone else, he would have attributed that lack of boredom to a dull, unimaginative mind, but not Cecily.

He watched as she raised her rifle—the one she'd taken out two nights ago to defend against bears—and set it to her shoulder. She shifted position slightly, lowering her cheek to rest above the stock, right eye aligned with the scope. She was focused and alert, yet calm and perfectly controlled. He had no doubt that she was absolutely aware of his position, even though almost a hundred feet separated them.

When the shot rang out, Ian couldn't help but twitch in surprise. The echo filled the forest with sound. Two seconds after the shot, she lowered the rifle to hang across her chest on its sling. Her stillness drained away, and she grinned over at him, expression shadowed by the fur-edged hood for a moment before she pushed it back and ran a gloved hand through her hair.

As he walked over to her, she asked, "Care to help, or are you sore from this morning's exercises?" She picked up her frame pack and started walking toward the buck she'd shot.

Curious, he followed, jogging to catch up. "I'm fine." She'd finally bullied him into doing the stretches on his physical therapy worksheet, most of which involved him lying on the hard wood floor and wishing for wall-to-wall carpeting. "What about a second deer? You said you can take two."

She laughed, looking up at him with a grin that seemed to chase away the cold settling into his extremities. "As soon as I took the shot, the others were already running away. Besides, do you really want to try to carry two deer back? We'll come out again tomorrow."

"I can think of better things to do tomorrow," he hinted, grinning back at her.

Mock-cheerfully, she answered, "Yes, and then we can spend all of January starving." She elbowed him and then pulled the rifle sling over her head, offering the weapon to him. "Here, you can carry this. I need my hands free."

"For what?" He pulled the strap over his shoulder, trying to find a comfortable way to carry the rifle. He hadn't held anything bigger than a .22 for over twenty years.

"Field dressing. We need to remove the lower GI tract to prevent contamination, and we want the meat to cool as quickly as possible. Tastes better that way."

"Martha Christie," Ian muttered, thinking back to one of his earliest clients.

"Hm?"

"Reminds me of Martha Christie. She called the police on her fiancé, who hired me to defend him after his arrest. She found a collection of knives and guns in his closet, along with traces of blood." He huffed in remembered irritation. "It was from hunting. He forgave her, and they got married later that year. Sent me a duck in thanks."

She laughed, leaning companionably close for a

moment before the terrain forced her to step around a half-hidden branch, parting them. "I have a waterfowl license. We could go out to the lake tomorrow, if you'd rather," she offered.

He glanced thoughtfully at her, barely noticing that they'd reached the fallen deer. "Preston goes hunting every year," he said with a falsely casual air. "Deer, birds, all of that."

She dropped her pack next to the deer and crouched down to open it. "Can you help? If not, don't worry. I'd rather you not throw up," she said as she took out a coil of neon orange rope and a black plastic trash bag.

"Not a problem. I've sat through postmortem examinations," he said with more confidence than he felt. Postmortems were clean and clinical and scientific. Minutes ago, this deer had been standing and breathing. Thank God she'd felled the deer with a single shot. He wasn't certain he could stomach tracking a wounded animal through the forest.

Unaware of his thoughts, she looked at him across the deer, her grin a bit awed. "Postmortems? You really don't live a very normal life, do you?" It didn't sound like a criticism or accusation.

He grinned back. "Normal is—"

"Boring. Yes, I know," she interrupted with a laugh. "Right, help me get this fellow on his left side, and drag his feet off to the right a bit."

Bracing himself, he lifted and moved the carcass as she directed. "You're not."

She glanced down at the buck, frowning. "Not? Not what?"

"Boring."

Releasing the deer's weight with a grunt, Cecily straightened and took a folding knife from the outer pocket of her parka. She used a lever to open it without having to take off her gloves. "Thanks," she said quietly.

Ian smiled.

—⁓—

It was almost an hour before Cecily finally made it back inside the cabin after butchering the deer and hiding the antlers in the quad. Though she usually didn't take hunting trophies, she had plans for the antlers. She went to the sink to wash off her gloves, sniffing at the stew bubbling away in the Dutch oven.

"God, that smells good. I'm starved."

"I thought so." Ian leaned on the counter beside her with lazy grace, a smile playing at his lips. He'd showered, leaving his blond hair streaked dark. The cabin was toasty warm; a glance told Cecily that Ian had restocked the rack of firewood beside the kitchen stove.

"How's your back?"

His smile turned into a grin. "Up for anything you'd like."

She laughed and dropped her clean gloves on the counter to dry. Turning away to hide her blush, she went to hang her parka by the back door. "I meant, you were carrying firewood. Did you hurt yourself?"

"I'm fine. I suppose," he admitted with a dramatic sigh, "that all the walking we do out here is good for me. Back home, the only exercise I got was in the gym, on the rare mornings when I had time."

Cecily huffed, warming her hands at the stove, thinking of the *other* exercise that he hadn't mentioned.

Of course, he probably didn't lack for partners back home. Unreasonable jealousy twisted through her.

At a touch on her arm, she turned and looked up into Ian's eyes. "I also didn't have much time for dating."

Startled, she blurted out, "How did you—"

"Logical next thought," he said reasonably, running his fingers up to her shoulder and back down in a soothing motion. "But really, there wasn't time for much of anything besides work. How do you think I got myself into so much trouble?"

Cecily smiled at him. "I think you attract trouble, and work has nothing to do with it at all."

Eyes bright, he ducked to brush a soft kiss over her cheek. "I got you, didn't I?"

Laughing, she swatted at him, and he backed away, wincing when he twisted out of reach. Worry spiked through her playful mood. "Go sit down," she told him. "I'll set the table."

Unable to surrender gracefully, he smoothed a hand over her hip and only retreated to the table when she poked at his arm again. "If I wasn't at the office, I was investigating my cases, searching records, even attending autopsies."

Somehow, she wasn't surprised. "That explains why you handled the deer so calmly."

"I'm not usually *that* close, but…" He shrugged and sat down. "Sometimes, my cases require specialized information. And it helps me think."

She set two bowls on the counter and ladled stew into each one. Ian had used a bag of the venison stock she kept in the freezer, and had added potatoes, onions, and stew meat. "What do you mean?"

"It's not always the actual examination results that matter so much as the process. It's methodical and precise — a tool for advanced thinking. Yes, sometimes something interesting is uncovered, but most often, a murder is a gunshot or stabbing or blunt trauma. But watching the examination forces me to think properly. It's about focus, not the postmortem itself."

"That...makes sense," she admitted slowly, picking up her bowl with both hands to carry it to the table. "I never thought lawyers and scientists would have so much in common."

"Logical thinking."

"What about your brother? Is he just as logical?"

He took a deep, thoughtful breath. "He's more passionate, I'd say. Impulsive. Growing up, he rarely did anything with much planning or foresight, though that's changed now."

"Fortunately for me," she said, spooning up some of the stew. She blew on it to cool it. "I'd probably be dead without him." She sipped at the stew, letting the taste help ground her here, in the reality of her safe, warm cabin on the other side of the world from her nightmares. "I still don't know how or why he sent a team after me."

He dropped his spoon with a loud clatter, splashing stew onto the table. "My God."

She looked up; he was staring at the table, frowning in thought. "Are you all right?"

"I'm...I'm fine." He darted a glance at her. "Preston broke the rules for you."

"What?"

"Rules. Battlefield customs, whatever they're

called," he said, picking up his spoon to give an irritated wave. "Shortcuts. I remember it now. He flew out to Iraq unexpectedly, at Christmastime. Our parents were furious."

"What do you mean, though?" she pressed.

"The Marines were looking for you. They don't leave their own. But Preston's soldiers found you before they did. *How?*"

He broke the rules, she thought, remembering the harsh reality of warfare and how frustrating it sometimes was to be hampered by military law. "But his troops were there on a military contract."

"Not all of them. That *has* to be it." He leaned back in his chair and gestured with the spoon again. "Samaritan has contracts all over the world, primarily to provide security for civilians in hazardous areas. I've done contract review for them. *Private* security doesn't need to follow military law. He must have gotten the video and sent the intel to one of his private groups."

"He... That was incredibly risky. Even passing intel like that..."

"Right after 9/11, Preston was briefly sent to Israel. He...met someone. Her name was Lilit. She was IDF — the Israeli Defense Force. She was in the intelligence branch, training for Mossad. She died."

"I'm sorry," she said automatically. By the look on Ian's face, the woman's death hadn't been an accident.

"It was because of red tape. Government negotiation and interference. They couldn't rescue her in time." He held out his hand to clasp her fingers gently. "That's why he intervened to save you. He won't let that happen to anyone again—not if he can prevent it."

A tiny thread of guilt wove through her. She was alive because another woman had died. "I'm—"

"There's no record of the organization that took you. They're gone. Entirely eradicated, as though they never existed at all, except perhaps in some buried government record."

Something inside her came undone, a little knot of fear deep in her gut, carried with her since she'd been taken. She closed her fingers tightly around his hand, letting the touch anchor her.

"I'm sorry. I should have told you sooner, but…"

She shook her head and gave him a forced little smile. "No. It's… It's fine. I didn't choose to live out here so they wouldn't find me. It's not like I've been living in fear of them."

Carefully, he moved his other hand over hers, fingertips rubbing little circles over her wrist. "But you feel better, knowing they're dead."

"I do," she admitted. "Maybe it's wrong, but I—"

"No. You're a survivor, Cecily. It's not wrong at all—not after what happened." He smiled softly and squeezed her hand.

She sighed, remembering the dead and the dying, the fear of captivity and the elation of rescue. She nodded, and this time, her smile was more genuine. "Thank you."

He eased his grip to rub his fingers gently over her skin. "How would you like that massage tonight?"

Her words lodged in her throat. The thought of Ian's hands soothing away her tension was nice, but the promise of intimacy was enticing and terrifying in equal measure. And her scars…He'd seen some of them, but not all, and she wasn't ready to show him.

"Rain check?" she asked, smiling weakly.

He nodded, gently smiling. "Anytime."

Chapter 15

October 31

CECILY LOOKED OUT THE EXPANSIVE WINDOW AS IAN walked through Marguerite's yard, heading for the river. He was bundled against the cold but walking smoothly in the snow. She couldn't help but wonder if he could be content here in the woods, away from Manhattan, even though she knew it wouldn't happen.

Marguerite turned to take the next piece of venison from the box she had strapped to the quad early that morning. "You two are adorable together," she said, fitting the meat into her freezer.

"Thanks," she answered automatically, hiding her flinch. She turned to the bundle she'd brought with her—the antlers, wrapped in canvas. "Do you mind bringing these with you to the Tuckers?"

Mags slammed the freezer door shut and joined Cecily at the counter. "Trading them away?"

"Actually, I was hoping to get them mounted."

"Really? Since when do you do trophies?"

Cecily glanced at the window, though she couldn't see where Ian had gone. "I—"

"Oh, no. Say no more," Mags teased, nudging Cecily with one elbow. "Should I ask them to get it done in time for Christmas? Two months should be enough time."

Hoping Ian would stay that long, Cecily nodded. "Please."

Mags laughed and hugged Cecily quickly. She went to the stove, picked up the kettle, and then carried it to the sink to fill, saying, "I'm so happy for you. You've been alone too long, you know."

"Mags…" Cecily gave a smile. "He's only here for the winter. He'll be back in Manhattan before spring."

"You say that, but I saw the way he watched you through lunch," Mags answered slyly. "You can't tell me there isn't *something* between you two."

Cecily nodded, caught herself at it, and shook her head instead as bands of tension locked around her chest. "It's just…casual," she insisted, and her smile turned brittle, because it *wasn't*. Not for her.

Ian talked about Manhattan all the time—his cases, his social circle, his clients. But Cecily…somewhere inside, she'd still been living day-to-day, and he had just slotted into her life as if he'd always belonged there. She felt *better* now, better than she had in years, as if a part of her from before the war was slowly reawakening.

She didn't allow herself to think about what would happen when he went back to Manhattan. He would pick up the pieces of his old life, and Cecily…Cecily would go back to the cabin, back to surviving instead of really living, back to being alone, and all the work she'd done to fortify herself would be gone, leaving her raw and condemned to her self-imposed isolation.

Mags's quiet voice intruded on her bleak thoughts. "Cecily?"

She gave a quick, forced smile and shook her

head. "Sorry," she said, hearing the unsteady edge in her voice. "I'm just—I should go check on Ian. The weather. Unpredictable."

Mags's brown eyes went soft and sympathetic. In the years they'd been friends, she'd grown accustomed to Cecily's mood swings. She'd once asked what was wrong, but she hadn't pushed for an explanation. "Let me. The tea is almost ready."

Cecily thought about going to find Ian. She could imagine how his eyes would sparkle with pleasure at the rare day of sunshine, and she flinched inside. Unable to answer, she nodded gratefully and was relieved when Mags left without another word.

⁓

The day was gorgeous, bright and brisk. Ian squinted against the glare that came through his polarized glasses and threw another rock into the river. This really was paradise, the sort of place city dwellers dreamed about one day having—somewhere to get away from it all, where life moved slowly and there was no constant buzz of cell phones and typing and shouting and traffic. Even his back felt better, despite the bumpy ride on the quad.

He should have hated it, but every time he felt resentment creep up at the thought of his willing exile, it died out at the thought of being here with Cecily.

Footsteps crunched through the snow and leaves. He turned, grinning with anticipation, and then blinked in surprise to see Marguerite, rather than Cecily. "You have a great view of the river," he said conversationally.

"Thanks." Mags came up beside him, hands shoved into her pockets.

Like Ian, she had her hood down, though her scarf was tucked high up under her chin. He glanced at her elegant profile, noting the way the sun brought out light shades in her rich brown hair. He should have been attracted to her. In Manhattan, he would've approached her anywhere, whether in a bar or nightclub or even the courtroom. Now, though, there wasn't a hint of interest—not when his thoughts were full of pale, freckled skin and short red hair.

A hint of accusation crept into Mags's voice as she said, "We were talking about you."

"Me?"

"You." She tossed her head and said, "She said you're leaving her."

The words hit him like a punch, stealing his breath. "What?"

Defiantly, she crossed her arms and said, "I thought lawyers were supposed to be smart when it comes to people."

He sighed. "I've heard *every* bad lawyer joke—"

"She loves you!"

He froze, staring at her, convinced he'd misheard.

As though his silence gave her courage, she turned and snapped out, "You're breaking her heart."

He actually backed up a step, scrambling to try and rally himself. This was ridiculous. Cecily was affectionate and friendly, yes, and she smiled more often now than she had just a week ago, but *love*? They were nothing more than friends, as much as he might have liked it to be otherwise.

"You don't even care, do you?" Mags pressed. She stabbed a finger into his chest, hard enough that it actually hurt, and demanded, "If you don't care, why don't you just go back to New York now? Maybe give her a chance to get over you?"

"Whatever you think is going on, you're wrong," he insisted, going automatically on the defensive. He looked around at the trees, hoping to see Cecily coming to his rescue, but he and Mags were alone.

"At least tell her now, so she—"

"Tell her *what*?" he demanded, glaring at her so fiercely that it was her turn to back away.

Then she rallied and snapped, "That you *don't* love her! It's not fair, leading her on like that."

Icy cold calm settled over him—always a dangerous sign when it happened outside the courtroom. "Please do me the courtesy of staying out of our private affairs. You have *no idea* what's going on between us."

"She's been my best friend for seven years."

"And what have you done to *help* her?" he asked sharply.

Apparently, she wasn't expecting to hear that. She stared at him, her angry expression melting into surprise, and he took advantage of her silence to leave the riverbank.

Anger carried him across the yard, though his steps slowed as he approached the house. A hint of worry and doubt began to creep through his confidence. What if Marguerite was right? She couldn't be. Ian would know if Cecily was in love with him.

Cecily came out of the house, bundled in her parka, ready to go. After ten days, he could read her mood almost perfectly. He could see the first hints of tension and anxiety before they even registered in her consciousness. He knew when she was bored or tired or frustrated with her writing. He knew how to provoke a smile or that dark, needy shade of brown that came into her eyes when they touched.

She wanted him. But love? He knew how *he* felt. He knew he wanted her to come back to Manhattan with him—to see if they could have something more together—but Cecily... She didn't love him.

Cecily joined him at the foot of the stairs up to Mags's back door. "You all right?"

"Yes." He fussed with her scarf to have the excuse to touch her face and watched as her smile bloomed. "Are you?"

Her smile faltered a bit. "I'm fine. You'd better put your gloves on," she said and went to say good-bye to Marguerite, who'd followed them back to the cabin. He looked at her, noting the mix of guilt and stubbornness in her expression, though she didn't say anything to Cecily, as they hugged good-bye. Perhaps she was re-thinking her assessment of their relationship, or perhaps she just felt guilty for interfering. Either way, she said nothing, and Ian breathed a sigh of relief when Cecily climbed onto the quad for the ride home.

"It's Wednesday, isn't it?" Cecily asked a couple of hours later, breathing deeply as she walked into the cabin. Before leaving, she'd filled the Dutch oven and buried it in the coals of the wood-burning stove. Now, the smell of onions and garlic and rich broth made her stomach growl.

"I think so, yes," he answered as he followed her inside.

"Halloween, then. God, I used to love Halloween," she said idly, leaning against the archway between the kitchen and living room. She didn't expect a response—he wasn't one for idle conversation—but when he ignored her completely to go into the living room, she couldn't help feeling a little bit alone. She glanced back to see he'd sat down to open his laptop.

Wonderful. So they weren't talking at all. Or was she just being oversensitive? A week ago, she'd been glad he was quiet company, not placing demands on her time. She needed to find that detachment again. In a few months, he would be gone.

Fuck. She needed to stop thinking about it.

She got rid of her jacket and went to the kitchen to make coffee. She focused on tonight, looking forward to a hot meal and Ian's attentions and maybe, just maybe, having only one nightmare. He'd enjoy tonight and not think about next week or next month, and it would all be fine.

"Dinner should be ready by now," she said.

"Bring it here," he answered, never looking away from his laptop.

Forgetting her resolution to enjoy their time together, she snapped, "Do I look like a waitress?"

His head came up, and he frowned. "I'm sorry. I'm just…distracted."

She met his eyes and felt a twinge of irrational guilt. He was probably anxious to get back home and get back to work. Not wanting to ruin what little time they had left together, she shrugged. "It's fine," she said and went to go serve up the roast that had been cooking all day.

She came back to the living room, carrying his plate, just in time to see him shut his laptop and flip the switch that turned off the satellite receiver and the modem. Irritation spiked through her, and she asked, "Change your mind, then?"

He caught her hand before she could move away. Her fingers were warm, and he pressed a kiss to the tips, saying, "I'm sorry. I didn't mean to…" He gestured at the laptop. "I'm sorry."

He didn't belong here. He had to be feeling edgy, needing any connection to the outside world. She looked into his blue-gray eyes and saw only contrition. She leaned in and kissed him, nothing more than a brush of lips. "It's all right. Do you want to eat here?"

"Kitchen table, like sane adults?" he suggested.

She laughed. "Sane adults. Sure, we can pretend, for the night."

Through the ride home from Marguerite's, Ian had tried to figure out a way to spark Cecily's interest in coming to Manhattan with him, even for a visit. But after a painfully slow crawl through event websites for the tri-state area, he realized that luring her to Manhattan surely wouldn't be as simple as buying tickets to a museum showing or the symphony. But what *did* she like? Reading and writing, yes, but how could he use that? Offer a tour of Manhattan's libraries? A shopping day to find treasures in little bookstores?

"Dinner okay?" she asked as he finished the last bite.

He smiled, brushing his leg against hers beneath the table. "Very good. I haven't eaten this well since I lived with my family. Our cook won awards before he retired and came to work for us."

"Wow. Count yourself lucky, then. I lived on noodles and pizza through college," she answered with a laugh.

She stood to gather the dishes, and Ian caught her hands and rose with her. "Let me," he suggested. He gave a tug to pull her close, though he didn't put his arms around her—he didn't trap her. Instead, he rested his hands on her hips and suggested, "Why don't you go relax in the shower? I'll clean up here."

Her smile turned curious, and then pleased. "Thank you," she said, giving him a quick kiss.

Feeling better, as if he'd redeemed himself for his earlier rudeness, he listened to the water heater gurgle as he washed up after dinner and put away the leftovers. Then he went to the living room and built up the fire.

She came out wearing jeans and a button-down shirt hanging untucked over her hips. He didn't think she was carrying her gun, and he counted that as a positive sign that she was relaxed and happy. She sat down at the desk and took her clunky laptop out of the drawer. "Let me just check my email real quick."

He decided to take her words as a good sign, and he considered building up the bedroom fire as well, but decided not to push his luck. Instead, he arranged logs and listened to her start up her clunky old laptop. When he heard her start typing, he rose, wincing at the residual ache in his back, and went to stand behind her. Instead of watching what she was doing, he combed his fingers through her wet hair, enjoying the silky soft feel. She didn't use product that made her hair crunchy or sticky, which was one more appealing difference between her and the women he used to date back home.

Her sigh was nearly a purr. She closed her laptop and shut everything down, and he leaned close to brush a kiss against her ear. "All done?"

"Mmm. Yes." She tipped her head back against his shoulder. Then she rolled the chair two inches back and turned to rise. He stopped her carefully, resting his fingertips lightly on her shoulder. He was wary of triggering another attack, but he needed to push her boundaries. There was no other way to prove to her that she was strong enough to leave the cocoon of the cabin and go back into the world, at his side.

"Stay," he suggested, circling around in front of her. He stayed slightly off-center, leaving one side clear—a reassurance to her subconscious that she could walk away at any time, if she felt the need. Slowly, he moved his hand from her shoulder to her chest and down, fingers catching on the buttons and dipping into the gaps to brush soft skin underneath.

Tentatively, she leaned back again, eyes fixed on him. She licked her lips, and he couldn't resist leaning in to chase her tongue back into her mouth in a kiss that seemed to catch her off guard. Her hands skimmed up his sides, holding him close with a light touch.

He caught her face much more firmly, biting at her lower lip before he swept his tongue back into her mouth. He lowered himself to kneel upright in front of her, body pressed against her right leg. He lifted his hand and touched her chest again.

This time, when he followed the trail of shirt buttons down, she shivered and whispered, "Ian."

"Don't talk," he said, kissing her into silence. When she relaxed, complying, he kissed her again and brushed his fingertips over her eyelashes. "Keep your eyes closed for me."

Tension rippled through her, but she nodded, her expression taking on an air of determination. She licked her lips again and opened her mouth as if to speak, then closed it again.

After one more kiss to reward her self-control, he knelt back on his heels, resting his hands on her thighs. Immediately, her legs parted just slightly, the movement so subtle as to be subconscious. He smiled, watching her expression as he trailed his hands down to her inner thighs. He pressed her legs open a bit more, taking the subconscious movement and making it his own.

He moved his hands up the insides of her thighs, reading the subtle responses on her face. He lightened his pressure as he ran his fingers over her fly, following the contours of her jeans. Cecily shifted her hips but made no effort to move away, and her eyes stayed closed. Her breathing was loud over the ever-present crackle of burning wood.

The quality of her tension had changed. He considered drawing this out, but the sight of her tongue as it darted out to wet her parted lips shattered his patience. He unbuttoned her jeans and drew down the zipper, watching for any sign that he should stop or slow down. He wanted her to want this as much as he did.

But she didn't object. She bit her lip, hands tightening on the seat of the chair.

"Lift," he said, his voice lower and rougher than he'd anticipated. His own body was reminding him of his desire, but he pushed it aside to focus solely on her.

Without hesitation, she shifted against the chair,

bracing her feet on the floor. She lifted her hips enough
for Ian to work her jeans down her legs. She let him pull
them off her feet. He considered taking off her socks,
but there was something adorable about her in thick
socks and an oversized button-down. Instead, he took
off his glasses and set them on the desk. Then he leaned
over to press his mouth against her cotton panties. He
breathed through the stretchy fabric.

She moaned and whispered, "Fuck," under her breath.
She slid one hand into his hair.

He lifted his head to look up at her face. "Shh," he
reminded her, smiling when he saw she'd kept her eyes
closed, as he'd asked.

She exhaled softly, jaw going tight. She scratched her
fingers over his scalp. Seconds ticked by. Entranced, he
watched her struggle against her own impulse to speak
or move or pull his head back down, and he saw the
moment that she surrendered. She relaxed, waiting for
him to continue or not, as he chose.

Heat blossomed deep in his gut as, for one moment,
he mentally abandoned his plan. He considered picking
her up and moving her to the desk, or laying her down
on the sofa to take her slowly, lavishing attention on
her body until her self-control broke. He thought about
two nights ago and how he could lie down on the sofa
instead and have her do all the work, giving him the
chance to watch her every reaction.

Only the fact that he had a goal kept him on track. He
pushed aside the fantasies, though not permanently—he
would indulge in every one of them, some other night.
Now, he leaned down again, pressing his lips to the
damp spot of fabric. Cecily's whole body reacted with a

twitch, and her hands dropped to clench the sides of the chair. He hid a smile and opened his mouth, pressing his tongue to the fabric as he exhaled slowly and listened to the quiet sounds she made.

With slow, teasing motions, he worked his fingers under the waistband of her panties. Almost immediately, she went to lift her hips, until he let go of the elastic to press her back down. "Don't move," he warned.

She growled under her breath, knuckles going white on the seat of the chair. She added a huff to express her displeasure, but she was still playing by the rules. Mostly.

Quietly laughing, he eased the waistband away from her skin and leaned over to lick at her abdomen. Her breath hitched; she wasn't ticklish there, but the touch had caught her by surprise. He slid his hands together, pulling the waistband farther away, exposing soft red curls to the cool air for a moment. Then he ducked his head and licked again, slipping his fingers down to tease over her clit.

With a broken sigh, she arched her back, pushing her hips forward against his touch. He moved between her legs to better tease, licking to the side, tasting the soft skin of her hip. Her breathing became ragged.

When he finally said, "Lift up," her movement was so abrupt that the chair rolled back three inches until he caught it by the base. She swore under her breath, but he let it pass, amused by her overwhelming arousal. She was usually the model of self-control, which made its loss to pleasure that much more appealing.

Once she conquered her fears, Ian would be free to push her further than she'd ever imagined. The thought of bringing her such pleasure was intoxicating, stealing his breath away. He knew it would be glorious.

———— ∿ ————

Cecily's head rolled back against the chair when Ian finally—*finally*—licked over her clit and slid a finger inside her body. She bit her lip to keep quiet, thinking only that if she said anything, he might stop, and she might well die on the spot if he did.

It wasn't possible that he had her so on edge now, with virtually no actual foreplay. The only explanation was that she'd somehow reverted to being a teenager. Two nights of mind-blowing sex, a night off in preparation for a predawn deer hunt, and now she was right back on the edge of desperation again.

For now, though, she lost herself in the feel of his mouth and fingers, the teasing brush of teeth, the hard flex of his tongue. It took an eternity for her to remember that the condoms were still in the other room.

She let go of the chair to reach for his shoulder. "Stop. Ian—"

He backed away and lifted his free hand to touch her lips. "Trust me."

She hesitated and started to say *condom*, but he turned his hand to cover her mouth.

"Trust me, Cecily."

She did. It wasn't his gorgeous baritone or commanding voice or the fact that her body was screaming for release. She had no reason to trust him, except that he had yet to betray her trust, and she didn't think that he ever would.

She trusted him, so she pushed aside her concerns

and nodded, realizing only then that her eyes were still closed. The thought made her want to open them, to look down into his eyes and watch, but she didn't. So she tried to relax—to show, silently and without moving, that she was complying.

It felt like forever before he finally took his hand away. She pressed her lips together to keep from speaking. She had no idea if she'd insist he get a condom or if she'd plead for him to continue. But a moment later, the point was moot. He licked a broad stripe up over the center of her panties, tearing a moan from her throat. Then he tugged down her panties and teased his tongue over her clit, lighting fireworks behind her eyes at the hot pleasure that coiled deep in her body.

He was far too good at this, she decided. It was impossible, the way he knew *exactly* how to bring her to the very edge before he backed off again, lightly sweeping his tongue down over her heat as the urgency receded. Then he moved back up to her clit with a hard, intense lick, and her world narrowed down to the effort not to grab his hair and hold him to her.

When he pulled back, she made a sound suspiciously like a whimper. She nearly let go of the chair, and her eyelids fluttered, almost opening. Then he pushed a second finger inside her, curled and pressed up, and licked over her clit all at once. She bit her lip, catching skin between her teeth, as he brought her to the edge and pushed hard, sending sharp heat to spike through her in waves of pleasure that left her breathless and tingling.

She forgot about silence, forgot about stillness, forgot about keeping her eyes closed.

Forgot about everything for a moment.

Breathless, she looked down, feeling the little after-shocks of her orgasm settle into her gut and chest, warming her. She met his beautiful blue-gray eyes and saw nothing but rapt pleasure. No demands or expectations.

"You're amazing," she whispered, cupping his cheek with one shaky hand, knuckles aching from the strain of clenching the chair.

Ian closed his eyes and pressed into the touch like a cat needing to be petted. With a soft smile, she leaned down, brushed his blond hair aside, and kissed his forehead. At some point, her growing affection had crept up behind her, evolving into something deeper, something far more powerful, and she had to close her mouth to keep from saying something she might well regret.

He's leaving, she reminded herself, sliding her hand to the back of his neck. In response, he drew close, chest pressed to her legs, fingers curved over her bare thighs.

Now that the desperate need had been sated, she had to work to fight off a growing sense of loss. They had one less time together in the future, one more memory that she knew wouldn't be enough to hold her steady, once he was gone. She swallowed, throat tight, and closed her eyes against the growing pressure that she couldn't face.

When she finally could speak, she asked, "Bed?"

In answer, he drew back to look at her, eyes flicking over her face. His eyes went wide, and his stare turned disconcertingly intense. Remembering his unnatural ability to read every one of her thoughts at a glance, she looked away and rose, pushing the wheeled chair back to make room. She pulled up her panties and tugged down the hem of her shirt so she wouldn't feel quite so exposed. "I'll be right in," she said. Then, cowardly as it was, she retreated, crossing the bedroom to go into the bathroom.

There, she closed the door and leaned back against it, trying to convince herself that she couldn't be falling in love. Not just after ten days. And definitely not with Ian, who was going to leave, whether she loved him or not.

Chapter 16

October 31

TOO STUNNED TO MOVE, IAN WATCHED CECILY disappear into the bathroom. He could still feel her hand on his face, the kiss she'd pressed to his forehead. When he closed his eyes, he could see, with perfect clarity, every detail of her expression as their eyes had met, and he could hear in his imagination the three words that she hadn't spoken.

So many times before, he'd faced his colleagues and schoolmates and clients and the police, and he'd told every single one of them that they were all too blind to see properly. Too rooted in expectations to accept the truth, simply because it didn't fit in with whatever stories they'd constructed in their minds. Sir Arthur Conan Doyle had once written, as Sherlock Holmes, "When you have eliminated the impossible, whatever remains, however improbable, must be the truth." Ian had lived by those words since he'd been old enough to understand the basic principles of law and reason.

In this case, her tender expression and gentle touch left no room for doubt. He couldn't even lay blame on the haze of post-orgasmic neurochemicals. The look in her eyes had been far too eloquent for anything other than a genuine emotional reaction.

No... Not that look. The fear that had followed—fear of loss.

Marguerite had insisted Cecily loved him. Was she right?

He rose, back aching as if it were on fire, and let himself out into the night. It was freezing, but he needed the cold to help him think. The taste of her body was like a drug, turning his thoughts slow and lazy with satisfaction at how completely she'd given herself to him.

"*Trust me*," Ian had said, and she had, beautifully.

Shivering, he looked at the sky, searching out the stars between the clouds that were rolling in.

Cecily loved him. It struck him as unlikely and probably unwise, but it was apparently true.

Cecily was afraid of him—afraid of losing him.

But that was a false fear. He didn't want to leave without her. All she had to do was be willing to take a chance—to follow the courage that was an intrinsic part of her psyche—and they could be together, which was what she wanted. What *Ian* wanted, too, more than he'd ever wanted anything before.

Was it love?

Yes.

When Preston lost Lilit, he'd told Ian to harden himself against emotional attachments. He had been young enough that Preston's rebellion caught fire in his mind. He'd taken Preston's word as law, finding emotional distance no handicap at all to getting whatever he wanted.

Early on, Ian had learned how to read people, how to manipulate people, and he'd always thought that was enough. Free of emotional entanglement, sex had been an easy distraction during school or a way to celebrate courtroom victories. He'd prided himself on being immune to the emotional vulnerability that others seemed to seek out recklessly, no matter how often they paid the price in breakups and divorces.

Now, he closed his eyes and thought about Cecily, recognizing that he'd entirely lost his objective distance. He laughed softly, a bit bitterly, and breathed in icy air. All the while, he'd been trying to encourage her to trust him, to let him help her heal, and instead, he'd let her become a part of him. He would sooner cut off a limb than lose her.

As the cold settled into his bones, turning the ache in his back into a bonfire, he tried to find answers. He had no plan for how to proceed—no past experience to draw upon. It seemed inconceivable to consider walking up to her to say, "I love you," with no warning. He'd too often seen those three short, ridiculous words turn into an emotional minefield of misunderstandings and expectations.

No, *saying* it would be too dangerous—even pointless, except perhaps for the momentary self-gratification of expressing himself. Even thinking those words provoked a physical reaction that entirely eclipsed the sexual desire he had for her, filling him with an all-consuming warmth.

He went back inside, and the warmth of the fires hit him like a truck. Cecily was still in the bathroom, so he went into the bedroom, closed the door, and went to build up the fire. As he stirred up the embers and coaxed the fire to catch, he considered fetching drinks for them both. After his unintentional addiction to painkillers, he was still wary of alcohol, but one glass would help her to relax. Then he pushed the idea aside. He wanted her trust, and that meant conscious, fully aware consent, not trust born of artificially relaxed inhibitions.

The bathroom door clicked, hinges squeaking softly as she entered the bedroom and closed the door again. "Need help?" she offered. Her voice was two steps higher than normal; she was still anxious but hiding it as best she could.

Deciding that the fire would do for now, he shook his head, rose, and turned to look her over. She'd changed her button-down for a T-shirt, but her legs were still bare. "Get under the blankets before you freeze. The room hasn't warmed up yet," he urged, pulling the stacked blankets back for her.

With a muttered thanks, she climbed into bed and slid across to her usual side, avoiding looking at him. The evasion hurt; it was his turn to retreat to the bathroom, where he closed the door and hid like a coward, trying to figure out what to do next.

~~~

Ian was in the bathroom for almost ten minutes, leaving Cecily to anxiously wonder if she'd finally ended up pushing him away. She hoped not, but...in a way, ending things now would be easier on them both. They could develop a distant friendship and part without any pain later.

Then he came out, and she forgot her good intentions under the sight of firelight playing over every inch of beautifully bare skin. Idly, she thought she could really learn to hate him for being such a gorgeous, perfect bastard. Half-remembered sayings flitted through her mind, things about love and loss and how experiencing one day of love balanced out a lifetime of loss, and she decided that all of that was bullshit.

Seven years ago, she thought she'd lost everything there was to lose. Then Ian Fairchild had swept into her life and turned everything upside down, and she realized she hadn't been living at all until now. And soon it would all be gone again, except the emptiness would be that much bigger.

Casually, he threw an armful of clothes into the laundry basket and got under the blankets. He didn't fuck around with staying on his side of the bed or waiting for her to close the last foot of space between them. He worked his way across the mattress and worked one arm under her pillow as he settled down on his back.

"Cecily," he said quietly.

"Ian," she protested, wanting to turn her back and curl up and try to stop hurting. Anticipation of pain was sometimes worse than the pain itself. That lesson had been cut and burned into her flesh, and now she was learning it all over again in a way that couldn't be stitched or bandaged. She *needed* to roll onto her left side, facing away from him, and pretend that the emptiness was already there, just so she could start trying to acclimate to it.

"Trust me," he said, as seemed to be his habit for the night. But then he added, "Please," and while she could have resisted the first, she had no defense against the second.

She moved close enough that her T-shirt brushed against his side whenever he inhaled, but that wasn't enough for him. The arm snaked out from under her pillow, circling her back, and she fought the instinct to flail and get free. The pressure was gentle, not stifling, and soft touches guided her to roll over until she was lying on top of him.

She thought about protesting—she hurt too much, deep inside her chest, to have any interest in sex. But his hands settled lightly on the small of her back, and he looked up at her with a serious, thoughtful expression that silenced her.

"I will never be bored of you," he said quietly.

She stared down at him, trying to think of how she could possibly respond to that, but there were too many layers of meaning hidden below the outwardly simple phrase. She studied his expression, half-hidden by the shadows. Her right shoulder started to give out under her own weight, and she shifted more weight to her left arm.

Ian frowned and ran his hands up her back, pressing more firmly between her shoulder blades. "Lie down before you hurt yourself," he insisted.

"You're—"

"Cecily." He sighed, pulling her close, for the first time in days taking choice away from her. Fear rose up, choking her from the inside, and her pulse hammered in her ears. Right as she neared the breaking point where she'd *have to* get free, at any cost, his arms relaxed and fell aside.

It was like sunlight breaking through clouds. She drew in a deep breath that was almost a gasp and felt the panic start to drain away, like water trickling through a clogged pipe. His hands moved down to rest lightly on her ribs, idly tracing ticklish little circles on her sides. It took some time for her to realize those circles were drawn to the rhythm of her breath, and she fixed her attention on them, consciously trying to match the movements. She didn't know which changed first—her breathing or the movement of his fingers—but soon she was relaxed enough to inch down so she could rest her head on his perfect, unscarred right shoulder.

His left hand slipped up, fingers combing through her hair, and though she wasn't precisely comfortable, fighting to balance on his too-thin frame, hip bones digging into her abdomen, she stayed. She didn't have this closeness in her life—not with anyone—and as much as it would hurt to lose it again, now she wanted to stockpile the memories, to arm herself against the coming loss.

"I won't hurt you," Ian said, his voice a deep, resonant rumble that seemed to sing along her bones.

She closed her eyes and curled her fingers over his shoulders. The feeling of fingers in her hair was hypnotic. "I know."

"I will push you, though never more than you can endure. I promise."

She sighed and moved, fighting his arm for a few seconds; he relented and let her go. She rolled onto her back a foot away, kicking to sort out the blankets tangled around her legs, and pressed her hands to her eyes.

"You're not here to analyze me."

"I'm not analyzing." Ian twisted up onto his side to face her. His right hand slid across under the blanket to settle possessively on her hip. "I want you with me."

She went tense and still, her mind thrown back to the times when a shot rang out from nowhere, echoing through the maze of twisting streets and tall buildings, and all you could do was drop for the nearest cover, never knowing if you were on the right side of the wall to hide from the sniper or if he was somewhere behind her. She wasn't infantry, but that had been no protection then, and she was equally defenseless now.

"Always," he promised.

Her mind shattered, not into darkness but into a war against itself, a war she could never win, between the side of her that wanted to believe that *always* meant what she thought it meant—what she hoped it meant— and the other part, the part that found safety in the shadows and solitude.

She knew better than to hope that this was his awkward way of offering to stay in Canada, but she wanted to cling to that tiny hope anyway, because the alternative was impossible. She couldn't go to Manhattan, not even with the temptation of Ian to lure her there. She could barely stay in Pinelake for more than a few hours, and she knew every single resident. Even the trip to Little Prairie had strained her self-control, leaving her with two solid nights of nightmares. If a tiny town in the middle of nowhere could put her on edge, Manhattan would leave her catatonic. She'd end up living in his closet like some sort of strange monster, creeping out at night to feed herself, returning to her lair without anyone ever seeing her.

"Cecily." Ian snapped out her name like a verbal slap.

Recognizing the signs of panic growing inside her, she lowered her fisted hands from her eyes and slowly worked her fingers open. Her palms stung from where her nails had dug in, and her chest burned as though she'd stopped breathing.

She turned to look at Ian, who took the slight movement as an invitation to inch closer. "I can't—"

"No, not yet," he agreed steadily. He deliberately moved his hand from her hip to her heart.

She caught his hand, clenching tight around long, fine fingers. Her grip must have hurt, but she couldn't stop herself, and he made no protest. "I can't," she repeated.

"You *will*, though." He held his hand steady over her heart, so she could feel warm skin through her T-shirt. He lifted up onto his left elbow to look down into her eyes. "You're strong, Cecily. Stronger than anyone I know."

The kindness stung more than the fear and loneliness did. She closed her eyes, swallowing, her throat painfully tight.

"Have I given you any reason not to trust me?" he asked.

She didn't want to have this conversation, but he wasn't going to let her escape. She shook her head, hoping to get it over with quickly. Sleep wasn't painless, but at least it was an old, familiar pain. Even her nightmares would be easier to endure than this.

"Then trust me now," he continued relentlessly. "Say you'll let me help you. Please, Cecily."

"Fuck," she whispered raggedly. She opened her eyes, blinking rapidly for a second. "Why?"

"Because if you can't—if you try and you still can't come back with me—then I'll stay here with you."

Her world tilted as his words left her disoriented, scrambling for balance, because what she'd heard couldn't possibly be right. Ian loved Manhattan. Every time he mentioned it, his eyes lit up and his voice filled with excitement and life.

"You hate it here." She shook her head and rolled over, twisting around to face him. She didn't dare let herself hope that this wasn't some huge misunderstanding, because this *couldn't* be happening to her.

"And deep inside, so do you," he said with a dismissive half shrug. He brushed his fingertips over her jaw and pressed a thumb to the corner of her mouth.

"But—"

His thumb swiped over her mouth, pressing gently to silence her. "Tell me that you trust me, Cecily."

"Ian…"

"Say it, Cecily. If you really do trust me, then say so."

She closed her eyes and lifted her hand to take his. She pressed her lips to his palm and quietly said, "I trust you."

He sighed as though relieved, as though there had been any doubt at all. "Thank you." He spread his fingers to catch hers, lacing their hands together. He ducked his head to brush his lips over her knuckles, and when he spoke again, his voice was subdued, almost hesitant. "I have to tell you something, but I don't want you to say anything until you've made your decision."

Anxiety twisted through her as she tried to anticipate his words and failed miserably. She'd been disoriented since this had all started, and she could still hardly believe he would give up Manhattan, just for her.

"What decision?"

"I want to be with you, Cecily."

Her heart leaped. "I—"

"Cecily," he interrupted. "Please, don't say anything. You need time to think, and you need to know… You have three choices here." He squeezed her hand and met her eyes. "We go to Manhattan, together. We stay here, together. Or you tell me to leave."

"Fuck. Ian—"

"Cecily," he interrupted. "Three choices. One day, when you're ready, I'll ask which one you choose. Then, you can tell me—but not until then."

She took a shaky breath. "Tell you what?" The obvious answer was which choice she would pick, but he wasn't one to ever choose the obvious answer.

"How you feel about me."

The anxiety evaporated into a sense of desperate relief. She knew how she felt. She'd been wrestling with that realization for what felt like days now, though she couldn't say exactly when it had started. "But I know—"

"Not until then, Cecily," he interrupted gently, "and you're not ready now."

She folded her arm beneath herself and lay back down on her pillow. Ian mirrored her movement, and they looked into each other's eyes in the faint glow of reflected firelight. She smiled slightly. "This isn't how a normal relationship is supposed to work, you know."

"I don't want normal. I want you."

From anyone else, that would have been an insult, but she knew him too well to take it as such from him. "And how am I supposed to stand Manhattan for thirty seconds without 'normal'?"

He huffed and untangled his fingers so he could brush her hair away from her face. His hand slipped down to the back of her neck, holding her steady for a brief kiss. "You're not meant to be a tourist, Cecily. Anyone 'normal' venturing into *my* New York would be eaten alive. I want you strong and in control, but you will never, ever be normal."

"How is that *possibly* a compliment?" she asked, trying for indignant, though she ruined it with another smile.

"I already told you. Normal is boring."

Chapter 17

November 1

"DO YOU *EVER* SLEEP?" CECILY ASKED, HER VOICE A low, lazy growl. She didn't open her eyes, but her fingers, resting on Ian's arm, lifted to slide forward over his wrist.

"Not much. I spend a lot of time just thinking. Still, I've slept more here than I ever did before," he admitted, studying the subtle changes to Cecily's face as she awoke fully.

She laughed quietly, barely more than a huff of air and a smile. "Sleep okay when you did?"

"Fine." He wanted to lift his hand to touch her face and smooth down her hair, but he held still. Her fingers moved and shifted aimlessly over his wrist.

"I didn't wake you up?" she asked self-consciously. "My nightmares and all…"

"You had two, but I was able to interrupt them." He gave in to temptation and moved closer, shifting from his pillow to share hers. "Does it help? Do you feel better today than most mornings?"

She closed her eyes, considering, and slowly her lips turned up in a smile. "I think so." She lifted her head enough to briefly kiss his lips. "It's barely dawn. Want to go back to sleep?"

"Cecily…"

Grinning now, she sat up and arched her back, eyes closing as she stretched. He admired the strength of her shoulders and back just as much as her curves, half-seen through her T-shirt. "Waste of time, right."

He couldn't resist reaching out to smooth his hand up her back, careful not to disturb the T-shirt too much. "You know me so well."

She pushed back against his hand and lowered her arms, rubbing briefly at her right shoulder. "Coffee? Breakfast?"

"Mmm." Ian lay back, twisting to watch as she slipped out from under the blankets, trying not to disturb them too much. She circled around the foot of the bed, pausing for a few seconds to throw another split log on the fire, and then disappeared into the bathroom.

Sleepily, he looked up at the ceiling, thinking back to last night. Cecily had been restless, waking him every time she moved, and he'd finally given in to the impulse to spend the night watching her instead of sleeping. Observing her, he'd begun to categorize the signs differentiating her dreams and nightmares, and he'd carefully experimented with gentle ways to interrupt the nightmares before they took hold.

Then he smiled as he realized she hadn't expressed any concern for his presence during her nightmares. There was no warning that she might hurt him. Knowing she trusted him turned his smile into a grin.

He listened to the sounds of her morning routine, noting when the toilet flushed and how long the water ran in the sink, distinguishing the hot water tap by the rattling pipes from the water heater. Most of his thoughts, though, were caught up in the hazy, wonderful fog of affection—of love—that consumed him. He'd seen people in this state before, smiling at everything as if their private, personal emotions somehow made the whole world brighter, but only now did he actually understand it.

Somehow, just knowing that she was in the next room made even this boring, primitive cabin into something wonderful.

He rolled onto his side to face the bathroom door, thinking that the person he'd been just a month ago would have looked at this future-self in horror. Well, even he had his moments of idiocy.

She returned to the bedroom and gave him an odd, amused look, full of affection. She'd started toward the closet but diverted to the bed, where she leaned down, weight on her left arm, to give him another soft kiss. "Bathroom's yours," she said unnecessarily, breath smelling of toothpaste, freckled skin flushed from a splash of warm water. "I'm going to fry up some eggs."

"You could just come back to bed," he suggested.

She grinned, the expression lighting up her whole face. "Or I could feed you up to a healthy weight, and then we could *both* go back to bed."

Idly, he considered suggesting breakfast in bed, but she stood back up and walked to the closet, leaving him to silently admire the view. He let his eyes trace down what he could see of her back, over the curve of her ass, down her strong legs. He thought about his past girlfriends who did yoga or Pilates or rotted their brains with mindless jogging on treadmills. Not one of them could possibly compare to Cecily.

"Have you been to Greece?"

The apparent non sequitur didn't even get a strange look. She was accustomed to his habit of skipping the boring parts of conversations. "No. You?" she asked, taking far too many clothes out of the closet: jeans, a T-shirt, a button-down shirt, and a sweater. She draped everything over her arm and went to the dresser.

"Years ago. Family trip." He curled around, bringing the pillow with him, so his view of Cecily continued without interruption. "They don't allow cars on Hydra Island. All travel is by foot or bicycle."

She glanced curiously over her shoulder as she found socks, panties, and a bra. "Sounds different."

"We could lease a villa there, on the beach. We'd never have to see anything, and you wouldn't have to put on all that clothing," he said a bit petulantly.

She laughed and tossed her clothes on the foot of the bed. She crawled up over the covers to trap him under her weight. "How exactly are we supposed to lease a villa on some primitive Greek island?"

He freed his arm from the blankets so he could take hold of her hip, hoping to coax her into staying for at least a little while. Coffee sounded appealing, in a distant way, but she belonged here with him, not out in the kitchen. "I have my passport and credit cards. What else do we need?"

Grinning, she leaned down to kiss his nose, startling him. "Small steps, Ian. Let's start with coffee," she said and got back off the bed, to his infinite disappointment.

———

Winter weather at the cabin was nothing if not unpredictable. By the time Cecily had the breakfast dishes

washed and a second pot of coffee brewed, the clouds
had dissipated, leaving the bright sun to melt through the
thin crust of ice and snow. She dried her hands, looking
out the kitchen window, and thought absently about all
the things she'd normally be doing to prepare for winter.
She had to check the snowmobile now, in case something had gone wrong while it sat idle over the summer.
She could go look for more deadfall; there was never
enough firewood. She could inspect the fuel lines to the
generator for any cracking or brittle spots. She could try
to catch her second deer.

Instead, she fixed up two mugs of coffee and carried
them into the living room, where Ian was sprawled over
the sofa, right arm draped out as though reaching for
the fire. In his left hand, he held a paperback. The book
didn't register at first; she had stocked the cabin with
every book that caught her eye at various used bookstores, thinking it wise to have years' worth of winter
reading materials on hand. Ian had dived into the collection without waiting for an invitation, so the sight of
him reading was nothing new.

Then she saw the cover art: a giant wolf-man with an
ax, a swordswoman in chain mail armor, and a leather-
wearing man with two wicked daggers. It was *her* book,
the first in a series she'd started two years ago.

"You know the target audience for that is age twelve
to eighteen, don't you?" she asked self-consciously.

"So I gathered." He rolled onto his side and pressed
back against the cushions, making just enough room for
her to perch on the edge of the sofa. "I've never read
much fiction."

She handed over the mug with three sugars, having

learned not to mix them up. She didn't know which was worse: accidentally drinking sugar-laced coffee or Ian having a sip of straight black. "Don't feel obliged to read it."

"I never feel obliged to do anything," he said bluntly, grin flashing to life. He sat up, managing to take off his glasses, curl around her, and press a kiss to the back of her neck, all without spilling a drop of coffee. He settled at her side, pressed close from shoulder to knee, and set her book gently down on the coffee table. He put his glasses on top of it and rested his mug on his knee. "What about your other book?"

She hissed in a breath, closing her eyes. She'd known that he would have found those pages by now, but she hadn't really allowed herself to think about them. "It's not for children."

His fingers pressed gently over her pulse. "At the bottom of the pages…"

"The X. I won't…I can't publish them under my name." She laughed uncomfortably. "Cecily Knight is too…cheery. It's not a very pleasant story. God knows I wouldn't want to read it."

"Does it help to write it?"

She shrugged. She turned the mug and took the handle with her left hand so she could drink without pulling away from his touch. "I don't know," she finally admitted. "I haven't made it far enough. Thirty-something pages is barely the first couple of chapters."

"Are you—"

She shook her head, rising abruptly. "We should go," she interrupted. "The sooner we get that second deer, the better. Towing the trailer with the snowmobile is a bitch."

Ian looked up at her with those too-sharp eyes, and she could almost see his brain analyzing her reaction. For one icy, suffocating moment, she thought he might push to keep her talking. But then he nodded and rose, fixing her with a wicked smile as he asked, "Care to help me change?"

She laughed, relieved, and pulled him down for a kiss, careful not to spill his coffee. "I'll help you warm up later. How's that?"

"I'll hold you to it."

—⁓—

When successful, deer hunting was an acceptable pastime, if the alternative was sitting alone in an isolated cabin with terrible Internet speed and several thousand chewed-up paperback books. When unsuccessful, though, deer hunting was cold, boring, and frustrating, even with the distraction that Cecily presented simply by existing. In a rare moment of empathy, Ian recognized that he was close to snapping and tried to look for any distraction, but none of his usual coping mechanisms were available. His mobile was a dead lump of plastic with no signal, his guitar was at the cabin, and his last resort—idiot-baiting—was entirely out of the question, given that she was the only living creature in earshot. There certainly weren't any deer.

So Ian trailed through the little piles of snow and mud puddles, staying well behind her, and tried to be patient, but finally the cold and silence got the best of him. He stomped forward to where she was standing under a tree, surveying their surroundings with her field glasses.

"We're not going to starve," he said, his voice sounding

absurdly loud in the silent forest, though he kept to a normal speaking volume. "Is there any sensible reason for us to stay here, when we could instead be back at the cabin, having sex?"

Cecily had begun to turn, most likely to reprimand him for startling the game animals who weren't there anyway. Then she dropped the field glasses, leaving them to swing against the strap around her neck, and started to grin.

Ian glared.

Instead of backing down, she laughed. "I take it that counts as a romantic proposition, coming from you?"

The laugh seemed to slip beneath his skin, winding through his ribs and around his heart, pushing away his boredom and irritation.

Ignoring his fierce glare, she set her gloved hands on his waist, compressing the down parka to pull him close against her body. Her kiss was cold and hot at once, soothing his mood that much more. As if of their own volition, his hands came up to circle her shoulders, and the last of his pique slipped away under the teasing swipes of her tongue.

When the kiss ended, he asked, "Does this mean we can go back?"

To his limitless frustration, she shook her head. "No, but I think I owe you for last night."

He blamed the cold on his inability to immediately see her intent. When she pushed him back, he almost tripped, startled. He scanned her face for any hint of anger or panic, but all he saw was sly amusement. Then his back hit a tree. Drops of water fell on his hood and rolled down the waterproof fabric, and the thick layer of down cushioned him from feeling the bark.

She kissed him again, pressing her chest against his, rising up on her toes to better reach. Despite heavy boots, he slipped on the tree roots and caught her arm for balance, remembering at the last moment to avoid her right shoulder. Then he almost slipped again as she dropped to a crouch in front of him, and her hands, now bare of gloves, slipped up under his hip-length parka to find his belt.

The last of his irritation vanished in a white-hot flash. Cecily was wonderful and brilliant, and even Ian could never predict what she'd do next. He dug his boots into the dirt between the tree roots and let his head fall back against the bark, closing his eyes in anticipation.

Then he almost yelped in indignant surprise. "Cold hands!" he snapped, sucking in his gut to avoid the icy touch.

She laughed, looking up at him. "I wasn't planning on using my hands."

Oh.

Ian's shiver had nothing to do with the cold. He thought about asking if she'd changed her mind about the condoms, but then decided there was no sense in talking at all. She opened his jeans, used icy fingers to tug down the waistband of his boxers, and licked at his cock just once. The contrast of freezing air and her hot tongue sent liquid fire boiling up from his gut, up through his spine, and into his brain, destroying all rational thought.

He reached down to touch her hair, but couldn't catch hold with his gloves on. Her laugh drove away the chilly air before her mouth followed, taking his entire half-hard cock into her mouth at once. Then she had to draw back as Ian went from halfway to entirely there in what felt like a single heartbeat.

"You're perfect," he whispered, fighting to keep his balance only because falling would mean she'd *stop*. "Cecily, you're wonderful. Oh, *fuck*."

She laughed without stopping, hands clenching on the backs of his thighs for balance. She was in an awkward crouch, not on her knees on the damp earth, and she kept having to pull back to breathe through her sniffling from the cold. He didn't dare move, though all he wanted was to thrust forward into her mouth. He had no idea how he'd gone so quickly from fatally bored to so aroused that he wouldn't notice if a bear attacked, except to ask it to wait and let him finish.

Then she found her balance, resting one knee on his boot, and it hurt enough to momentarily distract him until she took his cock deeper, fighting her gag reflex and swallowing until her nose pressed against his body.

"Oh, fuck. God, Cecily, don't stop. Please," he grated out, aware in some distant way that his voice had taken on overtones of pleading. "Please, don't stop."

Thankfully, she didn't even hesitate but kept at it instead, letting the gentle press of his hand guide her to move faster, taking him another fraction of an inch deeper into her mouth. Ian tried to gasp out a warning, but his mind had stopped functioning.

He came in a flash of blinding pleasure and affection he'd never even imagined, because love had never been tied up with sex for him. If he'd been able to speak, he might have let his thoughts—his feelings—escape, but it was all he could do to breathe. He didn't even flinch when cold fingertips brushed his abdomen as she pulled up his boxers, fastened his jeans, and then fumbled to get his belt buckled in place.

Cursing the gloves that made his fingers clumsy, he tried to help Cecily to her feet, but just ended up uselessly petting her parka. Laughing at his efforts, she fisted her bare hands into his jacket and kissed him, slow and sweet, filling the air with the warmth of their mingled breath.

"Thanks for last night," she whispered against his lips.

All but purring inside, Ian crossed his hands at the small of her back, holding her close, ignoring the rifle and field glasses trapped between their bodies. "Can we go hunting again tomorrow?"

Chapter 18

November 2

AS THE LITTLE AIRCRAFT TAXIED TO A STOP, IAN glanced sidelong at Cecily, who was busy with the controls. Tension had crept into her body and expression over the last hour as Little Prairie Air Traffic Control had guided them through the crowded airspace—well, crowded compared to Pinelake. Now, he could almost see the protective walls surrounding her. Necessary as they were, he hated them. He wondered if they'd ever truly be gone, or if she would simply learn how to better hide them.

"You don't have to do this," he insisted.

"After yesterday?" She laughed tightly and shook her head. Then she unlatched the door, letting a blast of cold air into the warm passenger compartment. Quickly, he zipped up his parka and exited his side of the plane.

He huffed, breath steaming in the frigid air, and fumbled his gloves out of his pockets as the chill settled into his fingers. Little Prairie wasn't nearly as remote as Pinelake, but that meant nothing when it came to fighting against the bitter chill. They'd discussed the trip to Little Prairie last night and this morning, and she'd absolutely refused to change her mind. She'd even gone so far as to tell him he could stay back at the cabin—as if he'd send her off alone?

Absolutely not. Especially not when she was doing this for *his* benefit, not her own.

So he walked beside her, trying to find the right space to offer comfort and support without crowding her. She led the way to the small terminal, where a security guard checked their identification and allowed them to enter. She looked around, then headed in the direction of a sign that promised car rentals. "You have a driver's license, city boy?"

Ian grinned, wishing she'd take off her sunglasses so he could see her eyes. "Yes, though driving in Manhattan is a futile effort. Makes it easier to steal Preston's car when I go on vacation, though." He was relieved that her answering laugh was a bit closer to normal.

Soon enough, they were in possession of a set of keys to a Ford Taurus and a paper map. Cecily followed him out to the parking lot and opened the map. He stopped looking for the car and glanced at the map. He'd been carrying his cell phone out of habit. Now, he powered it up and was relieved to see he had signal. As his phone started syncing with a backlog of emails and messages, he opened his navigation and said, "GPS. What's the destination address?"

"GPS? Really?" She turned away from the map to stare at the phone.

With anyone else, Ian would have asked sharp questions about living under a rock or in a dark cave. "Don't you have a—of course you don't," he said, momentarily caught off guard at the idea of someone in this modern age who owned an airplane, even a little one, but not a smartphone. And with no television and minimal Internet access, it was all too possible that she'd never even seen one.

He handed the phone to her, hit the lock button on the key fob, and then followed the sound of the horn to their car. He unlocked the doors and opened Cecily's. She gave him a tense smile of thanks, offered him the phone, and got into the passenger seat.

As he circled around to the driver's seat, he scanned his notifications. Over forty texts and twelve voice mails. He got into the car with a sigh and started the engine, reopening the navigation app. "Just put the health clinic address in here, and it'll tell us where to go."

"Civilian GPS," she said with a little shake of her head. She prodded uncertainly at the on-screen keyboard. "I never thought it would happen."

—⁓—

"This is the only reason to come to civilization," Cecily declared as she pulled open the door to an unfamiliar fast food restaurant.

Ian glanced skeptically at the gaudy red scrawl on the side of the building. He'd never been one for fast food, even in college. "Who's Tim Horton?" he asked, following her inside.

"Poor thing, you," she said mock-sadly. Despite the fact that the unremarkable beige restaurant was crowded, with three-quarters of the plastic tables occupied, she walked right in without hesitation.

Noticing that she was rubbing at her arm, he asked, "Did they take blood?"

She nodded, darting a glance at him as she got into line. "Yeah, but that was easy. You get used to it in the military. I ended up getting a birth control shot instead of pills. It's a little sore."

He moved a hand to the small of her back, and gave her a grateful smile. Despite having lived in isolation for seven years, she'd insisted on STI testing for herself. At the rehab clinic, the doctors had taken his blood every week, or so it seemed, and STI testing had been part of his intake screening.

The smell of coffee distracted him. They moved up the line to the counter, where he was faced not just with coffee but with an array of doughnuts and pastries. Fifteen minutes later, he was riding a fantastic sugar high, washing down the remains of his third doughnut with rich coffee. Cecily grinned at him, having taken the more traditional route of starting with chili, saving her doughnut for last. Faced with a boring chicken panini of his own, he eyed her doughnut and lifted a hand.

"Yes," she said, giving him a warning glare.

"Hm?"

"Yes, I am going to eat that." She kicked his shin under the table. "Eat your lunch. We'll get more to go, if you want."

He turned and smiled at her. "You know me so well," he said and picked up his sandwich. A bite proved it to be almost as good as the doughnut had been, which seemed somehow *wrong*. "Is this why you chose to come to Little Prairie?"

"Hm? Oh. No, this is a chain. They're all over Canada," she said, scraping her spoon in the bowl to get at the last of her chili.

"And yet, you live in the one town in Canada that *doesn't* have these?" he asked, using the sandwich to point at her still-untouched doughnut.

With another affectionate nudge, she promised,

"We'll come back whenever you like, at least until the snow sets in."

"Do you need to come back for the test results?"

She shook her head and tucked a strand of hair behind her ear. "We'll go to Pinelake Monday or Tuesday and use the phone at the airfield."

Ian nodded, hiding his disappointment at having to wait—though when he thought about it, the shot would require a week or so to take effect. So he finished half of his sandwich, and then changed the subject, saying, "I spoke to Preston."

She swallowed her bite of doughnut. "Oh? How is he?"

"Good. Meaning overworked, but he's not happy unless he's busy," Ian said with a wry smile. "He also said that if I didn't pass on his greetings and gratitude, he'd shoot me, so there's that."

She grinned. "He's a sweetheart."

"That's one word for it."

Chapter 19

November 7

CECILY BAGGED HER SECOND DEER BARELY AN HOUR into the hunt, thanks to an unlikely shot of opportunity. She'd been just ten yards away from the group of does when the wind blew just right and the snow cleared enough for her to see the herd, brown fur blending seamlessly against winter-bare brown trees. This time, she let Ian field dress the carcass, and he took to the task with grim determination.

By late afternoon, they were back at the cabin, carcass dressed and butchered, meat packed away in the deep freezer. Cecily made tea and set a pot of stew to reheat. When she heard a slap on the table, she glanced over at him and saw he'd dropped her paperback onto the kitchen table.

"There's a sequel. There has to be, with that ending," he complained as he sat down. He twisted so he could put his feet up on Cecily's usual chair. "It's not the one you're writing now, though."

"I finished the sequel this summer. Don't have a final copy yet," she answered apologetically. "I got the proof but had to send it back."

He huffed in irritation. "And you don't have an electronic copy."

"Actually, I do. It's—" She blinked, watching as he

pushed his chair away and left, long strides taking him back into the living room. A moment later, she heard the desk drawer open. "—on my laptop," she finished, amused, and pulled the tea bags out of the mugs.

"The battery's dead!" he called. "What's the point of having a laptop if you're going to let the battery run down?"

"I don't actually use it, in case you haven't noticed, except to email my publisher." She frowned, stirring sugar into his tea with loud clinks of the spoon. She'd set up a new email account for her writing, mostly so she wouldn't have to deal with messages from old friends from her past life.

She checked the fire in the stove, trying to gauge if it was hot enough to scorch the bottom of the stew, and then brought the tea out to the living room. Ian had made a mess of the desk, stacking his laptop on her in-progress stack of manuscript pages to make room for the second laptop, with the power cord draped over the box of blank paper on the other side.

"You don't even have a password?" he asked.

"Why bother? You're the first person to touch the thing beside me since I bought it, and you'd probably guess any password I thought up," she said, finding a clear spot for his tea, well away from the manuscript.

"True." He smiled at her. "The code for your gun safe is three-one-oh-three-four-six-one-six. Does it mean anything?"

"Other than the fact that you're terrifying?"

With a huff of amusement, he turned, saying, "It's a simple trick. One of my clients showed me. I'll show you."

Thinking it involved the laptop, she leaned in just as he rose. His elbow hit her arm, jostling her, and hot tea splashed everywhere, soaking through her button-down shirt and jeans and his sleeve.

The cup fell from her hand. She backed away and hit the couch with bruising force, overwhelmed by the memory of hot pain searing through her, pain she couldn't control, couldn't stop. She clawed her shirt away from her skin, panic rising up in her chest. She heard a footstep. Harsh voices shouted at her too fast for her to understand their words, every shout punctuated by more heat. More pain. She lashed out with a clumsy kick as she reached back, shoving something out of her way to make room to fight or escape.

"Cecily!"

The sound of her name—her first name, rather than her rank—cut through the suffocating, disorienting fear that gripped her. *Ian*, she thought, and the panic receded a notch. Dizzy, she crouched down so she could sit on the floor before she lost her balance and fell. She took a deep breath and heat seared into her skin, over her ribs, threatening to drag her under again.

"I'm fine," she said tightly, more for her own benefit than Ian's. Her fingers burned, clenched around the cooling fabric, but she could breathe. She knew he was nearby, just a few feet away, giving her the space she needed.

She opened her eyes, staring at the floor, and took a few more breaths. Her pulse started to slow, and a tiny, incredulous part of her mind thought that this hadn't been so bad. Her shirt was still warm under her hand and cool where she'd pulled it away from her body, allowing air to flow. It couldn't have been more than two minutes, start to finish. Maybe less. That was a hell of a lot better than two hours.

He moved, not to approach Cecily but to leave the room. She closed her eyes and leaned against the wood slats forming the back of the sofa. She had to find a way to stop this from happening. Ian would only tolerate this for so long before he left, and she'd be alone again. She was alone *now*—a thought that threatened to pull her under once more.

Then he returned, settling down on the floor nearby, a foot of space carefully left between them. "Take off your wet shirt," he said, holding out her warm bathrobe.

Her hesitation lasted less than a second. She tried to undo her shirt buttons, but her hands were shaking from the adrenaline still flooding her system. The harder she tried to steady herself, the worse the trembling became, until finally, embarrassed, she said, "Ian…"

Without a word, he leaned over and unbuttoned her shirt. He let her pull it off and took it. Cecily fought to tug the robe over herself, shivering from the cold air on wet skin.

"Do you need help standing?"

The denial was on her lips, but that, too, was pointless. She nodded and held out a hand, not meeting his eyes. "Please."

He took her hand and steadied himself, offering her balance without trying to guide her or cling to her. Embarrassed, hating that this kept happening to her, she murmured apologies which he ignored in favor of keeping her upright. When she was standing, he tugged the thick terry cloth closed, holding it at the waist with his free hand.

"Did it burn your legs?"

"No. Maybe. Shit, I don't know," she admitted. She thought about the effort it would take to get through her belt and jeans, and she was still wearing her boots. She gave up on the idea. Instead, she buried her face against his chest, breathing in the smoky wool of his soft sweater.

He let go of the robe and gently took her by the arms, making no move to hold her, to trap her, until she pressed closer, as if she could burrow into his warmth. Then his arms closed around her, and he pressed a kiss to her hair, offering a silent, comforting presence and demanding nothing in return.

Inside, Ian berated himself. He should have been more careful. He kept any hint of his thoughts out of his body language, knowing her senses were heightened on a subconscious level. She'd be looking for any hint that he was disappointed in her lack of self-control, and he was determined that she wouldn't see anything she could possibly misinterpret that way.

It had to be ten minutes before Cecily tensed, lifting her head fractionally. "This isn't going to work," she said, striving to control her voice. She was good enough to fool anyone who wasn't Ian. "I can't—I wouldn't make it even a day in Manhattan."

"Not like this, no," he agreed. He felt her surprise in the way she drew back just slightly, a shift of weight onto her heels. "I'm not asking you to leave now, though. I'm asking you to trust me—to let me help you. That's all."

"What's the point?" she sighed, breath warm through

the layers of shirts he wore. She leaned into his arms again, resignation heavy in the slump of her shoulders and the way her head bowed.

"Must there be a point? I want to do this."

"I'm not one of your clients, for you to figure out if I'm guilty or innocent."

"No, you're not." His arms tightened protectively, possessively—two new feelings that he was discovering he liked. "It *is* a scientific process, though. I'm not some"—he cast his mind about, trying to find just the right words to express his feelings about the doctors back at rehab—"some *witch doctor* stumbling about in your mind. I'm trained in logic. That's what you need, not voodoo."

Her tension disappeared in a snorted, choked burst of laughter. "Voodoo?" She leaned back enough to look up at him, grinning a bit desperately. "*Voodoo?*"

He shrugged dismissively. "I understand you. The more I get to know you, the more I can see what should have been so obvious to whoever failed to help you before. Let *me* help you."

"Why?" She reached up to touch his face. "Why is this so important? Three weeks ago, you didn't know I existed."

"Three weeks ago, neither of us had a future worth living for," he answered, feeling a little shiver crawl up his spine. A month ago, he would have killed someone to escape rehab and go back to Manhattan, even though he knew that Preston was right. The pressure of a career he loved would have driven him to take "just one more" painkiller.

He tightened his arms around her, ducking his

head down to kiss her. "Tell me this isn't better," he
said, drawing back only enough to speak, lips brushing against Cecily's with each syllable. "Tell me you
couldn't be content like this. Even happy."

She shook her head, sliding a hand around the back
of his neck to hold him close. "You'd just know I was
lying, if I tried," she whispered. "Trust you. That's all?"

He laughed quietly. "That's all."

"You know that's not... Trust doesn't come easily for
me." Her expression went distant as she looked down
so she could tie her robe closed, though she didn't step
away from him. "I can say 'I trust you' all day, but..."

"I know. But that's only here," he said, touching her
forehead. "Inside, you already do trust me."

With a faint smile, she challenged, "Cocky, aren't you?"

"I'm right." Then, in a rare fit of modesty, he corrected himself. "I'm almost always right."

That got a laugh. "Humble, too."

He grinned and touched her chin to lift her face,
meeting her eyes. "Look at the evidence. You fell asleep
beside me. I woke you from your nightmares, and you
barely moved. You didn't try to attack me or defend
yourself. You already trust me."

She took a deep breath and tipped her head back,
eyes falling closed. "Okay. Okay, I can see that," she
said slowly, opening her eyes again. "But look at this. I
mean, it was a fucking cup of tea, not—"

"Sensory association." Ian stepped back, sliding his
hand down her arm so he could lace their fingers together. He lifted his other hand to touch her chest, just
above the collar of her bathrobe. "Heat. Burns. I should
have been more careful."

The tension returned to her body, though she didn't pull away. "How could you possibly have known how I'd react? Even I wouldn't have guessed I'd—"

"I don't *guess*," Ian corrected, flattening his hand to feel her heartbeat. "It's an obvious mental connection. I'll be more careful in the future."

"I don't want you treating me like I'm made of glass."

"I wouldn't want you if you were." He looked into her eyes, searching for that strength, and quietly asked, "You don't see it, do you? You don't know how strong you actually are."

This time, she did pull away. She turned and walked for the bedroom, head bowed as she unbuckled her belt. "Strong enough that I live *here*? I'm not exactly impressed."

"Strong enough that you're alive at all." He followed, resisting the urge to chase her down and pull her close. The sight of her wasn't enough to soothe his irrational fear at the thought of losing her.

With a bitter little laugh, she said, "Yes, well. They did a good enough job of drumming that into my head at the hospital, even if they didn't accomplish much else."

"What?"

"'Suicide isn't an answer,'" she quoted.

Ian had known that she must have considered suicide, though only in a distant, rational way. Actually hearing her say the word was enough to break his resolve, like a knife in his heart. He crossed to where she stood by the fire in four quick strides. Startled, Cecily looked up, meeting his eyes for an instant before he pulled her into his arms. He told himself he shouldn't be holding her like this—that it would be too much, especially with the heavy emotional darkness pressing in on them from both sides—but he needed to feel her breath and heartbeat and warmth, to reassure some primitive corner of his mind that she was safe and alive. His breath came in strained gasps, and something in his chest shattered into spikes of hot pain.

Then her arms circled him, holding him just as tightly. "It's all right," she said softly, pressing a kiss to his throat. "It's okay. I'm here."

Of course she was. He wanted to snap at her for being so transparent, but he couldn't breathe enough to speak. He couldn't let go because he *needed* her in his arms, though all he could do was cling to her in silence as her hand pressed gentle circles against his back, as though he were the one in need of comforting.

Chapter 20

November 20

"YOU CAN'T KEEP SECRETS FROM ME," IAN SAID AS SOON as he circled the tail of the aircraft to Cecily's side. Cold wind swept across the airstrip behind the cabin and tugged at the hood of his parka. A painful chill settled into every inch of exposed skin. He sniffled and cupped his hands in front of his face, blowing on them to try and trap warm air.

"Oh, I'd say I can," she teased as she twisted around in the pilot's seat. She maneuvered a large canvas bundle to the passenger seat, and then lifted the cardboard box tucked into a corner of the cargo space. The mysterious packages had been the sole purpose of their trip to Pinelake. He didn't even know where she'd gotten them. She'd left him at the airport trailer while she went to do her shopping. Borrowing Mark's landline to call Preston didn't make up for not knowing where she'd gone.

To his infinite irritation, the box had been covered with butcher paper and securely closed with twine. Carefully, she handed it out to him. He gave it an experimental shake, but it was too well-padded to have any characteristic rattle or shifting weight. The bundle would have been much easier to identify, if he could just touch it. It was almost three feet across, with irregular lumps formed by layers of canvas and more twine.

"Get that inside before you freeze," she told him. "And if you open it, no sex for a week."

"Cecily—"

"No, make that *two weeks*," she threatened, waving him clear of the plane. She slammed her door and taxied the plane across the yard, toward the hangar.

Muttering under his breath, Ian carried the carton into the house and set it on the kitchen table. The package was small enough that it could have been delivered by regular post, though there were no shipping labels. There was no way he could get the twine unknotted, unfold the butcher paper, peek inside, and then put everything back before she was finished stowing the plane in the hangar.

Knowing her, she'd follow through with her threat, too. She wasn't the type to back down, once her mind was set on a course of action.

"Damn," he muttered, abandoning the box. He tossed his gloves on the table and went to the stove, building up the fire. They both needed something hot to drink.

By the time he had coffee brewed, Cecily was back inside. She put the canvas-wrapped bundle on the table beside the box and grinned at him. Then she pulled off her parka and draped it over the back of a chair. "Thanks," she said gratefully as she took the mug he offered.

"*Now* will you tell me what's in there?" he demanded, circling around behind her. He pressed an encouraging kiss to the back of her neck, brushing aside the strands of hair that were starting to grow in.

"Why should—" The word *I* trailed off into a moan as he closed his teeth on a lock of her hair and pulled sharply. "Fuck," she whispered, shivering back against him.

"Box first," he insisted, trying not to sound too smug.

She decided to cheat in retaliation, pushing back against him. She rose up on her toes, grinding her ass against him as if to suggest Ian forget all about the damned secret packages, because nothing in there could be better than the woman standing between him and it. He put his coffee safely on the table to free his hands so he could tug at the bottom of her old USMC sweatshirt. Happy to go along with the change of plans, she lifted her arms and turned as he got rid of the offending layer of heavy fabric.

"Box first, huh? Sure about that?" she asked, lowering her arms to circle his neck.

The sound he made as he ducked to kiss her was both a purr of satisfaction and a frustrated growl. He licked and nibbled at her lips until she was panting against him, fingers clenched in the back of his shirt, tugging the fabric out of his jeans.

"Show me," he whispered in the low, seductive tones he knew she couldn't refuse.

"No." She took a nip of her own, teeth closing on his bottom lip hard enough to make his whole body tingle.

"Stubborn," he complained, backing reluctantly away.

She grinned and said, "I have to be, to put up with you." Deliberately, she turned back and picked up her coffee again.

His huff of irritation wasn't very convincing. He wrapped his arms around her body and rested his head on her shoulder. "Then will you tell me what's in there?" he asked, flicking one finger in the direction of the canvas bundle.

"Nope." She tipped her head back and kissed his jaw.

"We'd be warmer if you went and built up the other fires. And if we were warmer, I could take off more than just my sweatshirt."

Smugly, he leaned forward against her and pressed kisses to the back of her neck. "Or I could do this," he murmured, licking the curve of her ear.

She shivered. This time, she put the coffee down hard enough to splash some out. "You're cheating."

"I am," he agreed, nipping at her earlobe. "You could show me what's in the box, or you could distract me. Your choice."

Shaking droplets of coffee off her fingers, she turned back to him and wrapped her arms around his shoulders. "Distraction it is," she said, and lifted up onto her toes to kiss him.

Surprising Ian was nearly impossible, but Cecily wasn't one to let "impossible" stop her from trying. She'd used the radio in the tiny attic to contact Mark and Marguerite, enlisting both in her plan. They'd cooperated enthusiastically, handling the purchasing and packaging, and Mark had kept Ian distracted at the airfield while Cecily picked up the surprises. Now, she just had to distract Ian until tomorrow.

Most nights, while dinner fried or simmered (or in one memorable case caught fire), Cecily sat down at the typewriter and wrote, keys out of sync with the rhythm of his guitar. She was finally back on schedule and had sent the first few chapters of her new novel to her editor. Tonight, though, she was too twisted up with anxiety to concentrate despite the soothing music.

Had this all been a mistake? Ian could be sensual and caring and sweet—and abrasive as hell, impatient, and childish. But he *wasn't* romantic, not by any stretch. She could barely imagine him signing an office birthday card much less thinking in terms of anniversaries. Certainly not anything as trivial as one month.

God, it was like Cecily was back in eighth grade, trying to work up the nerve to get Steve Matheson behind his dad's boathouse so she could try and kiss him.

She finally surrendered and turned away from the typewriter to watch him play. The light of the oil lamp was too harsh on his pale skin, so she turned the flame down until the only illumination was the warmer glow of the fireplace. Without pausing his playing, he opened his eyes and looked at her through his lashes.

Absolutely captivated, she met his gaze, making no attempt at all to conceal her thoughts or feelings. The words—those three little words—had yet to make their appearance, but she'd given up trying to control or hide how she felt. "*Trust me*," he had said, and she'd given him that trust, with equal parts excitement and terror.

She could believe, almost completely, that they would find a way to do this...*this*. Whether they spent next winter here at the cabin or made it to Manhattan by spring, they would be together, and her whole body ached with the intensity of her emotions.

His hands stilled on the strings, and he frowned at her. "What's wrong?"

Panic spiked through her, nothing to do with the war and everything to do with the unexpected, possibly irrational fear that he knew exactly what she was thinking and wanted nothing more to do with her. Sex was one thing; love was entirely different. And Ian had never said that word to her. Cecily *thought* they'd both been circling that declaration, awkward and tentative, but what if it had been her imagination? What if those three words never even entered his mind? There was a hell of a difference between "I'll never be bored of you" and "I love you," after all.

"Cecily," he snapped, his tone more worried than harsh. He set the guitar on the sofa and rose, eyes fixed not on her face but on the right side of her chest. "Are you in pain?"

She looked down, realized that she was rubbing the gunshot scar, and quickly curled her hand into a fist and dropped it to her side. "I'm fine."

"You're a terrible liar," he scoffed, not for the first time. He knelt down in front of her, touching the exact spot where she'd been rubbing. "Tell me."

She avoided his too-sharp eyes and looked at the fire instead. "I'm fine. Really."

He made an unsatisfied sort of sound. "Please?" he asked, and it was his turn to look away, eyes fixed to her shirt. "It's important, whatever it is. I was trying to help you write, and it didn't work. Why not?"

Confused, she turned back and lifted a hand to brush her fingers through his long, soft hair. "You were?"

"I don't just play random music like an iPod on shuffle." He pressed into her touch and smiled. "There are certain songs that help you focus when you're writing."

She smiled, some of her fears receding. Maybe he hadn't said it, but he *behaved* as if he cared for her, and that was what counted. Wasn't it?

She tugged on his hair, encouraging him to kneel up

for a kiss, soft and sweet. "You really are wonderful. I hadn't noticed—the thing with the music, I mean."

"You weren't meant to notice. It's a technique I use when interviewing clients and witnesses." He grinned and said, "Now you'll be conscious of it, and you'll try to analyze your writing based on my playing. That might invalidate my efforts completely."

Laughing now, she kissed him again. "Thank you."

Catlike, he knelt back down and twisted sideways so he could lean his shoulder against the seat between her legs. He tipped his head, resting it on her thigh, and said, "You still haven't told me why it wasn't working tonight."

She didn't answer right away. She combed her fingers through his hair and thought about the packages in the cellar and finally said, "Tomorrow it'll be one month since we first met."

Ian turned just enough to look up at Cecily without interrupting the petting. "Is that all? It feels like forever."

"Sorry if I'm boring you," she snapped, though she immediately regretted her tone.

With an irritated huff, he twisted away and rose, catching her hand to pull her to her feet. "Stop making assumptions—especially incorrect ones. I told you, I could never be bored of you," he insisted. His coldly logical tone was at odds with the gentle way he wrapped his arms around her body to hold her close.

She sighed and rested her forehead against his shoulder. "I never thought I'd have anyone for a single day, much less a month. It's…"

"Important."

"Yes."

"Then it is to me, as well," he said, his deep voice taking on a sly edge. His hands slid down her back, fingers pressing to either side of her spine, catching on her belt before dropping lower. He dipped his head and pressed hot, openmouthed kisses to her throat. When he nipped sharply at her jaw, her knees almost buckled. "I believe a celebration is traditional in Manhattan. Does the same apply to Canada?"

"You talk too much," she complained.

"Not tonight," he purred against her skin, clipping the last *t* sound with another bite. "We should save our energy to properly celebrate tomorrow. If we're going to celebrate tonight, then you'll need to get those packages out of the basement so we can do this properly."

Oh, fucking hell, Cecily thought. She'd expected— feared—that he would be contemptuous of a little one-month-anniversary surprise, disdaining as too feminine or some quaint country custom. She'd never imagined that he'd put that brilliant, absolutely evil brain of his behind the idea and come up with something far worse than a couple of surprise packages picked up in town.

"Tonight. Canadian tradition," she lied. "Celebrate tonight, gifts tomorrow. Like Christmas."

He laughed and licked and blew gently, freezing the warmth right out of her throat as chills shivered deliciously up and down her spine. "Liar."

"It is. Historical basis," she said, shivering again as he nipped her earlobe. "You know. In case we freeze to death before the actual date. Can't die without celebrating."

Ian's breathing turned into snorts of laughter that he failed to completely muffle against her shirt. "Forget everything I've ever said about lying to me," he invited, grinning so hard that she could hear it in his voice. "Your lies are ridiculously entertaining. Keep trying."

"Entertaining? You want entertaining?" she growled in mock-anger. She backed away just enough to get a hand down between their bodies, fingers teasing over his jeans.

To her surprise, he took one long step back. His blue-gray eyes had gone dark with lust; he grinned at her and tossed his hair back, saying innocently, "I thought we were saving that for our anniversary, remember?"

"We? I didn't agree to any 'we' in that," she complained.

His innocent act was no longer even remotely convincing. "Oh? Well, I suppose we could celebrate early. Need help carrying the packages?"

Two could play at that game. Determined not to let him win, she gave him an icy smile. "Right." She deliberately walked to the couch and settled at one end. "Tomorrow it is, then. You can go back to your playing," she added sweetly, gesturing at the abandoned guitar.

His eyes narrowed. He made a thoughtful, frustrated sound and then picked up the guitar. He set it on the floor and took his place on the far side of the sofa. The firelight gave a devilish gleam to his eyes, shadow filling the hollows beneath his sharp cheekbones, highlighting the gloss of his lower lip as his tongue swept over it. The bastard was absolutely gorgeous and knew it.

Twelve hours, she thought, letting her eyes sweep over his body. The thick cable-knit sweater added minimal bulk to his lean frame, and his tight blue jeans hid almost nothing that her imagination couldn't fill in with toe-curling accuracy. He wasn't just sitting; he was *posed*, fully aware of how the light played over him and the angle at which she sat.

Ian was an arrogant, clever bastard, but Cecily was determined. She hadn't made all her careful plans just to have them undone by lust. If he wanted sex tonight, she was fine with that. More than fine. But the surprise packages were staying in the cellar, no matter what persuasion he attempted. She'd just have to keep him distracted and off-balance.

There was only one way she was going to make it through until tomorrow, and that was by playing dirty. *Time to cheat*, she decided and unbuckled her belt.

The subtle metallic rattle and leathery rasp of Cecily's belt was a familiar sound, one that never failed to rouse Ian's interest in a Pavlovian response based entirely on what inevitably followed. He glanced to the side before he realized he'd moved, ruining the attempt to capture her interest with his profile. She had her belt undone, and now her fingers, strong and sure, worked to unbutton the waistband of her jeans.

His brain shut down like a computer program locking up, error messages flashing on screen. They were on the couch, not in bed, and while they'd kissed and very rarely cuddled and once she had gone to her knees and given him a truly breathtaking blow job on the couch, the sight of her stripping in the living room was new, outside all previously established behavior patterns.

The sound of her zipper was deafening.

He knew she was trying to provoke him. He knew he should turn away and look back toward the fire, summoning up an air of lofty disdain. He tried to focus on the puzzle of what was in the packages, but there was no hope for it. He could barely even remember what they'd looked like, much less speculate on the contents.

Then Cecily sat forward to pull off her shirt, and he wondered if he was going to lose this battle after all. She took off not just her sweatshirt but her T-shirt, leaving her in a plain cotton bra that was more alluring than any scrap of lace and satin had ever been. The firelight touched her scars with highlights and shadow, and he couldn't help but stare. She'd been less self-conscious about her scars—just in time for the snowy season to bear down on the cabin with relentless force, driving them both to pile on layers of warm clothing.

She lifted her hips just enough to push her jeans down past her hips. They fell to the floor, followed a moment later by her heavy wool socks.

The cabin was silent, save for the soft crackle of the fire. He didn't move, didn't make a sound, irrationally thinking that if he did, she might get dressed and leave.

Then she turned sideways to lean against the arm of the sofa, reaching back to arrange the throw pillows more comfortably. She put her right foot on the cushion and slid it forward until her bare toes just touched his thigh. Her left foot hung comfortably down, touching the floor, and her legs were spread invitingly wide.

She reached down, letting her right hand rest on her own thigh, fingers curling slowly over her skin with a soft touch he could all too easily imagine. Almost casually, she moved her hand up until her fingers were just barely resting along the edge of her white cotton panties.

"Since you're not doing anything, care to build up

the fire?" she suggested casually, toying with the edge
of the panties where the threads were just beginning
to fray.

His first instinct was to refuse; he wasn't about to be
complicit in her plan to break his resolve. If she wanted
sex, all she had to do was to show him what was in the
packages hidden away in the cellar.

But only on the surface was this about sex or the
mysterious packages they'd picked up in Pinelake.
Beneath it was her desire to celebrate their meeting.
The cardboard box and the canvas-wrapped bundle
were surprises. Gifts. While all gifts came with costs
that far outweighed their value, in Ian's experience, he
suspected that she would once again prove the excep-
tion. She hadn't arranged this surprise with an ulterior
motive. There was nothing of his that she couldn't have,
simply by asking.

She could have ended this all by giving in, either
graciously or in a fit of ill-temper. She could have
stormed off, slammed the bedroom door, and refused to
have anything to do with him until her self-appointed
deadline of Anniversary Day had dawned. Instead,
she'd taken the one route that he hadn't predicted: a
playful escalation of the conflict, done not out of mal-
ice but affection.

Ian was completely disarmed.

He rose, moved the guitar aside, and spent a few moments rearranging the logs already on the fire. Conscious
of how her scars ached in the cold, he took his time,
even though all he wanted was to go back to the sofa.
In a month, he'd become adept not just at keeping fires
alive but at learning how to stack the logs to reflect more

heat into the room. When he was finally satisfied by the warmth, he sat back down and turned sideways, making no attempt to hide his interest.

Cecily's smile went from sly to genuine. "Thanks," she said, sliding her right foot forward another inch, tucking her toes under his leg. He reached down and rested his hand on her ankle, only to have her pull her foot back with a scolding look. Then the sly smile reappeared. "Thought you were too distracted by your surprise?"

Never boring, he thought, hiding his affectionate smile. He faked an irritated huff and deliberately draped his arm across the back of the sofa to remove the temptation to reach for her again.

"By all means, feel free to make yourself comfortable," he said dryly.

She grinned, shifting down a bit more. With her right leg bent, foot flat on the cushion, her hips were canted invitingly up. One fingertip slipped beneath the elastic. Then one more, disappearing under soft cotton that shifted as she deliberately brushed her fingers over the soft, dark red curls shadowed against her panties.

Refusing to be baited, Cecily asked, "Are you going to make me do this alone?"

Ian loved games, especially clever, intelligent, engaging games. His gaming board was the office, the courtroom, even the bars and nightclubs where he socialized with his colleagues and competitors. Once engaged, he had a reputation for being absolutely cutthroat. He played not only to win but to destroy the competition, using any means necessary.

But this game, he cheerfully threw after only a token show of resistance. Pushing all thoughts of the box aside, he lowered his hand to her thigh, feeling the strong, sleek muscle under soft skin. "No."

She gave him a stern look softened by the heat in her eyes. "The packages stay in the cellar."

"Take those off," he countered, glancing at her bra and panties.

"Only if you agree. No stopping in the middle to renegotiate. No sneaking downstairs after I'm asleep. I expect you to play fair."

"I never play fair."

"You will, with me."

Despite all of his practice at theatrics, his sigh didn't come close to sounding genuine. "You're very stubborn," he complained, lowering his head to press a kiss to her knee. "Fine. I agree."

Cecily didn't fall for his irritated act. Laughing, she combed her fingers through his hair. Her voice was full of amused affection. "I'll just have to keep you from getting bored."

Ian smiled, pressing up into her touch, and met her gaze. Warmth filled him, not only from desire but from the powerful love that stole his breath. He ducked to kiss her knee again and closed his eyes, surrendering to her game. "Please do."

~~~

November 21

The next morning, Ian awoke alone, which was nothing unusual. Cecily rose before him most days and did her best to sneak out courteously without waking him, no matter how often he'd tried to explain that he didn't need that much rest. Sleep was just a remnant habit formed during the mind-rotting boredom of his recovery in the hospital, physical therapy, and rehab.

Knowing there was only minimal chance of luring her back to bed this early, he slid out from under the blankets and dressed in warm layers. The smell of coffee lured him to the kitchen by way of the bathroom, where he hurried to take care of the necessities. Warm tingling filled him, body and mind, as though he were still caught up in last night's sexual high. Keeping the same partner for more than a few weeks at a time had always been boring, but not Cecily. Not even after this long...

One month, he remembered as his sleepy mind finally woke for him to recall the surprise packages. He finished brushing his teeth and threw open the door to the kitchen, taking note of the relevant details: Cecily, still wearing her usual morning outfit of sweats and a bathrobe; smell of ham and coffee, sizzling sound of pancakes; electric lights on, rather than the oil lamp she usually preferred. *Cardboard box and canvas bundle on the table*.

It took all of his self-restraint to go to her rather than the packages. When she turned to look at him over one shoulder, mouth quirked up in a grin, he threaded his fingers into her short red hair, pulled her head back, and kissed her. The tingling warmth of well-being alchemized into a rush of pure, fiery love that had nothing to do with sex and everything to do with *Cecily*, and all he wanted to do was to keep her close and never let her go.

He finally did, though. He relaxed his fingers to comb through her hair as he looked down into deep brown

eyes, smiling at how they'd gone wide. With a lazy, satisfied grin, she invited, "Tell me what brought that on,
so I can do it every morning."

Ian laughed and nipped at her lip, casting a glance at
the skillet. "You burnt breakfast."

"I'll never undercook pancakes again," she promised.

He rolled his eyes, let her go with one last kiss, and
surrendered to his curiosity. He left her to burn breakfast
all she wanted and walked a slow circle around the table,
studying the packages. Last night's urgency had given
way to an unhurried sense of curiosity.

"Your presents are *in* the packages," she said, sounding both puzzled and amused. The frying pan sizzled as
she scraped the last of the pancake batter into the pool of
oil. "You can keep the box, too, if you want…"

With another laugh, he decided to start with the irregular package first. He wondered how she'd managed to
arrange this sort of surprise. He'd been with her almost
every minute of the last month. Someone must have
helped her. Mark, at the airfield, definitely. Possibly
Marguerite, too.

He tugged at the twine and unfolded layers of canvas
and crumpled newspaper, revealing a pale, sharp tine.
Antlers.

He pulled away the rest of the packing material. The
antlers were mounted to a small wood plaque, meant to
be hung on a wall.

"This was from your stag. The one you hunted," he
said as he counted the tines. But she didn't take trophies.
She'd once mentioned that she usually traded everything
away for food or supplies she'd need to get through the
harsh winters.

"It is."

"But—"

"I want you to have it," she said, a hint of uncertainty slipping into her voice. "If you want. It won't be easy to get back home, and Manhattan—"

He turned, one hand resting on the antlers, and touched her mouth with his fingertips. "Yes," he said, barely talking about the antlers at all. He watched her pleased smile reappear, and he answered with a smile of his own. "I know just where to hang them," he said, thinking of a place of honor in his living room, currently occupied by a trendy piece of modern art that he'd bought as an investment.

She smiled, eyes bright, and ducked to kiss his fingertips. "Breakfast is getting cold."

"I thought you burnt it," he said innocently.

Laughing, she smacked his arm and turned back to the stove. "Hurry up, or you starve this morning."

He grinned and dug into the box, tossing aside the twine and butcher paper. A bright, silvery gleam caught his eye, and he lifted out a pie wrapped in foil and plastic wrap.

"That's for dessert tonight." She took the pie out of his hands and gave him a quick kiss on the cheek. "There's more in there."

The lure of "more" made him look back down into the box, where he found another layer of butcher paper. He pulled it out and found a small, narrow cardboard package in the corner. He lifted it out, surprised at the weight.

The box was wrapped in more butcher paper. Ian ripped it free, and the lid came loose, revealing turquoise tissue paper. Inside was a matte black knife with bright steel hardware, the grip textured and notched in the front. One side had a metal belt clip. He pressed the safety button and eased the blade out of the grip. The mechanism was stiff. The blade was slick with oil, and it locked firmly into place at full extension.

She nudged him aside and set down two breakfast plates, nervously asking, "Is it all right? After you helped with the deer, I didn't know if—"

After carefully setting the knife down, he wrapped a free arm around her body, pulling her close. He captured her gasp with a kiss that said all the words he couldn't force past the tightness in his chest.

"It's perfect," he whispered as the kiss ended. He leaned his forehead against hers, loving the feel of sleep-mussed, soft hair against his skin. "You're perfect."

Cecily pulled him close, strong arms around his waist, and rested her cheek against his shoulder. "Happy anniversary, Ian."

Chapter 21

December 20

"GOT AN EMAIL FROM PRESTON. HE SENDS HIS REgards," Ian called from the front room of the cabin.

Cecily sat up, back aching from being hunched over the kitchen table. She'd been editing for hours, ever since they'd finished lunch. She put down the pen she'd been chewing and rose stiffly. She hated editing by hand, but it was part of her process. Write on the typewriter, transcribe to the computer, email to her editor. When she got the manuscript back, she'd print it out in Pinelake so she could edit by hand. Then she'd transcribe everything back to her computer, doing another pass as she typed.

"How is he?" she asked as she went to the living room archway.

Ian sat at the desk in front of his laptop. He looked back over his shoulder and said, "He's asking if I want to come home for the holidays."

No.

She felt panic rise up in her chest. Her fingers scratched over the riverstone archway as she fought to breathe. She wasn't ready. She didn't want him to leave without her, but *she wasn't ready*. They were supposed to have more time. Tomorrow was their two-month anniversary. Two months was *nothing* after seven years.

She heard the rattle of the desk chair. Then long, cool fingers closed around her hands. She took deep breaths and tried to ground herself in the present, telling herself that she was safe and Ian was here, and that was all that mattered for now. Distantly, she felt him leading her through the living room before giving her a little push toward the sofa.

Realizing just how shaky her legs were, she sat and tried to relax her death grip on his hands. He sat down beside her and quietly said, "I'm not going anywhere, remember? Not without you."

Her heart thudded into her ribs, but she pushed away the reminder. She let go of his hands and said, "You'll have to, though, one day. If you—"

"*Don't.*"

Ian's arms came up to circle her body tightly, and it was a measure of how far she'd come—how much she trusted him—that the panic was barely a whisper in the back of her mind. She let out a shaky exhale and got one leg over his, holding him more tightly. They both shifted and leaned back into the cushions until they couldn't get any closer together.

"Whatever you decide, I'll be right there with you," he said, stroking his hand down her back. "I came this far for you. I'm not leaving you."

"You came to get away from Manhattan," she said with a little smile. She lifted her head from his chest, and warmth curled through her at the way he smiled back at her. "You didn't even know I existed until you first saw my death trap of a plane."

"Either way, I found you, and now you're stuck with me." He kissed her forehead and dragged his fingers up her spine to tease at her nape, making her shiver. "But I think you might be more ready than you think."

"What?"

"Hear me out." He turned slightly, so they were sitting sideways on the couch, facing each other. His hand slid from her nape to her shoulder and down her arm. "We're humans—creatures of habit. It could be that you're wary of leaving simply because you're *used to* being that way. It's a pattern of behavior you've created."

"Is this something you learned from your addiction counseling?"

"No. Well, yes. Sort of." He gave her a wry smile. "What I actually learned was that even the experts don't have all the answers, and what works for one person won't necessarily work for another. But look at me. All the programs helped, sort of, until I returned to work. Then I was right back at it again."

She frowned, sitting up a bit. "What happens when you go back this time?"

"I'm not worried about it," he said reassuringly. "The circumstances are completely different. I've had time to physically recover, which was half the problem. The painkillers were masking what I was doing to my body before I was fully healed." His grin flashed to life as he added, "I plan on being able to keep up with you on your morning jog by summer."

She couldn't help but answer with her own grin. "It'd be nice to have company," she admitted. "But—"

"But," he cut in, "I had *habits*. Going to work too early, staying too late, ignoring when my body needed rest. Once I broke those habits by changing the circumstances—by leaving the city—everything changed."

"And you think my"—she faltered, unable to articulate her fear—"*this* is because…what? I've made isolation my habit?" It sounded ridiculous.

"Exactly." He brushed his knuckles over her cheek. "For me, it meant walking out of rehab early. It meant *not* going back to what I was used to. The city. My job. My apartment. It meant coming here, somewhere completely new, somewhere I had no chance to fall back into that habit. Break the habit, Cecily."

The warmth of Ian's touch disappeared under a cold chill at the thought. Her cabin was safe. No one came here. She wasn't in danger of being hurt—of hurting someone else.

But safety was a trap. Safety meant isolation. Not being with Ian.

To live—to love—meant taking a risk, and the woman she'd once been had never backed away from a risk.

"All right," she said, forcing the words past the lump in her throat. When Ian's eyes lit up, she couldn't help but smile and repeat, "All right. Let's give it a shot."

—✳—

Cecily wasn't one to wait. Once a decision was made, she acted immediately. No dithering, no backpedaling. She got up to start packing, pausing only long enough to put a pot of leftover stew on the stove to reheat. Then she went back to tearing through the living room, bedroom, and bathroom, occasionally throwing things onto the bed.

For Ian, packing was easy. He folded a mix of dress clothes and winter clothes into his one suitcase, packed away his laptop, and was done in under an hour. After he moved his carry-on into the kitchen, he went into the bedroom, where he found her crouched in front of the open gun safe. The drawer was open, and she had a stack of file papers on the floor beside her.

"Is there anything I can do?"

"I can't bring these to New York"—she gestured at the guns with one hand, never looking up from the papers—"and I can't just leave them here."

"Preston can help. He'd probably be willing to—" He cut off, realizing that while Preston would probably be happy to buy the whole collection, Cecily might not want to sell them. "You can probably store them in Virginia."

"And how do I *get* them there, from here? Do you know international firearms laws?" she snapped, firing a quick glare his way. "I'd probably have to find a licensed dealer to take delivery in Virginia."

Surprised by her sharp tone, Ian said, "I can find out—"

"Right." She nodded, swept up the papers, and stood. A hard kick closed the drawer, and then she slammed the safe door shut, engaging the lock. The papers went onto the bed.

Somewhat taken aback, Ian went into the living room and sat down. He was tempted to use her laptop, which was still out, but hers was intolerably slow. Maybe he could talk her into leaving it here so he could buy her a new one. If nothing else, it would save on luggage space.

He got out his own laptop instead. By the time he'd sent off an email to Preston, Cecily was in the living room, back to searching the papers she'd taken from the gun safe. Ian considered asking what she was doing, but her frown of deep concentration changed his mind. Instead, he decided to book plane tickets. Meanwhile, Cecily found whatever she was looking for and headed for the kitchen. The basement door creaked open, and Ian turned to look over his shoulder, listening as Cecily went downstairs.

Flights could be problematic. Assuming they were leaving tomorrow morning and not tonight, they'd get to Little Prairie by midday. They *might* make it to Calgary by nightfall, but the weather made scheduling unpredictable, and Little Prairie wasn't exactly JFK. Ian could all too easily imagine the airport closing down because the cows across the road got loose when high winds blew down their fence. Better to book a hotel room in Calgary and plan to fly out the next morning.

"If you're showering, do it now," Cecily said out of nowhere, her voice uncharacteristically tense.

Startled, Ian spun the chair around. Dust muted the colors in her fiery hair and turned her navy blue sweater to dark gray. "What?"

"I have to drain the pipes." She let out a huff and looked around. "Shit. I have to purge the gas lines." She crossed the living room and snatched her parka from the hook by the front door, only to stop again. "*Shit*. And I have to deal with the generator. And all the meat."

Ian stood, taking note of the tightness around her eyes, the sharp edge in her voice. She wasn't panicking, though; this wasn't a potential PTSD blackout.

"How can I help?"

"You can't." She snapped and glared at him for one brief, fierce instant before she turned away. "Okay, no. Sorry. There's too much to do. I can't do this."

Disappointment hit Ian like a punch, but he hid it. "Cecily, you're getting caught up in details that—"

"I'm *not*." She took a deep breath and shook her head, scattering dust from her hair. "There's too much to do, Ian. I can't just…pick up and leave."

It was on the tip of his tongue to ask if she was just making excuses, but he caught himself. Instead, he went to her and rested his hands lightly on her shoulders. She stared up at him as if braced for a fight.

Calmly, he said, "Okay. Then we don't go. What do you need?"

Her shoulders relaxed. "I'm not saying no. But I need time."

"Cecily—"

"This isn't about habits," she interrupted. She shook her head, and dusty hair wisped over her eyes. "I just need a plan."

Ian nodded, lifting a hand to brush the hair back out of her face. "Okay. Let's come up with a plan."

She smiled wryly and asked, "When's the last time you had to winterize a cabin in the middle of December while still living in it?"

He laughed and rubbed a finger over her nose, cleaning off a spot of dust. "Never. But I'm very good at taking notes and scheduling. You talk; I'll type."

―⁂―

By the time the to-do list was complete, they were both hiding yawns. "We're done," Ian said, flexing hands

that ached from the chill that had fallen. The fire had
died to embers.

"There's so much to do," Cecily said, raking her
hands through her hair. "We won't make it back by
Christmas. You can go. I'll meet—"

"Don't finish that sentence," he warned, giving her
a smile. "I'm happy to spend Christmas here with you,
draining pipes or boarding up windows."

"You really are crazy, aren't you?" she muttered,
smiling back at him. Then her eyes went to the laptop,
and she thoughtfully said, "I should go over the list one
more time."

"I've seen my brother do this, and even he admits
there comes a time when you have to stop refining the
plan and just execute it. And the middle of the night isn't
the time for either one."

She drew a breath to protest but apparently thought
better of it. "He's right. You're right." She got up off
the sofa and raised her arms, turning the motion into a
full-body stretch. Ian couldn't help but smile and think
just how lucky he truly was that she'd chosen *him*, of all
people. When she lowered her arms, she met his eyes
and gave him a curious little smile. "Let me just put
everything away, or we'll be eating paper for breakfast."
She brushed a kiss against his forehead and headed for
the kitchen.

He got up from the computer desk, back aching. For
once, it wasn't psychosomatic, and he felt no guilt in
taking a couple of ibuprofen before he went to shut
down his computer and the satellite modem. He'd been
trying to wean himself off the pills, thinking that if he
could do without even over-the-counter painkillers here,

in the cold and damp, he'd be just fine in Manhattan. Grudgingly, he admitted to himself that the morning exercises and gentle stretches seemed to be helping, too.

He went into the bedroom and built up the fire, listening as Cecily finished up in the kitchen and went into the bathroom. Once the fire was going strong, he stripped and got under the blankets. The sheets were like ice, and he curled up to try and warm the bed with body heat. If she wasn't ready to leave for good, maybe they could go somewhere for a vacation. Someplace with central heat. He could call Preston's travel desk and find an isolated cabin with proper heating, electricity, and amenities. Hell, he'd charter a damned plane to fly them directly, so Cecily wouldn't have to put up with being locked in a metal tube full of idiots for hours.

When she came out of the bathroom, she sat on the edge of the bed and set her gun on the nightstand. She stripped without hesitation and got under the blankets, avoiding his eyes. Usually, she curled up against his side, but this time, she lay down on her back and folded her arms under her pillow.

"You should know," she began quietly.

He rolled onto his side and rested his head beside hers, a careful inch between them. "Whatever it is, I probably already do."

She exhaled, a sound that might have been humor or irritation; it was too soft to decipher. "I need to say it."

"You don't have to say anything you don't want to."

"I do, though, don't I?" She sighed, and he slid his hand onto her chest, between her breasts, to feel her heartbeat. She covered his hand with her own, stroking down to his wrist and back to his knuckles. "I've wasted seven years of my life here, Ian. I'm not going to waste seven more years—of *both* our lives."

"If you hadn't, my brother wouldn't have sent me to you," he pointed out quietly.

"You're here now. That's what matters. But that's also why you should know…"

She fell silent, and this time he waited, feeling the unusually fast beat of her heart, at odds with her slow, carefully controlled breathing. The line of her back was rigid against the firm mattress, and her fingernails scratched short lines over his hand. The fire's warmth slowly stole over them, and he relaxed a bit more, easing his foot against hers to get that much closer.

"They had me for five days," she said softly. "At least, that's what they told me—the soldiers from Samaritan. I only really remember three, I think."

Heart pounding, Ian shook his head, suddenly wanting to find a way to silence her. In his career, he'd heard all manner of horrors, but this…this was too much. He'd seen the video. Bad enough that his imagination had filled in what might have happened before and after. He wasn't certain he was strong enough to hear it in her own voice.

"You don't have to go through this," he insisted.

"It's all right," she said, voice strained, making her words a lie. "They didn't have much in the way of medical treatment. There were three of us, all wounded. They stopped the bleeding, but that was about it. Then they— the video." Her fingers clenched tight around his hand. She stared up at the ceiling, expressionless. "I'd seen it happen before. We all had. Sometimes they'd release hostages—usually the journalists or contractors—but a lot of them ended up dead. Beheaded, mostly."

His heart leaped into his throat. "Cecily," he whispered.

Her hand held his even more tightly. "They usually filmed it. So when they pulled us in for the video...I thought that was it. I didn't know that much Arabic, so I didn't know what the hell they were saying. Then they shut off the camera—" She cut off, her inhale sharp and jagged.

"Did they..."

"No." She shook her head and met his eyes.

Guilty relief crashed through him. She'd suffered terribly at their hands, but at least she'd been spared the horror of sexual assault. He took a deep, shaky breath and tried to find something to say, but the words weren't coming to him.

She turned back to look up at the ceiling. "After the video... That's when *this* started," she said, gesturing at the blanket—at the scars hidden under the blanket. "I never figured out *why*. Ackerman and Dowd... None of us spoke Arabic worth a damn. We never knew what they were saying—what they wanted."

Ian went cold, rubbing his fingertips over the blanket as if he could erase the scars below it. She hadn't been interrogated. She'd been *tortured*, for no reason. They'd made their video and documented their brutality, but the torture had continued, possibly up until the moment the rescue team had arrived.

It was no wonder she hadn't healed after seven years. There wasn't a shred of logic for her mind to use, to rationalize the reason behind what had been done to her, except for the senseless cruelty of war. She couldn't even feel pride in her ability to resist them because they'd made no demand of her.

"You survived," he said, his voice rough, strained with the effort to sound comforting. "That's all that matters."

"I know." She sighed again and whispered, "I keep telling myself that."

Grief tore at him, though he tried to hide it. He let go of her hand because he needed to hold her. But just as he moved, so did she, thrashing at the blanket to roll over and face him. He ended up on his back, holding her close against his side, her head resting on his shoulder.

Cecily needed him. She needed him to be strong, not furious that she'd been targeted and hurt for no reason, not bleeding inside at the thought of what she'd endured. But he couldn't find the cool distance that had helped him through all the fights with his parents and the trials of college and law school. She'd slipped right through his defenses, and it felt as if he were sharing every one of her wounds somewhere deep inside, unseen.

Somehow, he kept from asking her what he should do. He couldn't put that burden on her, because she wouldn't have an answer. Maybe there wasn't any answer at all, except what he was doing now. "Being there for her" seemed a poor solution to Ian; he was accustomed to actively taking charge and *doing* something in the face of a problem. For now, though, it would have to be enough.

So he held her, patient and silent, and listened to the sound of her breathing for hours that felt like days.

Chapter 22

December 29

"YOU SHOULDN'T NEED TO DO ANYTHING," CECILY said, a tiny frown drawing her brows together as she stared across Marguerite's kitchen table. "We're coming back for a couple of weeks next summer, and if not, I can probably get someone from town to check up on the pipes and things."

Lunch had come and gone, starting with the venison roast she had cooked last night and ending with a pie Marguerite had baked. Outside, the weather was still cold but felt balmy in comparison to the long winter. The midday sun was painfully bright in the cloudless sky.

Last night, Cecily and Ian had driven the snowmobile to Marguerite's house, towing the trailer of luggage and essentials that would travel with them back to Manhattan. Ian had spent an hour carefully cushioning the precious antlers that had resided in a place of honor on the living room fireplace mantel. She'd insisted upon bringing her old manual typewriter.

They'd spent the night in one of Marguerite's guest rooms, and then packed her pickup truck that morning. The road to Marguerite's house had been buried under snow, but Ian had made a radio call to Pinelake a few days earlier and arranged for Mark to use the airfield's snowplow to clear the way. Marguerite would drive them to Pinelake, where Cecily had arranged for one of the residents to fly them and their luggage to Little Prairie.

Marguerite smiled reassuringly and said, "It's not a problem. And if you need me to ship you anything, don't hesitate to call."

"Thanks." Cecily smiled and reached across the table to take her hands. "You've been the best friend I could ever ask for, Mags."

Blinking back tears, Mags squeezed her hands and said, "I'm going to miss you two. You have to call me when you're settled in. It's been a long time since I've visited Manhattan."

"I'm not certain that's safe, turning you loose in my city," Ian teased. Marguerite's elegant beauty would turn heads in any nightclub—and no one would ever expect her sharp intellect or her solidly practical demeanor.

Cecily huffed, hiding a laugh. "For that, you get to help with dishes. I'll go finish packing the truck," she said, rising.

"Oh, he doesn't have to," Marguerite protested.

"Yes, he does. You're doing us enough of a favor, driving us to town again." Cecily leaned down to kiss his cheek before she left Marguerite's warm, cluttered kitchen.

After an entire winter of cleaning by hand, he started to scrub the dishes automatically, only to have Marguerite point out that she had a perfectly good dishwasher. He started to load it, listening as Cecily put on her boots and left through the front door.

As soon as the door banged shut, Marguerite walked up next to him. "Ian—"

"I'm not going to hurt her." He straightened and flexed his shoulders, feeling only the mildest twinge of pain in his back.

"Good. Because remember, she gave me her hunting rifle," she warned with a sweet smile as she started handing over glasses.

He laughed, glad Marguerite's loyalty was unshakable, and slid out the top rack of the dishwasher. "I won't let anyone hurt her. I promise. And if she needs to come back…then *we* will."

She avoided his eyes as she rinsed each glass and passed it to him to put on the rack. Only when she started handing over the silverware did she say, "I'm sorry. I've been meaning to say it for months, but…with everything that happened, with you both preparing to leave and then not leaving… I'm worried. But I know she'll be all right."

He nodded and closed the dishwasher. He reached past her for a dish towel to dry his hands. "You were right."

"I—I was?"

He waved a hand and dropped the dish towel. "You recognized what we had before I did."

Slowly, Marguerite smiled. "Have you told her?"

He shrugged and took off his glasses to brush off a stray hair on the lens. "She's not ready. I don't want to push her."

"How do you know?"

He smiled. "When she's ready, she'll tell me."

———ᴡᴡ———

They left most of their luggage at the Little Prairie airport, to be loaded onto the charter plane in time for their early morning departure. Cecily insisted on carrying their rucksack of clothes and toiletries out to the taxi to spare Ian's back. He started to argue and then stopped himself, kissed her cheek, and turned his attention to his phone.

She half listened to his call while staring out the windows, waiting for the anxiety that never came. She'd double- and triple-checked everything. The cabin was secure. Mags would check on things. Mark volunteered to go up there if she called and needed something. It was *fine*.

"Cecily?" She looked over at Ian, who was holding the phone out to her. "Preston wants to talk to you."

Surprised, she took the phone. "Hello?"

"Captain Knight," Preston answered. After months of living with Ian, she could hear the similarities in their voices. She suspected Preston was smiling.

"Cecily, please," she invited with a smile of her own.

"Then call me Preston." This time, there was a hint of laughter in his voice. "I haven't had a chance yet to thank you for letting Ian stay with you. This means everything to me."

She turned her smile on Ian, who looked curious, though he wasn't attempting to listen in. "Me, too," she admitted.

"I'm happy for you—for both of you," he said, his warm approval plain to hear. "But listen, there are a couple of things I want to talk to you about."

Apprehension teased at the back of her neck, making her sit up a bit straighter. "Go ahead."

Preston had been in the military; he knew how to skip past the bullshit and get to the heart of the matter. "First, if Manhattan doesn't work out, you've both got a place with me. Ian is licensed to practice law down here—he's helped out with a couple of contracts—and we could really use someone full-time. It's corporate, not criminal, so it's a little safer, too."

"My degree is in electrical engineering."

"I was thinking more about your marksmanship scores—and you've got training in logistics. You'd be perfect for new-hire training and mission coordination."

Interest sparked through her unexpectedly. She'd been so focused on the actual move that she'd barely given thought to what she'd do once she was in Manhattan. She could continue writing—she *would* continue writing—but she'd never be able to afford her fair share of the cost of living in Manhattan. For Ian, she'd try her best to make a new start of life in Manhattan, but she was a soldier. She liked having backup plans. But would Ian be willing to leave the city he loved?

"I'll think about it," she said, glancing at Ian, who was looking back at her steadily, without worry.

"Thanks. This next part, you can consider advance notice. As soon as our mother hears about you, she'll want to meet you."

"Is that good or bad?"

Preston laughed. "Good. We've had our differences with our parents, but…I'll leave it at that. She'll be thrilled to know he's found someone good for him."

A hint of guilt crept through her. "Am I?"

Instead of answering immediately, Preston hummed thoughtfully. "Ian and I have always been close—closer than we are with our younger sister, Amelia. He's passionate. Throws himself into everything he does. Just wait until you see him in the courtroom."

The thought made her smile. Ian had described a younger Preston the same way: passionate and impulsive. "I kind of picked that up," she said discreetly, wondering if Ian knew they were talking about him. Probably. Nothing slipped past him.

"He needs someone practical. Someone who's tough and smart and who won't take any bullshit from him."

She laughed and turned to look out the taxi window to hide the way her face had gone hot. "Practical. Got it."

"You'll do fine. And if you need anything at all, let me know, okay?"

She smiled at her reflection. Her free hand crept across to rest on Ian's knee, and his hand covered hers. "Thanks, Preston."

Warmly, he answered, "Welcome to the family, Cecily."

—◦◦◦—

"So, what did Preston say to you?" Ian asked as he pushed open the hotel room door. He suspected he knew the answer to that already; he knew his brother all too well.

She walked in, carrying the backpack she used in lieu of a proper suitcase. "Welcome to the family. That sort of thing."

"Did he warn you about our mother? She'll want to meet you." He abandoned his carry-on and caught Cecily around the waist, burying his face in her hair. "How tired are you?"

She hummed thoughtfully, covering his hands with her own. "Exhausted," she said, tipping her head back against his shoulder. She lifted up on her toes so she could kiss his jaw. "But not *too* exhausted."

He grinned playfully at her. "We could get doughnuts."

She blinked in surprise. "You—" Then she laughed and twisted in his arms, giving him a playful push toward the bed. "We are *not* getting doughnuts tonight."

He allowed himself to drop back onto the edge of the bed, pulling her down with him. "Then what are we doing tonight?" he asked.

"All I want is to spend the night right here, with you." She sat down beside him, then shrieked out a laugh when he rolled her onto her back. He propped up on his elbows and looked down into her eyes. There wasn't a hint of panic or tension in her, and he couldn't help but feel smugly proud of himself, knowing that he'd helped her just as much as she'd helped him.

"Preston reiterated his offer for me to come work for him full-time." He rolled off her to lie on his side, facing her.

She rolled over to face him, frowning. "What about your law firm? Isn't being a partner a big deal?"

"Well, yes. But I've been out for a long time, first with the accident, and then...everything else." He shrugged, remembering how proud he'd been to make partner. He'd worked himself half to death, and the price had been higher than he'd anticipated. Even now, a little voice in the back of his head was whispering that he'd need something stronger than ibuprofen to cope with this lousy hotel mattress and tomorrow's plane ride.

"Do you really want to work for your brother?"

"We actually get along very well. And he's making

ridiculous amounts of money ever since he branched out into domestic private security."

She nodded, moving a hand up his arm to brush her fingertips over his jaw. He hadn't bothered shaving that morning, mostly because he'd noticed that she couldn't resist touching his stubble. "Isn't Samaritan based out of DC?"

"Sort of. He has an office in DC, but the main head- quarters is in Virginia. It's nice there."

Her body went tense; her fingers stopped moving. "Nice."

"Nice," he agreed. "New building, training com- pound of—"

"Don't give me that," she snapped. "Virginia's all trees and hills. You *love* Manhattan. City boy, remember?"

"All I'm saying—"

"Is that you're coddling me?" She twisted away from him to lie on her back. "Screw that."

He reached out to catch her hand. "All I'm saying is that we have *options*. I'd probably end up working in DC at least part of the week, and DC *is* a city. Apparently one with traffic that's more fucked-up than Manhattan."

She narrowed her eyes, studying his face. Finally she relaxed and turned onto her side to face him once more. "You love Manhattan."

"And Manhattan is what got me into trouble in the first place," he reminded her. "Yes, I love the city, but Manhattan's only a train ride away from DC, so it's easy enough to come back. And for what I'm paying on this apartment, we could get a house with a huge yard down there."

She took a deep breath and squeezed his hand before

she intertwined her fingers with his. "We don't have to decide anything now."

"No, we don't. And it wouldn't be easy. I'm already allowed to practice law down there, but I'd probably have to go back to school. Take some more classes on contract law." He leaned in and gently kissed her. "We have time, Cecily. What I said hasn't changed. You're worth waiting for."

She squeezed his hand. "We don't have to decide anything now."

"No. No, we don't..." He took a deep breath and looked into her eyes, steeling himself. He'd never lacked for courage, but now he hesitated. He'd faced down death threats from convicted killers without backing down. Now, though, his chest went tight, and his eloquence failed him.

She tipped her head, looking up at him curiously. "Ian, is something—"

"I love you."

The words slipped out, silencing them both. Furious with himself, he looked away, unwilling to face the possibility of her rejection. For all those months, he'd held back, waiting for her to decide when she was ready, and now he'd gone and blurted it out without any sort of plan.

When he finally turned back and met her eyes, she smiled. "I love you, too," she said quietly.

"You've never said that before," he said inanely.

Instead of taking offense, she shrugged, a smile playing at her lips. "Neither have you. Both our faults, then."

Slowly, the fact that they were in accord filtered through his fear, and he reminded himself he was being irrational. He'd known for months that he loved Cecily. The words themselves were just that—words—even if hearing them from her somehow made it all *real*.

"Ian?" she asked tentatively, touching his face.

He shook his head, dismissing his thoughts, and kissed her fingertips. "Now you're ready to leave."

"What?"

"Remember I said when you were ready, you could tell me how you feel?"

Cecily's confusion melted away into understanding. "Yes." She brushed her fingers over his face, staring at him affectionately. "At first, it was there, but it didn't... I don't know. It didn't feel right to say it. And then, it was as if we both knew it."

"And now, you're ready." He leaned down to kiss her again, finally taking his time, thinking that he'd have to find ways to encourage her to say it more often.

She grinned and put one foot up on the bed. Then, with a single strong push of her leg, she shoved him over onto his back so she could roll on top of him. When she leaned down, her hair tickled his face. "It's too bad I'm so damned tired," she said, combing her fingers through his hair. "This is our last night together in Canada, at least for a while. We should celebrate."

All but purring with contentment inside, he asked, "Are you afraid of flying? Of someone else piloting, I mean. You were tense on the flight here from Pinelake."

She laughed. "I was tense because I kept thinking I'd forgotten something. No, Ian. Not afraid of flying."

His smile turned wicked. "In that case... It's a charter flight. We're the only passengers. If we can find some basic hand tools, I'm certain we can get the seats to fully recline."

Immediately, her eyes went sharp. "You are *not* taking our aircraft apart while we're flying in it," she scolded.

"But—"

"The rest of my life is going to be me stopping you from doing something dangerous bordering on suicidal, isn't it?"

"My mother always said I needed a caretaker," he said, lifting his hands to cup her face. He traced her freckles with his thumbs and looked up into her eyes, amazed at how very much in love with her he was. "Do you mind?"

With a delighted smile, Cecily shook her head. "At least I'll never be bored."

Chapter 23

December 31

"WELCOME HOME," IAN SAID AS HE UNLOCKED THE door and stepped inside to the sound of beeping. He pushed his wheeled suitcase aside and set down his guitar case. Cecily followed him inside, shoulders tense under the straps of the rucksack that had served as a carry-on bag. They'd shipped the rest of their luggage, including the antlers he'd refused to leave behind.

He closed the door and disarmed the alarm system, saying, "The code is 1013, then press Disarm."

"Thanks." She gave him a slight, fake smile and walked past him, through the foyer.

He followed, watching the tight line of her shoulders as she set down her rucksack. His own back was strained from hours of sitting on the plane and in the taxi from Newark Airport, but Cecily's tension was because of the trip itself—the crowds that had become unfamiliar after seven years of living in isolation.

"It's bigger than I expected," she said, walking forward in slow, cautious steps. She paused and glanced left into the kitchen, then right into the powder room, before continuing into the living room. "Is someone here? It's clean."

"Preston sometimes stays here. Otherwise, I have a service that usually cleans twice a week." He left his own luggage by the door, though he carried the old, battered guitar into the living room after her. "If you're hungry, I had them stock the fridge with the basics. Or I can get you something to drink."

"I'm okay, thanks," she answered distantly. Her attention wasn't on the sleek, stylish decor but the floor-to-ceiling windows that overlooked the Hudson River. The room was roughly square, with a small notch cut out of the far corner for a balcony just large enough for a small table and two lounge chairs.

She was still tense. Disappointed, Ian went to the couch and set down his guitar, thinking he might as well risk breaking the strings by playing it so soon after travel. His music helped her to relax, and he wanted her to be comfortable in his apartment. Their apartment.

Of course, it was nothing like her own cabin. Ian's apartment was built for company—anything from one-night stands to small dinner parties. The sofas were thickly cushioned black leather arranged on two sides of a luxurious shag carpet in a dusty olive green. The dining table had chairs at the ends and benches on either side. Two stools offered informal seating at the breakfast bar.

Only when he turned back to face her did he realize that she was still focused on the windows. Ian was so used to them that he rarely bothered closing the curtains in here and only closed the sheers in his bedroom. But Cecily was so private...

"Sorry. Here," he said, going right for the coffee table. There were two remote controls there—one for the entertainment unit, one for the household. He picked up the household remote, and with the press of a button, the blinds on the west-facing window began to descend. "Everything's automated. There are a couple of remotes floating around. I usually keep one in here and one in the bedroom."

"That's…" Cecily trailed off and gave him a smile that seemed easier. When he touched another button, turning the overhead lights to a dim glow, she looked up and gave a little laugh.

"Convenient?" he asked, walking over to her.

She tipped her head down enough to meet his eyes and rested her hands on his hips. "I was going to say lazy."

"I'm not lazy," he lied. He tossed the remote on the couch so he could wrap his arms around her. "I work hard for this lifestyle."

"Maid service twice a week, remote control blinds and lights?" she challenged. "Which part of the 'work' do you do?"

"The lawyer part," he teased, leaning down for a kiss.

But she turned away, smile fading, and wormed free of his arms. She took a few steps across the deep shag carpet and looked around. Her shoulders went tight again as she shoved her hands into her pockets. She still hadn't removed her parka; the waterproof shell rustled loudly in the silence.

"Your job." She looked down, scuffing her boot on the carpet, and shook her head. "I knew you lived well, but I didn't imagine… Ian, what am *I* supposed to do here?"

Ian's gut went tight. "You're a writer. We can build you an office, maybe overlooking—" He cut off, looking at the window that looked out toward the river, a window that was now covered.

He swallowed, wondering what he was supposed

to say now. Cecily was a writer, yes, but at the cabin, she had always been busy with the day-to-day need to survive. Firewood, food, repairs—all the critical things necessary to live in such an inhospitable environment. She needed to be busy. Useful. And here, she probably couldn't even afford to pay a tenth of the monthly bills, much less split expenses fifty-fifty.

She turned back to face him, hazel eyes dark with worry. "What am I doing here? I don't belong—"

"Don't," he interrupted. He went to her and put his hands on her shoulders, feeling the tension in her strong muscles. "Small steps, remember? You get a desk. You hook up your laptop. You write. Maybe go for a jog in Central Park one morning." He slid his hands up to cup her face, gentling his fingers over her soft skin. "And you give *us* a chance."

She closed her eyes, leaning into his hands. "I know. I'm sorry."

"And don't apologize." A touch under her jaw got her to look back up at him. "Do you think I want to go back to the office? To the courtroom? The hours suck. The stress of building a case, of dealing with clients and the DA and the damned press…assuming they remember who I am."

She exhaled warm breath over his hands. "You're not exactly forgettable." She straightened her back and looked around without breaking free of his gentle hold. "It really is nice. Not exactly my style."

"Your *style* involves freezing to death," he said with a smile. "And denying yourself."

"Denying myself?"

"Mmm. Living without life's little luxuries. Which reminds me, I have one last surprise for you."

Her eyes lit up with interest. "You do?"

"Give me ten minutes. Then I'll show you." He leaned in to brush his lips over hers and tugged at the coat she still wore. "Make yourself comfortable."

"Ten minutes," she agreed and took off her coat.

Cecily sank an inch deeper into the bathtub, opening her eyes just enough to see Ian leaning against the vanity. "I am never leaving this tub," she all but purred, lifting a handful of bubbles from the water's surface. For seven years, the closest she'd come to a bathtub had been midsummer swimming in the river by the cabin.

Grinning, Ian knelt down on the bath mat and reached out to comb his fingers through her damp hair. "I can get one of those bathtub trays for your laptop. You can write in here. I'll bring you snacks."

"I knew there was a reason I love you."

His touch went still, and she opened her eyes to look at him. Softly, he said, "I'll never get tired of you saying that."

She felt a blush creep up her face and hoped he'd blame it on the hot water. He'd covered every surface with candles, filling the room with flickering light that reminded her of her cabin. "Manipulative bastard," she accused fondly, turning her head to kiss his forearm.

His brows shot up toward his hairline. "What did I do?"

She laughed softly. "Just…you, with your candles." She turned, sending a wave of bubbles over the lip of the tub.

"Hey! Watch it," he protested with a laugh, swiping some of the bubbles back at her with his free hand. "What did I do?"

"Candles. Oil lamps and fireplaces, just like in the cabin." She sat up and pushed her hair away from her face. Bubbles trailed down her forehead, and Ian caught them with his fingertips, brushing over her eyebrow.

"Your hair," he said, moving his fingers to catch at the strands that fell back against her cheek. "Firelight brings out all these shades of gold and auburn. It's like…a little bit of you shining through."

She laughed again, throwing bubbles back at him, embarrassed at his extravagant words. "That's awful."

"I'm allowed to get poetic once in a while. It impresses juries." He leaned in and kissed her without a care for how his shirt got soaked. The kiss warmed her more than the bath, sending tingles through her body. As she wrapped her arms around his shoulders, he pulled back enough to ask, "It didn't impress you?"

"Not quite," she teased. "You'll have to try harder."

"Let's see about that." He ran his fingers down between her breasts, bubbles tickling her skin until his hand dipped into the water. She felt her body relax under his touch, and she smiled, thinking the bathtub was big enough for two.

"Were you going to join me?" she invited hopefully.

"Mmm, not this time. I'm not done with the surprises." His eyes lit up with a mischievous grin. "You relax. I'll lay out your clothes on the bed, if you don't mind?"

"My clothes—" Her face went hot as her imagination supplied images of lace and satin, things he couldn't have bought en route from Canada. Oh, God, had he had his PA go shopping for lingerie for her? She'd strangle him—if she didn't die of embarrassment first.

"Trust me." He kissed the tip of her nose and got quickly out of reach. He was gone before she could demand answers.

She sank back into the tub with a groan, but the hot water and bubbles soothed her irritation. Ian was smart and caring. He knew how much she treasured her privacy. Maybe he'd ordered something online or over the phone, without involving anyone Cecily would ever have to meet.

So she allowed herself to relax and enjoy the bath until the water grew tepid. When she got out, she picked up one of the towels and found it warm to the touch. Leave it to Ian to have a heated towel rack in Manhattan. Laughing, she pulled the drain plug, dried off, and went into the bedroom.

To her surprise, instead of anything lacy or frilly, she found blue jeans, boots, and shirts meant to be layered. The bedroom door was closed, with a sticky note above the knob. Curious, she went to read it.

> *When you're dressed, follow the trail to your surprise.*

Delighted, she dressed quickly, trying to guess what he had in mind. He'd picked warm wool socks and a flannel shirt under a thick sweater. A late dinner on the balcony? She could probably manage that, even if the huge floor-to-ceiling windows were going to take some adjustment.

In the living room, she found no trace of Ian; instead, she found her parka and scarf arrayed on a chair near the door, along with another sticky note.

Come out to the hallway. Don't worry about setting the alarm. The door will lock automatically.

Maybe they were going out somewhere. A hint of trepidation crept through her, but she dressed warmly, zipped up the parka, and went out into the hall.

There, she found another sticky note, this one on the emergency door at the end of the hall. The sign on the door warned that it was protected by an alarm, but the door was open, just a crack.

Come upstairs. Hide the note. Don't let the door lock, or it will get very cold before morning.

"Sneaky bastard," she muttered, grinning now, and pushed the door open. He'd crammed the latch full of crumpled paper held in place with a strip of duct tape, like a college student holding an illicit party in the dorm rooms.

Laughing, she went up the stairs two at a time, following the signs to the roof. She pushed the door open and saw the city, alive with lights, interrupted only by the darkness of the river on one side.

A flashlight guided her to where Ian, bundled warmly in his Canadian outerwear, had set up a picnic on a blanket. The wind stole Cecily's laughter; Ian stole her breath with a kiss.

"You're mad," she accused, tears filling her eyes. She

could barely see him in the darkness, but she knew he was grinning proudly down at her.

"Which makes you equally mad, since you're here with me," he said, guiding her down to the blanket. "Are you warm enough? No, scratch that. You lived in the wilderness; you're fine."

"Yes, I am, thanks for asking," she said, nudging his shoulder. "I take it we're not supposed to be up here?"

"I would never admit to knowing how to pick locks," he declared. He turned the flashlight to shine into a brown paper grocery bag. "Sorry I didn't have time to arrange a proper picnic. The closest I could get to a picnic basket was this or shoe boxes."

"Looks like you'll have to owe me." She leaned against him, peering into the bag. She could see a bottle inside, and she heard the crinkling of wrappers. "Maybe the next one should be in summer."

"Only if it's somewhere other than the roof. It probably gets hot as hell up here. Aha! Not broken," he said, putting down the flashlight so he could take out two fine champagne glasses wrapped in paper towels. He shoved the paper towels back into the bag and offered her the glasses.

Happiness filled her all the way down to her toes at how utterly ridiculous and charming this all was. "Are we having champagne and potato chips for dinner?"

He froze.

"Oh, my God. We are."

"Pretzels, actually." In the darkness, she could just barely make out his sheepish grin. "The potato chips were stale."

She laughed as he opened the bottle of champagne.

"You're insane—*Careful!*" she yelped when he filled one glass to overflowing.

"Sorry," he said, clearly lying, and set the bottle down. Instead of taking the glass, he lifted her hand and ducked his head, licking slowly, sensuously over her fingers. The heat of his mouth sent shivers through her, and she leaned down to steal a champagne-flavored kiss from his lips.

"Careful," she whispered as the kiss broke.

"The night's not done." He filled the other glass without spilling any champagne, put the bottle aside, and took one of the glasses. "To you, Captain Cecily Knight, the strongest, most amazing woman I've ever met."

"Ian—"

He touched a finger to her lips. "Not done yet. I'm a lawyer. I can't resist a speech."

Grateful for the darkness that hid her blush, she rolled her eyes and nipped his finger.

"Where was I? Strongest, most amazing... Oh, right." His smile reappeared, this time warm and gentle. "To Cecily Knight, the only woman mad enough to put up with me at my worst, and I'll spend the rest of my life trying to be my best for her."

Her breath caught. "Ian..."

This time, he silenced her with a kiss. "You let me into your world. You let me touch you—not just your body, but *you*. And I'll never leave you, for as long as you'll let me stay by your side."

Even if she'd known what to say, she had no breath with which to speak. She lifted her hand to touch his face, and the skies around them caught fire in waves of color carried on muffled blasts of thunder, startling her for an instant. Shouts and honking horns filled the air.

"Happy New Year, love," Ian whispered over the sound of fireworks and celebration. "Our first, but not our last."

Tears spilled over her lashes as she looked up into his eyes. "Not our last," she repeated and forgot all about the champagne as she pulled him down into a kiss.

Acknowledgments

This book wouldn't exist without Cecily, Chris, Conor, and Nicole, who were right there with me for the early stages and answered my silly questions about life in Canada; and Jenny, Ray, Steph, and Summer, who held my hand during the tough rewrites. Leah believed in me and made my dream come true. At Sourcebooks, Deb and my editor, Cat, have given invaluable feedback and advice on making a pretty good story into a great romance. And I couldn't have done any of it without my wonderful agent, Jen at Donald Maass, who's gone above and beyond the call of duty to answer my questions, cheer me on, and save me when it felt like the plot hit a brick wall.

The McCauley Brothers

the hot new series by Marie Harte

—◦◦◦—

Meet the rough-and-tumble McCauleys, a tight-knit band of brothers who work hard, drink beer, and relentlessly tease each other.

The Troublemaker Next Door

Flynn never thought he'd fall for the girl next door. But when he's called to fix Maddie's sink, he's a goner. Too bad the fiercely independent interior designer wants nothing to do with him. Even worse, he's forced to rely on advice from his nosy brothers—and his five-year-old nephew!

How to Handle a Heartbreaker

It's lust at first sight for Brody when he sees Abby Dunn. But Abby's still trying to get over her last relationship, and he isn't getting the hint. It doesn't help that she keeps casting Brody as the hero in her steamy romance novels. Will Abby write her own happily ever after or stay safe in her shell?

Ruining Mr. Perfect

Vanessa Ann Campbell is a CPA by day, perfectionist by night. But she can't stop thinking about the youngest McCauley brother, even though they tend to rub each other the wrong way. Cameron's dying to get Vanessa to let loose—but if he succeeds, can he handle it?

What to Do with a Bad Boy

Mike had his soul mate for a precious time before she died giving birth to their son six years ago. He's sick of everyone playing matchmaker... until he meets Delilah Webster, the tattooed mechanic who sets his motor running. But the closer they get, the more the pain of the past throws a wrench into their future...

—◦◦◦—

For more Marie Harte, visit:

www.sourcebooks.com

Find My Way Home

Harmony Homecomings
by Michele Summers

She's just the kind of drama

Interior designer Bertie Anderson has big dreams for her career, and they don't include being stuck in her hometown of Harmony, North Carolina. After one last client, Bertie is packing up her high heels and heading for her dream job in Atlanta. But her plans are derailed by the gorgeous new owner of that big old Victorian she's always wanted to renovate...

He's vowed to avoid

For retired tennis pro Keith Morgan, Harmony is a far cry from fast-paced Miami—which is exactly the point. Keith is starting a new life for himself and his daughter Maddie, and he's left the bright lights and hot women far behind. Bertie's exactly the kind of curvaceous temptation he doesn't need, and Keith refuses to let their sizzling attraction distract him from his goals. Keith and Bertie both have to learn that there's more than one kind of escape, and it takes more than wallpaper to turn a house into a home.

For more Michele Summers, visit:

www.sourcebooks.com

About the Author

Kara Braden believes in fighting fire with fire. As she spends her days in the desert outside Phoenix, Arizona, she combats the heat with endless cups of hot coffee, setting her kitchen ablaze once or twice a week, and writing smoldering romance. Her hobbies include incessant reading and writing, video games, and hiking whenever it's not too hot outside.